THE LONELY GRAVE

KEITH DIXON

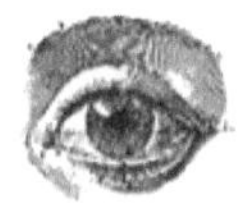

Semiologic Ltd

"The problem was to love people, try to serve them,
without wanting anything from them."
Ross Macdonald, *The Barbarous Coast*.

PROLOGUE

HE FELT IT before he heard it: a shift in the air pressure like the passage of a thought through his mind.

Someone had opened the front door, and though he was upstairs in his bedroom he knew someone had entered the house. Whoever it was didn't want him to know—there'd been no knock on the door, no ring of the doorbell. They either had a key or knew how to fool the lock. Now he felt the door closing again like a whispered threat.

He knew it was the men who'd come before, asking his house-mate Jack questions he didn't answer because he knew the men were trouble. Just the look of them, Jack had said. Scary and bizarre. He'd thought they'd return because they were unhappy when they left.

He picked up his laptop and rose from the desk where he'd been working and took one step to the bed. He reached beneath it and slid out the rucksack he'd prepared—a change of clothes and underwear, some cash, his study notes. He pushed the laptop inside the rucksack and unplugged the power cable, wrapping it in a coil before stuffing that inside too. His phone was in his pocket, the charger already in the rucksack. He grabbed his wallet from the table and crossed to the door quietly.

With Jack out of the house he felt more than usually alone. He pressed his ear to the door. He couldn't hear a thing. Perhaps they had already gone. Perhaps they were checking out the rest of the house …

He snicked the door lock to its closed position as quietly as he could.

Then stumbled backwards as someone hammered loudly on the other side.

"We know you're there, we just want to talk."

A man's voice, a rough accent, the voice of someone used to giving orders.

The bedroom window was already opened six inches, despite the cold. He opened the gap further, levered his leg outside and on to the ladder he'd propped there three days before, then descended rapidly. Once on the ground he pulled the ladder down and laid it flat so it couldn't be used by the pursuers.

Above him he heard the bedroom door splinter open but didn't look upwards.

He sprinted down the garden, yanked open the wooden gate and ran down the alley behind the row of houses, conscious of the slap of his rubber soles on the old tarmac. His heart was beating so hard he felt its pulse in his head.

Turning a corner he halted, catching his breath, and looked back for the first time, edging his face around the corner of a creosoted wooden fence.

Two men were framed in his open bedroom window, looking straight at him.

Jack was right—they were bizarre. Neither of them was older than thirty, maybe a little older than himself. One of them had black hair and was darkly tanned, but his skin was marked by a criss-cross web of scars that showed white against his dark complexion, as though someone had carefully scored his face with the point of a Stanley knife. The other man was shorter, with hair that was long and stood up in spikes and was bright yellow, a cartoon character brought to life.

They stared in his direction but he was certain they couldn't see him.

Then the dark-faced man raised a hand and pointed one finger at him, cocking his thumb to make the shape of a gun.

He mouthed, 'Boom,' then grinned and stepped back inside the room, into the darkness.

CHAPTER ONE

I DIDN'T WANT to be there.

Working for politicians is at the bottom of my list of Jobs I'd Die For. There were always so many considerations I couldn't ignore: Could I believe what they told me? Would they listen to a word I said? And worst of all: Would I get paid?

Planted in front of Giles Minton's fake-Tudor house in suburban Nantwich, looking up at a massive wooden door surmounted by a small security camera, I couldn't see me changing my mind. He wasn't a politician yet—he was standing for election in a month or so—but already he had the trappings: the elaborate house in its own grounds, the tended lawn, the double garage, the air of genteel respectability … and now, opening the door, the final signifier: the Party official, a large man with a frowning, dubious expression and wearing a waistcoat with ancestry in the 1930s. What gave away his status was the file of papers he held under his left arm. He bore the harried demeanour of someone with a lot to do and no time in which to complete it. This wasn't Giles Minton, who I'd researched online, or his wife, the person who'd spoken to me the day before and asked me to call. Nevertheless, the man sized me up and took charge like a head butler welcoming a new groundsman.

'You're Dyke,' he said, closing the door behind him and taking my arm with his free hand, leading me a short way from the house and on to the lawn. I realised the rustling I heard was the sound of his thighs rubbing together. His hand on my arm was soft, the fingers like trained slugs working as a team. We stood beneath a large oak tree that was several centuries older than the house. He looked around as if watching for intruders, his cheeks red, his eyes small but intense. He said, 'I checked you out. Quite a profile for someone who's supposed to be discreet.'

'Full transparency,' I said. 'Everyone can see what a sleazeball I am. It's not really my fault I'm in the public domain. And which sleazeball are you?'

I said it with a smile so sweet he couldn't take offence.

He'd removed his hand from my arm and now held it out to be shaken. I did so, warily. I resisted the impulse to count my fingers afterwards. He said, 'Tony Wolfe. You'll be seeing a lot of me. I take the shit Giles can't and shouldn't handle.'

This was the man I'd seen referred to online as Minton's Machiavelli—the agent whose job it was to get Minton elected by spending his election funds wisely. But Wolfe didn't look like someone to whom I'd entrust my piggy-bank, never mind several thousand pounds. He had the look of a down-at-heel lawyer which, I thought unkindly, is probably what he'd been before landing a rock-star gig.

NOW THAT WE'D established our bona fides he stepped closer, though his eyes wandered and looked past me at the house.

'Look, I know Carol called you in and there's nothing I can do about that. But between you and me she's taking all this too seriously. Alistair's practically a grown man, and if he wants to drop off the radar for a few weeks I don't see how that's a problem. What are your politics, by the way? You're from Yorkshire, aren't you? Does that mean you're a roaring lefty?'

'I've given up roaring. More of a polite whimper.'

'Good. We're tacking left, what with all this Brexit shite, but we can't be seen to be Mr Marx's poodles, can we? Not in Nantwich.'

'I didn't think we were going to talk about my politics,' I said. I was beginning to wonder what he was trying to tell me. 'Can I see the Mintons? Or are you going to keep me out here until we both freeze to death?'

His eyes narrowed, an almost impossible feat given their initial size. 'You know what's going on here, don't you? With the Mintons?'

'Only what I read in the papers. Your man Giles has given up a lucrative position in banking to stand for Parliament. I hope he knows what he's doing.'

Wolfe glanced worriedly over my shoulder again, like a man desperate to see the postman arriving while being fearful of what he might bring. He said, 'Don't under-estimate him. Most politicians have a few principles rattling around in the back of their heads, even if you wouldn't know it from listening to them talk. Giles believes what he says. He's from a modest background and he's done well for himself, but that doesn't mean he's forgotten where he came from. He's one of the few who *does* make decisions based on principles, not self-interest. So it won't do you any good if you go in there being cynical or defeatist.'

'Well there goes my unique selling point straight away.'

He poked me in the chest with a chubby finger. 'That's exactly the kind of thing I mean—flippancy doesn't go over well with these two. Especially when they're talking about their son.'

'Thanks for the advice but I know how to deal with clients. I don't usually need to go through an interview before I'm allowed to meet them.' He had no answer to this so I pressed my advantage. 'Now how about us going inside so I can start the charm offensive?'

Wolfe looked at me with calculation, like a head-waiter considering my suitability for his dining-room. It was the first week in November, heading towards nightfall, and the evening chill was seeping further through my jacket. Wolfe's attitude was almost as chilly.

He tried one more time. 'Remember what I said about Carol. It's her son we're talking about here and she dotes on him. Yes, there's a daughter, too, but I'm not giving away any state secrets by saying Alistair was the child Carol was devoted to.'

'Was?'

'He's not been seen for a month. What other tense am I supposed to use?'

Before I could answer that I heard the door behind me open and saw Wolfe's eyes move away from me and towards the house, satisfied at last that the worst had happened. I turned and saw a young woman standing hesitantly in the door, her arm raised towards us. She was perhaps twenty-two or -three and had neatly-combed blonde hair falling to her shoulders and a concerned frown on her face. She wore a white office blouse and black trousers. Her posture and deportment told me as much about her background as her tasteful clothes.

'Tony,' she said, 'Giles is looking for you.'

Wolfe seized my arm again in his soft grip and turned me to walk with him.

He said, 'This is Sally Collins, my assistant. Be nice to her. She does lots of running around for me.'

Listening to him as he wheezed across the lawn towards the house, I understood why he didn't do the running himself.

We approached the door and Sally Collins stood back to let us in, opening a wide smile in my direction.

It was the first human gesture I'd seen since I'd arrived.

CHAPTER TWO

THE HOUSE ITSELF opened out in several directions from the front door, but Wolfe led us confidently towards the back of the house as if he knew where the owners would be hanging out. As we passed I noted expensive-looking side-tables and rugs, a couple of original watercolours lit by individual down-pointing picture-lamps, a few Wedgwood figures and other pieces of pottery resting ornamentally on book-cases and shelves. There was no sound of movement in the house and the air smelled of furniture polish and faded scent, like a florist's workshop.

Giles Minton was standing in a large sitting room that looked out over a long and very green garden through a floor-to-ceiling patio window. He was of average height and build, with the sleek greying hair that seems to be handed out to bankers when they reach a certain pay-grade. He wore a casual cream jumper and brown corduroy trousers, standing with one hand posed strategically in a pocket, as if modelling for *MPs at Home* magazine. His wife, Carol, sat on the corner of a blue sofa as if she were afraid of it, her eyes when she looked up at me seeming hollowed-out and blank. She wore a cream blouse and neatly-pressed slacks and her hair was piled on her head in a swirl of blonde and grey. I could still see the young woman in her shape and posture. She and her husband were both attractive people in their mid-forties who had obviously done well for themselves but were now facing consequences they hadn't expected.

As if a starting bell had rung, Giles turned towards me and simultaneously Carol stood up and offered both a grim smile and her hand. Then we all formally uttered our names, Carol sat down again and Giles raised his chin towards Wolfe, though he spoke to me.

'Tony tells me you're very good at what you do, even if I'm still not sure what you can do for us.'

'Giles,' Carol said. 'We've had this conversation. You don't have to inflict it on Mr Dyke as well.'

She turned to me. 'Giles is of the view that because Alistair is twenty years old, he's a fully-functioning adult.'

'And you don't agree?'

'Well of course at one level he's perfectly capable of looking after himself. But wouldn't you worry if your son wasn't heard from in a month?'

I refrained from telling her I hadn't heard from mine in eighteen years … though admittedly the circumstances were different, neither of us knowing the other existed during that whole time.

I said, 'When we spoke on the phone you said he was a student—isn't it typical for students to ignore their parents for long periods? And actually, does a month seem that long?'

'That's what I think,' Wolfe said from behind me.

'Carol, you have to give the boy some freedom. Let go of the apron strings.'

Carol Minton's face grew dark and she glanced away. I suspected she'd been in this position before, and not just in relation to her son. I suspected she was surrounded by men who didn't listen to her but offered constant advice.

I said to Wolfe, 'Why don't you and Sally leave us alone for a while, so Giles and Carol can talk in confidence?'

'Tony's my right-hand man,' Giles said. 'You can say anything you like in front of him.'

'That's good—then he won't mind me telling you he's going to interfere in the conversation if he stays, will he?'

I noticed Carol Minton smirk at this and thought it likely she didn't approve of the influence the man had on her husband. Wolfe looked at Giles, who gave a small nod. Wolfe turned away, saying to Sally, 'Come on, let's go and do something more important in the office.'

They left and I sat at the other end of the blue sofa from Carol. At last Giles turned away from the contemplation of his garden and sat in a facing chair, folding his hands like a sinner finally submitting to the Inquisition. He said, 'Tony's using a spare room as an office when he's here. Saves travelling back and forth to the office in town just to print a letter. You should try to work with him rather than antagonise him.'

'I always like to start an investigation by upsetting someone. So why don't you tell me what's going on here?'

Giles gestured for Carol to take the lead. She too folded her hands together—perhaps it was a family trait—then said, 'I take on board everything you say about Alistair, his being a student and possibly unreliable and so on ... but he's not the kind of boy to stay out of touch like this. This is his second year at the university and he's always been good at telling us where he is and what he's doing. I suppose he knows I worry.'

'When was the last time you heard from him?'

'I'm not sure exactly. He went back to university mid-September and called me the first two Saturday nights he was there. That takes us to the beginning of October. Then nothing for a month. So here we are at the beginning of November and I have no idea where he is or what he's doing and it's killing me.'

'Carol ...'

'No, Giles, don't say a thing. Don't you dare. I'm all right.'

I caught a frowning glance from Minton and said nothing while his wife regained her composure. She wasn't crying but it was a possibility. This was her opportunity to lay out her case and she was going to do it clearly and without emotion. After a while she went on. 'The other thing is, he's not answering his phone. I didn't start to worry until two or three weeks of his being silent, but since then I've left dozens of messages and texted him but he's just not replying.'

'Have you spoken to the police? The university?'

Giles Minton said, 'Given my situation, we thought we'd hold off on that just yet. In my view it's not urgent so I'm afraid I convinced Carol to keep quiet, at least officially. That's where you come in. I hope we can be assured of your discretion.'

'Discretion would be my middle name, if I could spell it.'

'I hope you're taking this seriously,' Carol said, lifting her head sharply, and I remembered Wolfe's warning about being flippant. Too late.

I said, 'Once I've committed to working with you you'll get my full attention, don't worry.'

Just then another door opened and a young woman came into the room, staring at the screen of her phone. She was probably eighteen or nineteen, had short black hair dyed blue at the edges where it framed her oval face, and a blue nose stud. She was wearing black jeans and a loose black top with short sleeves. There didn't seem to be a lot of colour in her life.

The Mintons glanced at her and Carol said to me, 'This is Deborah, our daughter. Alistair's sister. Debbie, this is Mr Dyke. He's going to help us find out where Alistair's got to.'

The young woman continued staring at her phone, but said, 'Oh, Mum, are you still going on about that?'

'Hi,' I said.

She glanced up but didn't really see me. I was crushed but kept my feelings to myself.

Giles Minton said, 'Debbie, if your mother wants to do this then we shouldn't get in the way.'

Deborah put the phone in her rear jeans pocket, then threw herself into a large armchair. It didn't complain. 'Ali's all right,' she said. 'He's just off on one, moody bastard.'

'Have you heard from him?' I asked. 'I get why a youngster might not want to talk to his mum and dad … but has he spoken to you, or texted you?'

She stared at me. 'What makes you think he'd do that?

We barely spoke when he was home—why would he do it when he's off gallivanting around in sunny Stafford?'

I noticed she hadn't answered the question but I decided not to pursue it right now. I turned back to the adults.

'Where is Alistair living while he's at university—in halls?'

'No,' Giles said. 'We bought him a share in a house so he could have some freedom.'

'And get on the property ladder,' Deborah said. 'Let's start 'em early on the capitalist path to happiness.'

'Deborah,' Giles said abruptly. 'That's enough.'

She frowned at him but said nothing more. A minute or so later I noticed she'd left the room the same way she'd come in.

I said, 'A share in a house? So who's it shared with?'

'He has a friend called Jack he's known for years. We went in with his parents, fifty-fifty on the deposit and mortgage.'

'Have you spoken to Jack about Alistair's whereabouts?'

'We have,' Carol said. 'He knows nothing. He came home one day and Alistair had vanished. Now do you see why I'm worried?'

'And have you been to the house to see for yourself?'

Carol lowered her eyes. 'I'm afraid we've been too busy ...'

'It's me,' Giles Minton said. 'It's my fault. I asked Carol to be circumspect and we agreed she should be seen with me as often as possible. On the campaign, I mean. Carol's family is well-known in this area—better-known than I am, in fact—so we agreed she'd be seen at my side wherever I go. This seat is on a knife-edge as far as the Party's concerned, so every advantage we can squeeze out is important. That's right, isn't it, Carol? We agreed to this strategy.'

'Yes,' she said. 'We agreed.'

She said it, but I'm not sure she meant it.

CHAPTER THREE

I TALKED TO the Mintons for another few minutes but
realised they couldn't help me any further—I needed to
start seeing things with my own eyes. Before I left I asked
whether I could talk to Wolfe and Sally Collins again, in
case they had any ideas we hadn't discussed.

While Giles went upstairs to fetch them, I said to Carol,
'I'll do my best but don't get your hopes up. If his best
friend doesn't know where he is—or won't tell you—then I
doubt anyone else is going to let me in on the secret.'

'You're not exactly inspiring confidence.'

I saw that the reality of the situation was alien to her
and that she was prone to move straight to the worst
interpretation of every statement. She had stood up when I
stood up and had moved close to me. I felt as though any
minute she might pounce and hug me until I promised to
find her son.

'I'm sorry,' I said, 'I'm not being clear. What I mean is,
I'm confident he's okay. For example, it doesn't sound like
he's been kidnapped, which would be highly unlikely
anyway. To be blunt, you're not rich enough. And to be

even blunter, I haven't heard of any unidentified bodies being found in the last couple of weeks.'

Her mouth trembled and sagged in the corners. 'Please don't say that—you'll put ideas in my head.'

'I'm trying to tell you that's a worst-case scenario and it doesn't seem likely. What I meant was, he's probably taking time away, or perhaps he's struggling with the idea of going back to college. I understand that's a common complaint.'

She seemed to take this as a personal affront and withdrew, drawing herself up by stiffening her spine. More than most people, and like some actors I'd met, she seemed willing to use her body as a physical expression of her feelings.

'Do you have children, Mr Dyke?'

'A boy, a little older than Alistair.'

She paused, reconsidering what she was going to say.

'Then I hope you'll understand what it's like to simply not know. I don't really mind what he's doing, so long as it's nothing illegal. I just want to know he's safe. You'd think he'd extend me that courtesy.'

'Of course. Incidentally, do you have a photograph I can have?'

'In the last few years, since Alistair's been Alistair, there are only digital ones. In fact I need to go through our photographs again.' Her eyes became unfocused briefly and then she fluttered a careless hand. 'I don't think we have any in print. I'll email one to you.'

I gave her my card.

'All my details are on there. The sooner you can do it, the better. I'll start tomorrow morning.'

She nodded, then walked away absently as her husband came down the stairs, trailed by Wolfe and Sally.

WE ENDED UP in a small room that seemed to be a cross between a library and a TV lounge. One wall was filled with excitingly-titled business books while in the corner there was a mid-sized flat-screen Panasonic facing a single leather chair. I guessed Giles Minton watched business programs, or maybe golf tournaments, as a way of separating himself from his family. The room had the air of a masculine cave, dark wood and black leather and the husks of crushed nutshells scattered on the carpet.

Wolfe had decided to play along. He stood with his hands behind his back, pushing his extensive stomach into the space between us, and looked up at me with a resigned expression. Sally Collins stood behind him with the posture of an acolyte, head bowed. He took up so much space in the room, she had little choice but to shrink into a corner.

I said to Wolfe, 'I'm interested in why no one's made much of an effort to find Alistair before calling me in. Couldn't anyone find the time to drive half an hour to Stafford and knock on a door?'

'You're asking me? He's not my kid.'

'It's all politics, though, isn't it? You wouldn't want people to know the boy's gone missing and no one's made a short car trip to have a look around. What's your professional opinion of that?'

His expression didn't change, though a slight hardness came into his eyes. 'I'm here to look after the money. That's all. A bit of advice now and then, sure, but mainly I'm supposed to keep an eye on the ingoings and outgoings from the account.'

'How long have you known Minton?'

'I've known both of them almost twenty years. I used to do her father's books. Practically my first job when I qualified. My wife and I used to have dinner with them from time to time, before she passed away. We met at a Rotarian evening and hit it off.'

'As aspiring Marxists.'

He smiled. 'Keeping our powder dry.'

'When did your wife die?'

'Twelve years ago next month. Don't tell me you're sorry for my loss because you never knew her and it would be a hollow gesture, wouldn't it?' He added, 'It was cancer. Three weeks from diagnosis to death. We had no children. I live alone.' He looked at me as if daring me to find another set of questions.

Instead I turned to Sally. 'What about you? What do you think of the Mintons? Did you know Alistair?'

She glanced at Wolfe, who'd half-turned, and I sensed she was seeking permission, as if she didn't know what the rules were. She said, 'I've known them a while. I knew Deborah and Alistair at school. Though I didn't know Alistair well. We were all in different years.'

'And what did you make of him? Did he seem like the kind of son who'd leave his parents in the lurch like this?'

Now she blushed and I wondered what button I'd pressed. She came through with one of her winning smiles, though.

'Like I said, I didn't know him well. He seemed nice enough, but he was ... distant.'

'In what way?'

'Oh, you know, introverted. Like his dad. I shouldn't say anything—I'm just here to run errands, make tea, that kind of thing.'

Wolfe said, 'She's the daughter of a friend. Work experience, helping me out.'

'So do either of you know anything that might be useful in tracking Alistair down?'

'I thought that was your job,' Wolfe said. 'All the newspaper reports say you're Mr Shit-hot when it comes to hunting wild-eyed criminals.'

'Is that what Alistair is?'

'I have no idea, but I'm guessing not. My guess, if you want to know the truth, is that all this political business is driving him crazy and he's just keeping his head down. Reading his books. Sitting in the library. All that stuff that students do. When the election's over he'll come back wagging his tail and asking for money to buy a car or travel round the world. So if I were you I'd work as quickly as I could to find him, let Carol know where he is and what he's doing, then send in your invoice and bugger off. We've got too much at stake to be spending time on this. Lovely though Alistair is,' he added with a bland smile.

He was almost a head shorter than I was but I know when someone's trying to bully me. He said he'd known the Mintons for nearly twenty years, which meant he'd known Alistair practically all his life. But despite that lengthy acquaintance he was showing as little concern for him as he would for a stray cat—perhaps less. Being of a suspicious nature, I wondered whether he really thought Carol was being over-protective, or whether there was something he was hiding and so wanted me to wrap up the search quickly before it came to light. The idea that someone didn't want my involvement because they had something to hide was my general operating principle.

Or maybe recent history had just taught me to be suspicious of all politicians and their motives.

WHEN I'D FINISHED with Wolfe and Sally I returned to the giant living room and found the Mintons in almost the same poses as when I arrived. Their lives seemed to be lived glacially. Even the house seemed mired in time, each room a perfectly drawn image of a singular moment that had died as soon as it was created.

I broke the silence by telling them I was leaving and I'd be in touch when I had something useful to say.

Giles Minton raised his hand: it was holding a cheque made out to cover initial expenses. I had asked for this earlier, as I usually did, but I didn't always get it. Perhaps he was feeling guilty for arguing with his wife in my presence.

He said, 'I hope this covers it. I don't expect you to keep coming back for more.'

'For a minute there I forgot you were a banker.'

He almost smiled but thought better of it. He was a man of limited expressions and he harboured them zealously.

'I read about you after Carol contacted you yesterday. You're not exactly what I think of when it comes to private detectives in this part of the world. You seem rather more … explosive.'

'My clients haven't always been well-considered.

Perhaps I should vet them more carefully.'

'Perhaps you should.'

Then he seemed to lose interest in me and turned back to the panorama of his back garden, illuminated now by strategically-placed solar lights and a lamp-post similar to the one at the front. His eyes roved across the long lawn, the flower beds, now denuded of blooms, the wooden shed at its furthest end. Perhaps it reminded him of happier times, family times, when Other People didn't present him with so many problems.

———

CAROL MINTON SHOWED me to the door and I thought she was going to offer me another exhortation. But she walked me quietly across the entrance hall, her fingers light on my elbow, and closed the door behind me without saying anything except goodbye. I'd sensed a greater sadness in her the longer I was in her presence, as if she exhaled it along with her breath.

Now I stood for a moment looking at the stars, then set off down the drive. I'd almost reached my car when a voice called my name.

Deborah Minton was coming around the side of the house, walking with the heavy-footed lope you use when your boots are too big. She was smiling in the dark but seemed purposeful, as if she had something urgent to tell me.

She came close and looked up at me, her eyes large, the whites clear and moist against the encroaching night.

'Aren't you going to ask me any questions, Mr Detective? You seem in an awful hurry to get away from here.'

I leaned with my back against the door of my car, wondering where this was going. I reminded myself that the key is always to remain open to information.

'Just keen to get on with the job,' I said. 'A detective's life isn't all chat and social niceties, you know.'

'Oh I know! There's shoe-leather to wear down, bad guys to pin against walls, police inspectors to take the piss out of. All while screwing their beautiful clients. Or their daughters.'

I smiled one of my charming, lop-sided smiles.

'The daughters can't handle it,' I said. 'They run away squealing.'

'I've never squealed in my life.'

'I've only known you fifteen minutes.'

'How long does it take?'

'I've never run a stop-watch.'

She paused, still looking up at me.

'What are we talking about?'

'I have no idea. You started it.'

'I did, didn't I?'

She shifted her position and leaned next to me against the car.

'I was a bit rude in there,' she said. 'But really, Alistair never talked to me about things. You've met Mum and Dad—not exactly the most communicative family in the world. We all live in the same house but we go our separate ways.'

'What way is your way? What do you do?'

'Me? Why nothing, sir. Unless you count swimming. I'm doing a lot of swimming. I tried college for a year but I didn't like living away from home in a crappy flat, and I don't think the tutors were that wild about me anyway. So I'm having a gap year or two … or three.'

'What do you do for money?'

She shrugged. 'Look around you. We're drowning in cash. They don't let me starve. I've got a phone and there are some good charity shops in town if I need new clothes.'

'I noticed that black is the new black.'

'Your trained eye misses nothing. The truth is, I can't be bothered. It's all fashion, isn't it? "Fashion" as in, it'll go out of. Nothing's permanent today. I'm only nineteen and I'm already out of date.'

'I'm going to cry.'

'Oh for god's sake don't do that. We don't allow any emotion in this house. We have to be buttoned up and civil and never speak our minds. I'm going to be an MP's daughter, you know—I can't be seen to *feel* anything.'

I glanced at her. Despite what she'd just said, she obviously did feel something about her situation. And as a young person she felt the need to dramatise it. Perhaps she and Alistair had more in common than she thought. Perhaps he was simply acting out the same discontent she was describing verbally.

I said, 'Do you give your parents a lot of trouble?'

'Define trouble.'

I said nothing and eventually she smiled at me, as if I'd passed a test.

'Not for a year or two,' she said carelessly. 'Don't forget I'm a member of the idle nearly-rich. We've got to work to earn a living, but it doesn't have to be really stressful. And besides, there's always something to fall back on. A bank balance that magically doubles itself without any help from human hand.'

'Did Alistair feel the same way?'

'Who knows? Alistair was always secretive. Actually I'm not surprised if he's fucked off somewhere to get out of the way.'

'Aren't you worried something's happened to him?'

'Nah. He's a nerdy student. As far as I know he doesn't do drugs, doesn't drink to excess … he's absolutely wasting his student years by studying. You heard Mum—he always phones, always lets her know where he is and what he's doing.'

'You're presenting the case for your mother—if he hasn't called, he must be in trouble.'

She shook her head. 'No, I don't believe it. He wouldn't dare do anything to get into trouble. He barely casts a shadow. I think he's just pissed off with this whole political stuff so he's gone into hiding till it's over.'

'That's what Tony Wolfe said.'

'Oh fuck, don't put me on the same side as that creep.'

'You don't like him?'

'Put it this way, if he walks in a room I walk out of the other door. He's like that Shakespeare character whispering in Dad's ear all the time.'

'Iago.'

'That's the one.'

'So who's he poisoning your dad against? That was the point of Iago, wasn't it? He didn't like what Desdemona was doing to Othello so he turned him against her.'

She looked up at me.

I said, 'What? Can't a detective read Shakespeare?'

'It's not in the regulations, is it? You're supposed to

wear a long overcoat and carry a gun.'

'No overcoat, no gun. I'm a failure.'

She levered herself up from the car and pushed her hands into the pockets of her jeans. It was cold and I could see goose-pimples on her bare arms. She said, 'You should talk to Jack, see if he knows anything. Alistair preferred talking to him than members of his own family.'

I nodded. 'Thanks, it was on my list. Can you answer a question for me?'

'Depends. What is it?'

'Does it hurt to have a nose stud put in?'

She laughed. 'You thinking of having one?'

'I've always wondered whether it hurt.'

'Not so much that you'd notice. You hype yourself up for it and it does sting but it's finished in a second or two.'

'One little prick and it's over?'

'The story of my life.'

CHAPTER FOUR

IT WAS NEARLY midnight before the office door opened and Giles Minton walked in.

Wolfe thought he looked shattered, his skin dry and dark with the shadow of a beard, his eyes red in their corners. He knew Minton was having difficulty holding it together in these last few weeks. The strain of keeping up appearances for everyone you met, every day, all the time, was a burden that pressed you down like a physical weight.

Minton was holding two glasses in one hand and a bottle of Laphroaig in the other.

Wolfe said, 'I hope one of those is for me. I swear to god I'm eating paper mites in this fucking room.'

Minton set the glasses down and poured them an inch each.

He gave Wolfe one of the glasses, saying, 'How soon can we get Dyke to pack up and go? I didn't like him. Too cocksure. He came in and looked at me as if he wanted to throw me out of my own house and have his way with Carol on the living-room carpet.'

'Don't rush him,' Wolfe said. 'Remember we're doing this for Carol in the first place, just to show willing. You and I both know Alistair has fucked off somewhere so he doesn't have to speak to you, or me, or deal with the consequences of you being an MP. You don't like to hear it, but you and him are the same—neither of you likes change and would rather bury your head in the sand than face up to difficulties.'

Minton took a sip from his whisky and measured his words.

'I didn't have any choice. You've seen how she's been this last week, traipsing around the house like a moody cow. I had to do something or she might have burst into tears on stage right next to me.'

Wolfe cleared some papers off the single armchair in the room and sat on it. It sighed beneath his bulk. Minton took the black office chair, swinging it around to look at the computer screen and the figures it displayed. 'What's this?'

'Money stuff, nothing for you to worry about. Forget you were a banker for five minutes. You just need to get your head straight and concentrate on the next two weeks. A couple of big events are coming up and you need to be focused.' Minton continued staring at the screen until Wolfe said in exasperation, 'Giles—look at me. And listen. If Carol wants to waste time trying to find Alistair, let her. I don't like it and you don't like it but maybe it'll keep the peace.'

'You don't understand.'

'Believe me, I'm trying.' He lowered his voice, hoping that a show of intimacy would help. 'What does he have against you?'

'I don't know,' Minton said, 'but he doesn't trust me.'

'I can't understand why.'

'Don't be brutal, Tony. This is all a mess and it's partly of your making.'

'What do you mean?'

'Those people you sent to fetch him—it was only after they scared him that he dropped completely off the radar.'

Wolfe felt his face glowing red but kept his voice even. 'Don't blame me. How was I to know he'd do a runner? Did you tell Carol about the men?'

Minton looked at him derisively. 'Be serious. If she knew we'd sent two thugs to bring him back, probably against his will, she'd have a fit.'

Wolfe tasted his drink. Laphroaig wasn't his favourite whisky but it would do. He hated these conversations with Minton because they were vague and usually ended with nothing decided. He felt like a professional counsellor most of the time, just there to provide an ear for Minton to unload into. He preferred conversations that ended with a plan of action, something specific that you could tell whether you'd achieved it or not.

Minton didn't seem to understand that. Wolfe wondered what kind of Member of Parliament he would be if he preferred talking to achieving results.

A typical one, perhaps.

HE COULD SEE no way out of it—he'd have to bring up the Big Subject.

He said, 'Is this to do with that business when Alistair was a kid?'

Minton shifted in his chair and coughed and lifted his chin as if to clear any obstructions from his vocal chords.

'I don't know. I don't know what he remembers, what he saw—or thinks he saw. He's never mentioned it … besides, he was so young he couldn't have understood what was going on. Five years of age, for god's sake. I can still see his face poking around the shed. It's just … I've never felt comfortable around him, especially since he's been an adult. I catch him looking at me from time to time and wonder what he's thinking. But he's never mentioned it so I don't know whether he even remembers. Maybe he just hates me because of the politics.'

'Does Carol talk about it?'

Minton frowned. 'What do you think? We've tried our damnedest to forget the whole event. Why do you think I'm even running in this bloody election? It's all because of that … that … thing that happened. I feel like I've been escaping it all my life. I'm just hoping this is going to put it behind me forever.'

Wolfe realised Minton didn't want to pursue the conversation and *he* certainly didn't, even though he was the one who'd brought it up. It led to nowhere but grief and regret, which he didn't do. They didn't get you any concrete results.

He said, 'So what shall we do about Dyke? You realise he might actually find Alistair and even bring him back. I wouldn't put it past him to tie him in gaffer tape and throw him in the back of his car. We need to speak to Alistair and give him a good talking to before any of that happens.'

'I've been thinking about that.' Minton leaned over and made sure the office door was securely closed. His energy levels had risen, Wolfe thought. He really did like playing the game: politics. Minton went on, 'Carol wants to know Alistair is safe. I want that too, but I want him close at hand, if at arm's length. She wants him here so she knows where he is and can mother him. At least for a few weeks, until the election. As you said, I want to talk to him about consequences, for all of us. And to find out what he thinks he knows. Put him right, if necessary.'

'I'll see if I can organise a padded cell.'

Minton stared at him. 'So you see the last thing I want is for Dyke to bring him home in his present state of mind. Before we've had our conversation.'

'What state is that?'

'He's probably angry, upset at all of us. If he remembers anything concrete, we're fucked, and I'm afraid he'll want to betray me just to prove his point.'

'Christ Almighty—you're not asking for much, are you? Why on earth did you let Carol call Dyke anyway? It's complicating things way too much.'

Minton shrugged. 'I couldn't stop her. I'm taking away her normal life by doing this, even though she agrees with me it's the best thing to do, for us. Having Alistair in her pocket will make her feel better, even if he goes down to Stafford and comes back every night.' He paused and raised his eyebrows. 'What am I saying? I don't know what she's feeling and I doubt she could explain it. It's all a mystery to me, what women think and feel.' He sighed extravagantly. 'Now I've read up on Dyke I don't think it was a good idea to recruit him. He seems more competent and dogged than I'd like in this instance. Any suggestions gratefully received.'

Wolfe had tuned out, following his own line of thought. After a moment he said quietly, 'I've got an idea. I think it might work, but it's risky given the situation.'

Minton put down his whisky glass. 'What is it?'

'Okay, we've allowed Carol to have her way and hire an outside contractor to find Alistair. But we can't actually allow him to do his job because we need more control over the situation. What we need to do is keep Dyke out of circulation for a while. We've done the good deed by having him here and asking him to find your kid. But what if he were prevented from doing that job? I mean, physically prevented?'

'What are you saying?'

'I could get my people to rough him up, break a couple of extremities, perhaps, to keep him out of circulation. So he can't do what we've hired him to do.'

'That's a bit baroque, even for you.'

'We don't owe him anything. Hiring Dyke was done for Carol's sake. Now we just need to take him out of the picture for a while. And the beauty of it is, he won't know it's us behind it. We can plant the idea your political opponents heard a rumour he was working for you and some fanatics took it into their own heads to teach him a lesson. It's happened before. They've seen his picture in the papers and don't like the idea he's working for us. So they decide to beat him up. He might buy that. And if the press came sniffing around we could use the same story.'

Minton was already shaking his head, thinking through the consequences.

'So say the papers come around asking us for a comment about the famous Sam Dyke being beaten up while working for us. What do we tell them he's been doing? We've already told *him* we're operating under the radar so the press *don't* get wind of our problems with Alistair. If we admit to the papers he's working for us it would be waving it in their face, not keeping it quiet.'

'You don't understand,' Wolfe said patiently. 'This is just the cover story, *if* it got out that famous local detective Sam Dyke was working for us and got beaten up. In fact the priority is to convince him *not* to talk to anyone about it, tell him it's all politics, we don't want the wrong kind of publicity and so on. He has to leave the bad guys alone. On the other hand, if anyone gets nosey, we tell them it's our opponents who've done the dirty deed—but we didn't say anything because we didn't want to raise a stink until we were absolutely sure of our case. Mr Dyke was just working on some security issues for us until he was attacked because of his connection to the campaign.'

'Being beaten up might antagonize him, make him more determined to finish what he's been paid to do, find Alistair.'

'That depends on what happens to him, doesn't it? Not life-threatening, obviously, but serious enough to keep him out of action.'

Minton was quiet again, then said, 'So let me get this straight: we get someone from our side to beat him up so he can't carry on working for Carol. And if anyone asks questions we tell them it must have been the *other* side that did it for political reasons, because he was working on the campaign. Meanwhile we pay Dyke off and apologize and tell him to keep his mouth shut. Sounds shaky to me.'

Minton stared at the facing wall, a typical pose that

Wolfe knew indicated he was thinking it through. Finally
he turned his beautifully-coiffed grey head towards Wolfe.
'How soon?'
'Why hang around?'

CHAPTER FIVE

STAFFORD WAS A good half hour drive down the M6 and by the time I got there the chill of the night before had turned into a grey drizzle. I used my GPS to find the address Carol had given me and sat in the car for a while looking at the house Alistair Minton had shared with Jack Cooper. It was on a street of standard semi-detached red-brick houses, cars parked on what would have been the front garden thirty years ago and with most of the original windows replaced by uPVC plastic. There were little white porticos over each front door to add a sense of grandeur, and nests of aerials and satellite dishes vying for space on the roofs. The house the Mintons bought for their son would have been relatively cheap but was inoffensive enough to be a good investment.

I was still watching the front door when it opened and a stocky young man with red hair and wearing denim came out, locked it, and climbed on a push-bike that had been chained to the fence between the house and its neighbour.

He manhandled it down the short pathway and then took off down the street, turning towards the town centre when he reached the far end.

I followed at a distance.

———

IT TOOK US ten minutes to reach the town centre, which was smaller than I remembered, with narrow, twisty streets, many of which were inaccessible to cars. I was stuck at traffic lights when I saw him get off his bike ahead of me, walk it down a side street, and park it outside a café. I found a parking spot twenty yards on and walked quickly back to where I'd seen him.

Inside, he was sitting at a corner table with a latte and reading an economics text-book with a graph on its front cover. He had curly ginger hair that sprouted from the centre of his head like an unruly plant, and when he looked up at me I noticed first of all the forest of dark freckles beneath each eye.

I sat opposite him and he jolted upright, closing the book quickly.

I said, 'It's Jack, right?'

'Who are you? What do you want?'

'I'm a friend of Alistair's parents.'

'So what?'

'They've asked me to see whether I can find him—I mean, find out what he's up to.'

The mention of Alistair's parents didn't seem to relax him. He glanced over my shoulder, into the café, and took a tighter grip on his book. I had the feeling he'd have tried to run past me if he could.

He said, 'If you find him, tell him he owes me half the electricity for this month.'

'So you don't know where he is?'

'Who are you again?'

I leaned back in my chair so I wasn't crowding him. The café was fairly busy with a young crowd and Jack's nerves seemed to be on red alert, so I didn't want to give the impression I might create a scene.

'Look,' I said. 'No one wants to hurt Alistair—why would they? But his parents are worried because he's not been in touch. All they want is a phone call so they know he's okay. Can you get a message to him?'

'I don't know who you are and I don't know why we're having this conversation. Why don't you piss off and leave me alone?'

'Hey, don't be like that.'

'How did you find me here? Have you been following me?'

'That's a fair question.' I decided I needed to break the foot-thick ice between us. 'Incidentally my name's Sam. I live in Crewe. I drove down this morning to talk to you, but you came out of the house just as I was parking and I had to follow you into town, all right? I'm not here to scare you, just to have a conversation.'

'Do you work for the police? Has Ali's dad set you on him?'

I shook my head. 'I don't work for the police. Ali's mum asked me to come down and try and find him. You know how busy they are at the moment.'

He almost sneered. 'Yeah, all that election crap his dad's doing. I don't believe a word he says. Nor does Ali.'

'Is that why he's dropped out of the picture? Because he doesn't believe in his dad's campaign? Seems a bit harsh.'

His eyes fell to the table. He thought he'd said too much. He was trying to defend his friend and now he suspected he'd made things worse.

He said, 'I'm not his guardian angel and I don't know where he is every day. I said that to the two men his parents sent.'

'What two men?'

'A few weeks ago. Ali was out and these two weirdos came to the door asking for him. I didn't like the look of them so I told them I don't keep a record of where he goes and shut the door on them.'

'What did they look like?'

'Don't they work with you?'

'No, they don't. His parents didn't mention anything about this. They probably don't know. What were they like?'

Jack went on to describe a tall, thin man who had a dark complexion that was covered with white scars, and a shorter man with bright yellow hair.

'And they just wanted to talk to Alistair?'

'That's what they said. I wouldn't give them the time of day. Who were they?'

'I'll be fascinated to find out. Listen, get Alistair to call me. I'm not sure you're being completely honest with me about someone who's supposed to be your best friend.' I placed one of my cards on the table between us. 'Just tell him I want to talk. I don't mean him or you any harm. I'm just trying to find out where he is and whether he's okay.'

Jack had been looking at my card.

'It says here you're a private detective. I didn't think they really existed.'

'We don't in real life. I'm just a ghostly presence asking you to do your friend a favour. Enjoy your coffee.'

I stood up and left.

Jack had been more scared than angry at my following him. Whoever those men were they carried something with them that frightened the horses. It was the first hint I had that Alistair's disappearance wasn't just the result of a family dispute, and it made the case both more interesting and less straightforward.

I walked back to my car wondering whether I'd said the right thing—or if I even knew what that was. I hadn't pushed Jack too hard because I needed him to be on my side, and anyway, I sensed he knew more than he'd said.

In my line of work that was usually the precursor to a deep and meaningful relationship.

CHAPTER SIX

I'D DECIDED TO go home via the A34, avoiding the motorway, and I'd been in the car fifteen minutes when the call came through. I had an in-car system fitted so I didn't need to pull over to take the call, though I hated being distracted when driving. I braked and moved into the slow lane.

A voice said, 'This is Alistair Minton. I gather you want to talk to me.'

He was well-spoken, with one of those deep voices that wealth often seems to bestow on young men, as if they're made more manly by a large bank balance.

'Hi, Alistair, thanks for getting back to me so quickly.'

'Yeah, okay, whatever. So who are you?'

'I'd rather do this in person, if you don't mind. I'm on the road right now.'

'What if I do mind? I don't know you, I don't know what you want. Why should I meet you?'

'Okay, I understand that. My name's Sam Dyke. I'm in the phone book and Yellow Pages if you want to check me out. Your parents asked me to find you and talk to you.

They're worried because you haven't been in touch for a few weeks.'

'So what? I'm a grown-up, or hadn't they noticed?'

'Don't put me in the middle of this. I'm just the messenger.'

'Right, so you've delivered the message. Now what?'

'I'd still like to meet you face to face. Ask Jack about me. Ask him if I seemed trustworthy.'

'I don't know what you're talking about.'

And then he hung up.

FIVE MINUTES LATER the phone rang again.

'Where are you?'

'I'm heading to Crewe. I can turn round and come back if you like.'

'I haven't said I'd meet you yet.'

'So why have you called?'

'I'm thinking.'

'Haven't you taken this far enough? Just hang up and call your mother. That's all she wants. You can't blame her.'

There was silence at the other end. I'd come up behind a slow-moving lorry spouting black diesel fumes into my windscreen, so I slowed further.

'I don't have to talk to my parents if I don't want to,' Alistair said. 'And you can't force me or make me feel ashamed. It's my choice.'

'Okay, I agree with that. But can I at least meet you so I can tell your parents you're all right? No one else there but me, I promise. Tell me a time and I'll get there early and you can look around before you sit with me, check I'm not lying.'

Another pause. Then he said, 'The café on the railway station at Crewe. The outside one, on the platform going south. Do you know it?'

I told him I did and asked when he wanted to do it.

'Seven o'clock tonight. Do you know what I look like?'

'Yes. Do you know what *I* look like?'

'Yes.'

'Then we're not going to be talking to the wrong people, are we?'

Too late. He'd already hung up.

HE DIDN'T LOOK much like his photo when he came around the corner of the platform and stood inspecting the tables. He'd grown a straggly beard and his hair was longer than in the photo his mother had sent me. He'd turned into a student. He wore a blue cagoule and pale jeans. In that location he might have been mistaken for a train spotter. I'd taken the table furthest from the kiosk, so he could see there was no one with me. In fact, there was no one else in the area at all. I can have that effect on a place.

He saw me and wandered over, then sat down opposite me, keeping his hands in his pockets, as if to say he could take or leave this encounter. Then he relaxed and slid down the zip on his cagoule and opened it up.

I'd bought a flat white coffee which I kept in my hand to appear more casual.

I said, 'Hi,' but at first he didn't acknowledge me, as though he were still wondering whether to give me any of his precious time. I wondered whether he was embarrassed by the tensions he was creating at home, or the fact he was revealing the inner workings of his family to a stranger.

Then with sudden vigour he said, 'I don't know why everyone's so interested now. Nobody could give a shit before all this election stuff kicked off.'

'People are funny like that,' I said. 'They notice when people behave differently. Perhaps it's the change in your own behaviour that's brought on all this worry—not phoning your mother, hiding away and refusing to tell anyone where you are … and so on.'

His eyes were large and brown and now he put a little hardness into them, as if trying to persuade me he could be tough when he wanted. 'My family have had a hard time seeing what I am. You should try it some time, never being taken seriously for what you say, or think, as if you're an overgrown puppy sitting in the corner. I'm a grown-up, if you hadn't noticed. I don't have to answer to anyone.'

'People keep telling me you're an adult but I'm not seeing much evidence.'

'Fuck off.'

I'd been thinking how to have this conversation but already it was turning sour. I remembered what Jack had told me, and said, 'What do you know about those two men who came to your door and spoke to Jack? Do you know who they were?'

The eyes registered a tic of anxiety. 'They didn't leave a calling card so I don't have a clue. Do you?'

'Have they been again? Is that what this is about?'

He hesitated, then said, 'They came to the house and I left without talking to them.'

'What did they look like?'

'Bizarre … listen, I don't want to talk about them. I

want to know why my mother and father hired two men and a private detective to track me down. What's so important they can't leave me in peace for five minutes?'

I finished my coffee and placed the mug on the table. His eyes followed me as if I might suddenly smash it on the edge and use the jagged remains to attack him. 'Look, this is just a job to me. What's going on between you and your family is none of my business. As far as I know they didn't hire those other men—at least they weren't mentioned. I have no idea what that's about.'

'So you say.'

'I'm going to tell them you're all right, if a bit paranoid, and that everyone should just get on with their lives. How does that sound?'

He seemed to be considering the offer, but when he spoke it was obvious his mind had been elsewhere.

'It's the hypocrisy I can't stand,' he said. 'You don't know them. You don't know what they're really thinking. They're trying to put themselves over as on the moderate side of the party, keen on the EU, wishing nothing but happiness and good luck for all. But it's all bullshit. Look at the way they live, and where my dad worked before he gave it up for politics. And that wanker Wolfe—have you met him yet? He's someone you should be investigating, not me. Perhaps that's something you could do—see what he gets up to when nobody's watching. He's been around all my life and not once have I liked him. Even as a kid I knew there was something wrong about him, and I haven't changed my mind.' Shifting the topic of conversation had brought him to life, as though discussing his own experience hadn't been worth the effort. His skin had started to glow with an interior passion.

'Anything specific?'

'He only ever talks about money, or how to get it. You can't have a conversation without him bringing up the cost of something, or a deal he made, or how much money he's earning. I don't know whether he does it because Dad was a banker, so he thinks he'd be interested … or whether he's so shallow he can't talk about anything else.'

'People get fixated on the things that interest them.'

'I think it's psychotic.'

A train came in on the Manchester line and we watched as dozens of commuters got out of the carriages and headed towards the stairs and the outside world. A couple of people headed towards the café and took seats at separate tables, ignoring both us and each other, turning instead to their phones and the latest important bulletins from their social media.

When I spoke again I realised I was repeating myself, but I wasn't sure how much he'd taken in first time around. 'Okay, this is what I'll do. I'll talk to your parents and tell them you're okay. You're pissed off and need some time alone, but generally speaking you're doing all right. How's that?'

'You won't follow me or try to take me back to the house?'

'Not for the money they're paying me. Do you think that's what they want? To keep you wrapped up?'

The air seemed to leave him and he slumped, unable to keep up the victim act without real cause.

'Not really. But those men were scary. I still don't know who they were. I'd locked the bedroom door and they burst through it to get to me. You can't tell me my mother paid someone to do that, can you?'

'No,' I said. 'That seems a bit too … enthusiastic.'

But it *was* intriguing.

I WALKED BACK to my car thinking I'd done everything I could do. I'd left Alistair on the south-bound platform waiting for a train back to Stafford, standing with his shoulders hunched and his hands in his pockets and looking like any other miserable student with straggly hair and a half-formed beard.

If someone had asked me, I'd have said I wanted to get out of the situation altogether. The Mintons seemed like a family waiting for trouble to tear them apart. If Giles Minton became a Member of Parliament in a few weeks time I wouldn't have been surprised to see him resign after six months 'for personal reasons'. He didn't have the open-handed bonhomie I associated with successful politicians, his wife seemed passively resentful of the change to their lifestyle, his daughter had more energy and life than any of them but didn't know where to put it … and Alistair seemed haunted and somehow temporary, as if he wasn't fixed in time or place.

Looked at objectively, they were a mess, and I told myself I'd had enough of that in my own life to consider taking on someone else's.

I should have listened to the voice of sanity.

CHAPTER SEVEN

As MY CAR was parked only fifty yards from the main road into Nantwich, I thought I'd drive straight to the Mintons before going home. I soon left Crewe and let the car find its own way along the winding road out of town and past the large suburban houses that lined the route almost all the way to Crewe's snobbier neighbour. Cheshire's dark farmlands lay hidden in shadows to my left, breeding unhappiness and entitlement in equal measure.

It was still only nine o'clock when I rang the Mintons' doorbell, the moist darkness of the garden lit partly by an old-fashioned lamp-post placed in the middle of the front lawn and partly by a smaller version in the same design sited over the door. The house lay some distance from the main road, up a winding gravel track, and all I could hear was an insistent owl hooting forlornly in one of the trees behind the building. I knew how it felt.

Giles Minton opened the door and looked down at me along his straight nose. He wore a green Lacoste pullover and held a whisky glass in one hand, gripped as tightly as he might hold a weapon. After a moment spent in recognising me, followed by a second of obvious and almost insulting calculation, he said, 'Well this is unexpected,' and stood back to let me in. I brushed past him, catching a hint of an expensive aftershave, and waited for him to close the door. I found myself acting more formally, as if the Mintons' affectations of good manners were rubbing off on me.

Tonight there was a low throb of piano jazz coming from upstairs and the lighting was soft and welcoming, as though the house was relaxing after its emotional exertions of the day before.

Minton took me through to the same room we'd spoken in previously, where Carol was sitting at a polished table laying out photographs for a leather-bound album that was open to one side. Her hair was loose around her shoulders and the hollowness had vanished from beneath her eyes. I wondered whether I'd passed through some kind of Back-to-the-Future wormhole to a parallel universe where all the problems of its sibling realm no longer existed.

When she saw me, Carol smiled and put down the photographs in her hand. She stood and came towards me, bare feet riffling through the deep-pile carpet.

'Mr Dyke, you're back so soon. Do you have something to report? And would you like a drink?'

She'd come quite close to me and I was pleased by her physicality, though surprised it had arrived, apparently coalescing out of nowhere. I said, 'I'd love a drink but I won't, thank you.'

Giles Minton said, 'So what have you found out? Here, sit on the sofa.'

We sat in a cosy semi-circle with me in the centre, the

Mintons either side on the armchairs. You might have thought I was the vicar asking for assistance with the village fête.

———

I EXPLAINED WHAT I'd done that day and how I'd come to be talking to their missing son on Crewe platform less than half an hour before. Carol Minton breathed out audibly when I described his arrival and explained what I'd agreed to say to them: he was fundamentally all right and just wanted time to himself because the election hoo-hah was getting on his nerves.

'There you are,' Giles said, leaning back in his chair and striking a note that even I knew was too celebratory. 'We said all along he was fine. Blame me for his absence, if you must. He doesn't want his old dad to be a Member of Parliament and is sick of hearing me practising my speeches.'

'I'm sure it's not just that,' Carol said firmly, drawing a quizzical glance from her husband. 'We'd be lying to you, Mr Dyke, if we left you with the impression that everything's been sweetness and light in recent months — well, in years, really.'

'Carol—'

'No, I think Mr Dyke deserves to know. We should have said more yesterday, instead of sending him off with only part of the information he needed to do his job.'

'Mrs Minton, it's all right. I don't need any more information now. The case is closed.'

'No, it decidedly isn't. Do you know where our son is, if he's not in his home?'

'No.'

'Do you know how to contact him?'

'Not directly.' This was true inasmuch as Alistair had used a phone that displayed a different number to the one Carol had given me. That number was in my phone History but there was no guarantee it would reach him.

'Exactly,' she said. 'We have half of the information we need—*I* need, I should say. I'm grateful that you've found him and spoken to him, and that he seems to be well, but I'm left with a sense of anxiety. Can anyone explain that? Why do I feel no different than when you arrived tonight, Mr Dyke? What's the mechanism here?'

I noticed Giles Minton staring at his wife as if he didn't know who she was. He seemed to shake himself and took a sip of his drink, but said nothing.

Carol Minton looked at us each in turn but we couldn't answer her unanswerable question.

I WAS BEGINNING to see an old enmity emerging between them, not just based on their differing views of what to do about Alistair—it seemed to go back further and was maybe a defining element in their relationship.

Giles said, 'We can't instruct Mr Dyke to continue to search for Alistair if he's already found him. Don't you see that? What would be the point? We just have to accept the result of his findings and move on. Carol, please.'

I could see she was now close to tears. When I'd arrived she'd been almost cheerful, but what I'd told her about Alistair had made her feel worse.

She was shredding a tissue in her hand and now she

looked down at it like someone who realised she'd been tearing a kitten apart. She threw the wadded tissue on to the coffee table.

She said, 'Can we find something for Mr Dyke to do on the campaign? Perhaps he could work on security, for example. The police people we get are very nice, but it's a bit impersonal.'

'Out of the question,' Minton said, shifting in his chair. 'For one thing we don't need it. For another it sends entirely the wrong message if we're trying to tell people we're one of them, not an elite who've been sent in from afar to govern them.'

'Christ, Giles, we won't be hanging a sign around his neck saying "Stand clear of the bodyguard".'

I'd been looking for an opportunity to bring up the part of the story I'd kept from them so far. This looked like the chance. I said, 'I have to tell you something else about Alistair's story. I don't know what it means, yet, but I think you both should know.'

Alarm lit Carol's eyes and she tensed. 'What? What is it?'

I told them about the two men who'd been to see Alistair, worrying Jack initially and then almost chasing Alistair down.

'Great Heavens!' Carol said. 'Why didn't you mention this before?'

'Because I'm not sure what it means. These men haven't been seen again and we have no idea what they were after—though obviously they were serious.'

Carol was looking at Giles with urgency now. 'Giles—for god's sake say something. What do you think we should do?'

'How do I know?' Minton said, almost desperately, a man who'd suddenly found himself thrown into the deep end of a pool with experience only of the shallows. 'I can't think about all this right now, I've got too much on my mind.'

'Giles! It's your son!' Carol said, and for a moment I thought she was going to reach over and slap him across the face.

'I know,' he said quietly. 'I understand, of course I do. But Carol you know perfectly well I can only handle one thing at a time. It's in my personality. Let's ask Tony what he thinks before we do anything rash, can we?'

Carol Minton stared at him for a long time, then stood up and left the room without looking backwards at either of us. Minton and I avoided each other's eyes for a moment, then he too stood up.

'I'm sorry about that,' he said. 'I hope you understand she cares very deeply for Alistair. We'll need to think about this a bit more. Perhaps you'd better stay away for a day or two.'

I stood up but neither of us offered a hand to shake.

I think neither of us was happy with the way the day had ended.

BUT IT WASN'T ended yet.

It was almost 10.30 when I turned into the long driveway that leads up to my own, newly re-built house. It had been burned down by some Far Eastern thugs a couple of years ago but insurance and compensation paid out by the local police authority had allowed me to reconstruct it almost as new.

It wasn't the same. The original build had been over a hundred years old — the walls were out of true in places, the exterior brickwork degraded, the roof-tiles in need of repair. All of which had given it an almost Dickensian character that seemed to suit me. The replacement I'd built was like an impostor, superficially the same but missing something deeper in its bones.

I'd parked on the gravel outside and was searching my pockets for my front-door key when the first blow struck me from behind. It felt like a piece of wood or a baseball bat, catching me just below my right shoulder blade.

In these situations you need enough experience and savoir-faire to keep moving, even though you just want to double over to ease the pain. Fortunately, this wasn't the first time I'd been caught by surprise and I'd learned a couple of things.

I let the force of the blow knock me forward, but then I headed into a forward roll, moving away from the initial perpetrator and coming up to face him.

And discovered there were two of them: one tall, one short, both wearing close-fitting black outfits and balaclavas. One was carrying a piece of wood about two inches square and three feet long. The other was wearing some kind of brass knuckle-duster on his right hand.

They didn't hesitate but came straight towards me, perhaps not seeing that I now had my house key protruding between the fingers of my right hand. And they probably didn't expect me to step into them.

The man on the left, the short one, was holding the

wooden spar. I stepped inside his arc of swing and hit him with a straight left on the nose, knocking him back. I'd felt a satisfying crunch. The man on the right, the taller one, had already swung at me, but I turned my shoulder to him and ducked as he connected. My upper arm felt the stinging blow, like being hit with a brick, but I brought up my left hand again and clawed at his balaclava.

He knew what I was trying to do and raised both hands to protect his identity … which gave me the opportunity to raise my right hand, the key still between its knuckles, and slash it down across his face and fingers.

He yelped and stepped back and I glanced left, to the shorter man, who was standing staring at me, holding his nose, the wooden spar at his side. 'You fucker,' he said, breathing hard. 'You better stop working for that arsehole Minton. His politics are … are … all wrong.' Then he turned and ran away down the drive.

His partner was also turning away, his hands still at his face, and he added: 'You bloody right-wingers,' then stumbled after his colleague. I let them go.

I leaned back against my car and massaged my right shoulder, trying to get some feeling back into it.

At least now I knew what the two men who'd frightened Alistair were up to.

CHAPTER EIGHT

WOLFE HAD JUST switched on his electric blanket when he heard the banging on the door. He went downstairs, peered through the front window, and said, 'Shit.'

When he opened the door, Jordan and Stevie almost fell through it. It was close to midnight and the street behind them was empty, the blurry orange light from the streetlights falling on parked cars like mist.

'Fuck,' Wolfe said, 'what are you doing here? I thought you were taking care of that thing?'

'Yeah, well,' Jordan said, the older and taller of the two and the one who had less hesitation speaking his mind. 'You didn't tell us he'd fight back, did you? Just an investigator, you said, made me think he was one of those old guys with a pipe and a tie.'

'I told you to watch out for yourselves—you didn't fucking believe me, did you? You're so full of piss and vinegar you thought you could manage it standing on one leg.'

'I dink he broke my dose,' Stevie said, then added, 'Hey does by voice sound fuddy?'

Wolfe noticed that he was holding a bloodied handkerchief to his face. He said, 'No more than usual. Don't stand there like a prick, come into the kitchen. What happened?'

As they moved through to the back of the house, Jordan told him what they'd done and how Dyke had reacted. They'd said some political stuff, Jordan said, so he wouldn't guess they were acting for Minton. He'd blame it on the other lot.

Wolfe shook his head. These two were the only people he could use for work like this—unless he got really heavy—and they kept proving they weren't up to it. He'd known Jordan off and on since he was thirteen, and when he recently ran up enormous gambling debts in London Wolfe had offered to pay them off, in return for occasional bits of work. Jordan had spent a year in the army before they kicked him out so he thought he was tough, and he certainly wasn't afraid of anything. After the army he'd gone down to London for a while and got involved in protection racketeering for the Wo Shing Wo Triad. He'd come back north because his face had been cut when he'd failed to pay the first instalment of a debt, owed to a Triad member. The retribution for non-payment had been painful. He only stopped worrying about further attacks after Wolfe sent them the money. The lacerations criss-crossing Jordan's face weren't abstract lines, they were writing in Chinese calligraphy. He'd never told Wolfe what it said.

Wolfe said, 'Did he see you? Would he recognise you?'

Jordan avoided his eyes and said, 'We dressed like burglars, balaclavas, gloves—everything. He didn't see us.'

'Not even your face?'

'Nah—I had goggles on and a scarf round my mouth.'

'If Dyke saw you and then he hears something from Alistair about you, your face, we're fucked.'

'He didn't see us! We were protected!' Jordan looked to Stevie for support. 'Weren't we? It all happened so quick anyway.'

'I hit him a good one on de shoulder,' Stevie said, standing up from the sink, where he'd been soaking his handkerchief and then rinsing it out after applying it to his nose. His yellow hair looked matted and dirty. 'You'd dink he was ready for it, de way he come back at us.'

'He had a knife or something in his hand,' Jordan said. 'Tried to slash my face. Got my hands instead.'

He held them out so Wolfe could see. The backs of several of Jordan's fingers had been scored with something but probably not a knife, otherwise they would have been cut more cleanly.

He said, 'Tidy yourselves up,' and walked out, too angry to be rational.

THEY CAME INTO his sitting room five minutes later, smelling of testosterone and looking like a circus act in search of a circus. *Jesus Christ*, Wolfe thought. *My comrades in arms.*

He said, 'So he's not injured in any way, but you've turned up here acting like extras from Night of the Living Dead, right?'

Jordan sat down facing him. Stevie, as usual, didn't know what to do with himself so tried to sink into the background. He was Jordan's friend and did what he was told, but Wolfe had no belief he was trustworthy.

Rubbing the back of his hand, Jordan said, 'Look, just fuck off with all the jokes, will you? Why didn't you tell us he could fight? We were going in blind, on your word. I'm getting sick of this shit, chasing people around the country just because you paid a couple of my bills.'

Wolfe barked out a laugh.

'A couple of your bills? You'd be lying face down in a turnip field if it wasn't for me putting my hand in my pocket. What they did to your face is nothing compared to what they'd have done if you hadn't paid up.'

Now Jordan looked away guiltily. *He knows I'm right,* Wolfe thought, *fucking toe-rag.* He said, 'As long as he didn't see you there's no harm done. He'll probably put it down to a burglary gone wrong—is that right? Did you at least nick something from the place?'

'I broke a window,' Stevie said. They looked at him. 'Well I tried to. It was toughened glass or something. I put a dent in it, though.'

Wolfe closed his eyes.

Jordan said, 'So what's next? Do we have another go at him? How much more have I got to do before I've paid off what I owe?'

'No, you don't have another go at him, at least not yet. I'll talk to the boss and see what he says. Stay away from him, by the way. He shouldn't know who you are. Fuck it, *I* shouldn't know who you are, the amount of grief you're bringing me.'

'Thing is,' Jordan said, 'I've got no money. You haven't paid the petrol for us to get to and from Stafford, and that was weeks ago. If you want us to hang around just in case, we're going to need a bit of life-support, know what I mean?'

Wolfe felt his cheeks blooming red. 'Jesus Christ, you fuck up twice and still want paying? You should be paying *me* for keeping your head above ground.'

Jordan was nodding. 'I know, I know … but I've still got to eat and pay the rent on my shitty little flat in Chester. And if you want us to hang around, doing nothing like proper work so you can call on us when you want, then we need a … what do you call it, a retainer. Board and lodgings. Can't you get it from the posh twat you're working for? Doesn't he have money?'

Not yet, Wolfe thought. *Not yet.*

CHAPTER NINE

WHEN I WOKE up the next morning my right shoulder was throbbing and I had a massive bruise on my back, beneath the shoulder-blade. I gave up on my fitness regime for once and instead soaked in a hot bath. My mind had been working overtime on the two men who'd attacked me and I was certain it was the same men who'd tried to get at Alistair—whether it was for a conversation or something worse, I didn't know.

The tall one had looked like a 1930s aviator, with goggles worn over his balaclava and a scarf wrapped around his mouth, but it didn't matter. I'd seen enough of the skin around his eyes and his cheeks when my car-key had snatched down the balaclava that I knew it was the scarred man Alistair and Jack had both mentioned. The question was: who did the men work for? What did they want? They'd shouted some political phrases but they felt gratuitous, as if they didn't even know what they meant.

I realised I hadn't questioned Alistair enough on this. He said he didn't know them and I'd accepted his statement at face value. But perhaps I could have dug a little deeper and pushed him. So I needed to talk to him again.

———

I'D ALSO BEEN considering what to do about Giles and Carol Minton. The night before he'd asked me to keep my distance … but that didn't seem good advice to me, after the attack. If they were the same men who'd gone after Alistair, my time would be better spent trying to find them and unearthing the connections between all this underhand activity.

A Google search located Minton's election office and their telephone number. I had breakfast, then I called the number and it was answered by a well-spoken young man who said Giles was going to address a public meeting in Wistaston, and gave me the location of the event. It was a ten-minute drive and I thought it would be good to see Minton in politician-mode, so I got in my car and headed out through the sluggish morning traffic.

———

THE HALL WAS a single-story white building whose car-park was crowded and outside of which fifty or sixty members of the public stood around in thick coats, talking amongst themselves half-heartedly, like film extras. I drove past the building and found a parking slot around the corner then walked back towards the hall.

Wistaston is a fairly prosperous village and the vehicles in the car park reflected the income and taste of its inhabitants, including a number of low-slung sports cars as well as some larger BMWs and Range Rovers. The sky was grey and low and seemed barely able to maintain its altitude above the red-brick, semi-detached community it covered. The clouds looked ready to offer up their rain at the slightest hint of trouble.

As I arrived back at the hall the doors opened and the public started to filter inside. I hung back and eventually stood against the rear wall, looking at the back of the well-coiffed heads of the audience and, at the front, a small stage on which Giles and Carol Minton were seated like nervous actors preparing for curtain up. A stick microphone waited for them at the front of the stage and I wondered how Giles felt about this kind of public display. The behaviour I'd witnessed from him so far had been reserved, egocentric and single-minded. I couldn't see him transforming into a barn-storming demagogue just because someone thrust a microphone in his face.

Now another man emerged from the audience, where he'd been talking urgently with Tony Wolfe, and stepped up to the microphone. His features went through several changes in a short period of time—a smile, a frown, a surreptitious glance at his notes, a cloud of confusion—then he found the expression he wanted and tapped on the microphone and called everyone to order. He was a man in his forties, slight and earnest and wearing a semi-professional outfit of tweed jacket and red knitted tie.

He began by welcoming us to Wistaston and to the local branch of the party, reminding us to take some of the literature when we left—to hand out to 'friends and foes alike!'—and gesturing to some vague offstage repository of the pamphlets in question. Then he briefly introduced Giles Minton before stepping back daintily, applauding as he did so, like the host of a second-rate talent show. The faithful in the hall picked up the applause and kept it going for fifteen seconds or so while Giles stood up and fiddled with the microphone. Finally he decided to take it from its stand and hold it under his chin.

'Well,' he began. 'This is a good turnout for a wet Tuesday morning, isn't it?'

There were some chuckles from the crowd and everyone smiled at everyone else, ignoring the fact that it wasn't actually raining outside. Perhaps Giles had been told the forecast was for rain and had built it into his ice-breaking comments …

He went on for a while thanking the local staff, the organisers of the event, the councillors who'd arranged for the hire of the hall … and then he seemed to run into a blank space where his speech was supposed to be.

He stared out at us, his grey hair glinting in the single spotlight the stage afforded, his mouth fixed in a half-smile. The crowd was still with him and smiled back expectantly, rustling slightly. The silence was on the verge of being awkward when at last he seemed to wake from whatever dream had been haunting him and he swallowed, licking his lips, glancing down to where Tony Wolfe was sitting on the front row. Next to Wolfe I saw Sally Collins' halo of blonde hair, tilted slightly back as she too looked up at Minton. I could sense both she and Wolfe urging him on silently.

Minton turned his gaze on us and said, 'I'm going to address the elephant in the room first of all. This party has not typically been associated with standing up for the rights of the foreign workers in our midst. But as you know, this is something I feel strongly about. I stand for self-determination, for fairness in employment practices and for the establishment of a business culture that encourages individual success—but not at the cost of social inequality.'

He paused and looked around the room and I think he saw me at the back, though he registered nothing. Perhaps I was just part of a general blur.

He went on, 'For too long we've been seen as the party of selfishness, as the party of resistance to change and, yes, resistance to the presence of foreigners in our midst. There are some who have called us racist. There are some who've said we're only here to enrich the top one percent of our population—the ultra wealthy—and if I'm perfectly honest, given my background, that's a charge it's hard to refute. But this is exactly why I'm running for office in this constituency. I understand the way our society works, what fuels it and how to make it run more efficiently.'

He paused and looked around again. The silence was as tense as that of an audience watching a high-wire act. I wondered whether they were as familiar with his policies as he seemed to assume.

'But I also know that we can't continue the way we have. We can't cut ourselves off from our nearest neighbours and expect to be taken seriously as trading partners. We can't renege on our financial commitments. And we certainly can't continue to put up barriers between ourselves and the other great nations of the world, either near or far. Immigration is a difficulty. But it's not a little, local difficulty. As the earth continues to warm we're going to be confronted by ecological disaster on an enormous scale. Immigration will be driven not just by wars, by people escaping their riven countries, but by sheer physical necessity. Their lands will be underwater. Or, conversely, will be so dry because of a lack of rain that they cannot support life any more. We will be a haven for immigrants from countries who have never before featured in the lists of immigrating countries—not just the Middle East, Syria, Turkey and so on. But the coasts of India, the Philippines. The Far East. And our job will be to find a way, with our continental neighbours, to make this new world work. If we don't we will literally be over-run. These people who have nowhere else to go will be here anyway. We can accommodate them. We *must* accommodate them. Or we as a nation, as a continent, as a planet, will die not through lack of water, or air, or sustenance ... but through lack of conscience.'

Now he looked down and seemed surprised to find he was holding a microphone. He leaned forward and placed it back on its stand, just as the first sounds of applause emerged from the front rows. Within moments the sound was taken up further back and those around me, at the rear of the hall, raised their arms and with shining faces and thunderous hands gave Minton their blessing.

He looked around and glanced shyly at his wife as the applause rang loudly off the walls.

Carol's face held a smile that was both slight and mysterious, as though she were thinking about something none of us could possibly understand.

———

MINTON WAS TAKING questions when a man in his thirties

with a sharp face, a haircut that made his head look like a peach and large black-framed glasses came up to me and nodded familiarly.

He said, 'You're Sam Dyke and I claim my five pounds.'

His grin was open-mouthed and over-friendly, as if we'd been mates for years. I felt my features pinch together as I looked down at him.

'Whatever you're selling, I don't want any.'

His mouth opened further in joy and now his eyes joined in the merriment.

'You don't know me, I can tell, but you're pretty well-known in my neck of the woods.'

'I gave up my subscription to Alcoholics Anonymous Weekly.'

He ignored this and turned to look to the front of the room, where Giles Minton was now engaged in a long description of his plans to revitalise the centre of Crewe. Good luck with that, I thought. The man said, 'It's all right, I'm not hurt. I'm a hack, I can take anything you can throw at me so long as I can write it down afterwards.'

I glanced at his profile. He'd been right, I hadn't recognised him. I thought I knew most of the journalists in the area by now, but not this one.

He said, 'My name's Forster.' He turned to look up at me. 'I know why I'm stuck in this living hell reporting on a boring wannabe crony politician, but why are you here? This isn't your beat usually, is it? No kidnappings, no bombs about to go off, no massive heists going down in the Town Hall ... or are there? What's going on?'

'If I told you I'd have to kill you.'

For a nano-second he was alarmed, then his curiosity

kicked in again and he leaned forward.

'Is it security? Is it the kids—Deborah, is she at it again?'

Now my curiosity was piqued. I grabbed his arm and took him outside, leading him away from the door where a group of smokers eyed us carefully, as if we'd come to confiscate their drugs.

I said, 'What are you talking about?'

'Okay, okay, go easy, jesus … I bruise easily.'

'What are you saying about Deborah?'

He glanced around and the amusement returned to his eyes.

'It's nothing serious,' he said. 'I'm not casting dispersions, everyone knew about it.'

'Like everyone knows I have a low patience threshold.'

'Okay, okay, she had a bit of trouble a year or two ago, didn't she? Got thrown out of college for some sexual shenanigans. That's all I know. I was just wondering if you were a chaperone or something. Though come to think of it, I haven't seen her this morning. They keep her on a short lead now, don't they? Is she here?'

'Even if I knew I wouldn't tell you.'

'Oh come on, don't be like that. You have to admit it's weird you being here. You can't blame a chap for pushing his luck.'

'Who was she was supposed to have been involved with?'

He was laughing again, his mouth open, his tongue working away behind his teeth. I'd never met anyone so enamoured of his job.

'Well not another student,' he said. 'Who'd give a shit

about that? No, she was having it off with one of her tutors. That's why it caused a fuss, even before Mr Holier-than-Thou in there had any prospect of running for MP. But of course as soon as he announced his plans, it all came up again. After we'd dug it out of the archives and plastered it over page 5 with a teasing headline. No names, you understand. Even we couldn't do that, without being one hundred and fifty per cent sure. But everyone knew who we might be talking about. It's a question of family morality, isn't it? They need to be squeaky clean.' He grinned again. 'That was our editorial approach—the dangers of what might transpire between tutors and students.'

'Do you know the tutor's name?'

'Not offhand.'

I thought about that for a moment, then said, 'What relevance do Deborah's problems have to her father making a good MP?'

'Oh, none, none at all.' He was all innocence. 'But it's interesting, isn't it? There might be some relevance eventually, once we've worked at it for a bit.'

'That's why you're so loved by your readers.'

He lowered his head briefly in a mock bow. 'Thank you. Now look, let me know if you need anything—anything to help you do your job, whatever it is. I can get you up to speed on all sorts of issues.' His hand slipped a business card into my jacket pocket.

'And what do you get?'

'What do you think? An interview. Gossip. Any tidbits you think our readers would be interested in. We're very flexible.'

'Well,' I said. 'I'm not. Don't talk to me again or you'll see just how inflexible I can be.'

I left him grinning at me and went back inside the hall.

INSIDE, THE MEETING was breaking up. Wolfe was up on stage talking to Minton while Sally Collins was talking to his wife, who looked exhausted by the whole thing. I made my way to the side of the stage and waited for either of the men to see me.

It was Wolfe who noticed me eventually, looking around to see if anyone had noticed and then walking towards me heavily, as if each step cost money. He said, 'Giles told me this morning what you said about those two men going after Alistair. I don't understand what's happening with that boy, but Giles said he asked you to stay away, at least for the time being. So given all that, what are you doing here?'

'Something interesting came up. Bring him over, we need to talk.'

'This is what I was afraid of—you get your hooks in and then we can't get rid of you.'

'Yeah, that's me. The sort of man who thinks ethics is a county outside London. Is that what you mean?'

I stared at him until he turned away and caught Minton's eye. Minton broke away from his conversation with an earnest woman and came over.

'I thought we agreed you were to keep your distance,' he said. 'Carol is under a great deal of stress. Look at her. Did we or did we not agree to that arrangement?'

'In so many words. When I got home, things changed.'

'What do you mean?'

I described to them the attack made on me by the two men, together with my conviction they were the same two who'd been tracking down Alistair.

Minton and Wolfe glanced at each other, then Wolfe said, 'How can you be sure it was the same men? You said they were wearing balaclavas and so on.'

'I saw enough of his face to catch sight of the scars Alistair described. And I think the other one had strands of yellow hair sprouting out of his balaclava. It's too much of a coincidence, anyway. Do you have any idea what the hell's going on?'

Wolfe said, 'Did you call the police?'

'No—do you want me to?'

'No, not if you haven't already done so. Are you hurt?'

'Just bruises. I'm hoping I might have broken the blond one's nose. And there's something else.'

'What?'

'They tried to make out they were attacking me on behalf of your election opponent. They spouted some nonsense, warning me off from working for you.'

Wolfe looked at Minton before saying, 'So you didn't believe them?'

'Not entirely. Why would they come at me, somebody who doesn't even work on your campaign? Not officially. How would they even know?'

'Politics is a small world, I'm sure they've found out through the usual gossip. Perhaps your notoriety angered them, or riled them up.'

'You're missing the point.'

'Am I?'

'If it's the same people who were looking for Alistair, why was I the next target? What did they want with him, and then me? What's he got to do with your politics? And what did they think they could get from me? It's all random.'

Wolfe put his hands in his pockets and watched two men stacking chairs for a moment. Then he said, 'So what do you want to do?'

'I'm thinking about it.'

Giles Minton was looking down, as usual, but then he pulled a face, as though he'd spotted something unsavoury on my shoes. He said, 'You must do what you think fit. As for myself, I can't see how this has got anything to do with us. Were you robbed? Did they break into your house? Perhaps they were just common-or-garden burglars ...'

I shook my head. 'No, you don't carry a piece of wood like a baseball bat if you're going to break into someone's house. Some tools and a swag bag, that's it.'

'And they didn't have a swag bag,' Wolfe said distantly.

There was a pause as we considered this, then Minton said, 'So what do we do now? I refuse to see this as having any connection to me or to Alistair or to my campaign. I think it's just a bizarre coincidence, perhaps stemming from your colourful recent past, Mr Dyke.'

Around us the party helpers were deconstructing the minimal set that had been built on the stage—the standing posters, the microphone, the two chairs on which Giles and Carol Minton had sat. Part of me wanted to be deconstructed too—set aside, put away, left to stand in a corner until next required. The environment around the Mintons was toxic, laden with poisons and chemicals that were proving bad for my health.

On the other hand, I couldn't get the image of Alistair out of my mind as he stood on the platform at Crewe, hands in the pockets of his cagoule, staring up the line waiting for a train to take him back into an unknown peril.

Nor could I quite forget the various expressions of pain, hurt and resentment that had flitted across Carol Minton's placid and regular features as she listened to the men arguing around her.

So I told Wolfe and Giles Minton that I'd be in touch. I'd found Alistair and spoken to him so I'd fulfilled one part of the contract. We could discuss any future engagement later, if they wanted to use me again.

In the meantime I told myself it was a tactical withdrawal only, and that if Scarface and Yellow Hair thought they'd got away with giving me a couple of bruises, they were mistaken.

CHAPTER TEN

Wolfe watched Dyke's back as the man pushed through the people remaining in the hall. *He's so superior,* he thought. *If I was six inches taller and a hundred pounds lighter I'd have punched him in the face …*

He turned to Minton and said, 'He's more of a fucking problem than I thought he was going to be. Don't talk to him unless you absolutely have to.'

Then he realised that Minton was staring at him in cold fury.

Wolfe said, 'What? What now?'

'Those people of yours,' Minton said. 'Where did you get them? Is there a special web site where you can recruit idiots and morons to screw up straightforward jobs? Or did you have to go to a head-hunting firm specialising in simpletons for hire? Idiots-R-Us?'

'That's not fair—'

'I don't care if it's fair or not, you're bungling this. And I don't even know what it is. I don't know what we're doing here, either with Alistair or with this man Dyke.' He glanced around and lowered his voice, noticing that Carol was alone on the stage, staring at him coolly. 'Can you tell me what the problem is, exactly? Why are we spending money on trying to prevent something that may never happen?'

Now it was Wolfe's turn to feel angry. He pushed close to Minton, letting his size intimidate him.

'Don't you say that to me, you shit. It was you who wanted to bring Alistair back in. You're the one who's worried about what the precious sunbeam might say unless he's kept in hand. I've run everything past you and you've agreed every step of the way, so don't try to come off all high-and-mighty and above the fray. You're up to your neck in it, my son, and if you don't get your head on straight I'll be walking out. I'm only doing this because you're a friend, and I'm beginning to wonder how deep that goes.'

Minton recoiled and Wolfe felt the man's fear coming at him like cold air from an open refrigerator.

Then Minton surprised him, saying, 'It seems to me that Dyke is not going away. He'll go home and lick his wounds and then he'll come back and talk to Carol. He'll get into her good books and find a way to keep digging. He knows as well as we do that what happened to him last night is connected to me, to the campaign. He doesn't know in what way yet, but he'll be looking at me and he'll be looking at you. Can you guarantee there's no official connection between you and these half-wits you're using?'

'Nothing official, no. I'll tell them to stop coming to the house. I'll get another phone.'

'Tell them to stand by but do nothing. For all we know Alistair will come to his senses and come home anyway and it'll all blow over.'

'Do you think?'

'Not a snowball's chance in hell.'

He walked away, leaving Wolfe again staring at a retreating back.

THE BUILDING WAS almost empty now. Wolfe looked around but couldn't see Sally Collins. Carol was still sitting on her chair, looking down at the floor as if expecting the floorboards to crumble beneath her.

Then Sally appeared at his shoulder. She looked even paler than usual.

He said, 'How's Carol doing?'

'She hates these things but feels obliged. I understand that—they can be dull.'

'Get used to it. You're going to hear the same speech a few dozen times before we're done.'

She was nodding. 'I agree with him. About immigrants, I mean. With global warming everything's going to get worse, isn't it? People are going to be on the move, and not just those he talks about in his speech. Anyone who lives next to the sea is going to be in danger.'

'Oh, for fuck's sake, Sally, it's a routine. He's a stand-up comedian going through a routine to please a crowd. It'll wash in Nantwich but let him say the same thing in Stoke-on-Trent or Burnley—he'd be strung up.'

He knew he was shocking her but he didn't care. Her face was like a perfect painting and he wanted to ruin it, make it cry.

'Are you saying he doesn't believe it?' she asked,

her voice sharp.

'You be the judge of that. What was he? A banker. What do bankers do, these days? Help rich people keep hold of their money while preventing poor people getting any of it. If you think he gives a toss about immigrants, you're deluded.' He watched her take this in, then added, 'I'm not trying to shock you, Sally—well, maybe I am. But this is politics and politics is PR. We're selling Giles Minton so that people will buy him. We have to stay above it and not get sucked into sampling the product ourselves. Do you understand? I'm teaching you a lesson that'll stand you in good stead in whatever you end up doing. Remind me what you did at university.'

'Languages.'

'Good. Learn the language of marketing—it's easy to pick up. You just take a turd, spray paint it and then dip it in Chanel No 5. Then you work hard to convince everyone it's an unusual and tasty slice of cake. It's not that difficult. People want to be sold to. They want to feel they're getting something special, something that's never been on sale before. The art is in finding the suckers, then adjusting your product so they really want to buy it.'

'I don't want to believe that,' she said, and he wondered why there was a sudden fierceness in her eyes.

'What's happened?'

'I heard you and Mr Minton talking. Some of it. I came out of the side door, looking for you, and you didn't see me.'

'What do you think you heard?'

'I can't say. It didn't make much sense. But I don't think you've been honest with me, Tony. I might have to quit.'

Wolfe put his hand on her shoulder and smiled. 'You say anything to anyone and you're in big trouble. Do you understand?'

She looked up at him with round eyes but said nothing.

CHAPTER ELEVEN

I WAS SITTING in my car outside the meeting hall, still thinking about my confrontation with Wolfe and Minton, when Deborah Minton rang. I presumed she got my number from her parents, but I wondered whether they knew she had it and, moreover, whether they cared. Her voice was quiet, almost apologetic, as though she was going to tell me something I needed to hear in spite of the pain it was going to cause. She said she wanted to see me as soon as possible and I asked why.

'I want to talk to you in private.'

'Can't you tell me over the phone?'

She hesitated. 'I could, but that's sort of impersonal, isn't it?'

'I thought you kids did everything by phone.'

'We do everything but talk, if you want to know the truth.' She named a coffee shop in Nantwich and asked how long it would take me to get there.

'Less than fifteen minutes,' I said.

'So you're close anyway.'

'Closer than I want to be.'

'You certainly know how to motivate a girl.'

'It strikes me you don't need any motivation.'

'That's for me to know and you to find out, isn't it?'

—————

WE MET IN the upstairs café of a bookshop in the centre of Nantwich. The windows looked out over the central square, a few dismal Tuesday morning shoppers heading into W.H. Smith for a newspaper or a birthday card. The rain had come and gone while I'd been driving here and the pavements glistened darkly.

Deborah had arrived before me and was sipping a short espresso, her demeanour laid-back, idly curious and amused. I bought a latte from the counter and approached. She watched me as I took off my jacket and draped it over the back of a chair. I felt she was sizing me up. She wore a short leather jacket and a thick woollen scarf wound tightly around her neck. As I sat down opposite her she shifted her position and became more serious.

'The ladies here don't like me,' she said conspiratorially. 'They think I'm letting the side down. They all know my dad and probably can't believe how he could have spawned someone like me. Alistair, on the other hand ...'

She let the thought trail away dreamily, wanting me to invent my own version of his masculine perfection in their eyes.

I said, 'Do you really care what other people think? It seems to me you like to challenge people, or even piss them off, just to get a reaction.'

Now she leaned back, her eyes glittering at the prospect of a competition. 'That makes me sound like a bored princess, doesn't it? Nothing better to do than tease the servants or throw red meat to the dogs and watch them fight over it.'

'Is that the image you've been cultivating?'

She laughed lightly. 'Do I look like a princess? Can you see me in spangly shoes and an evening dress?'

I took a sip from my coffee and watched her over the rim of the mug. Two nights before she'd seemed younger, a little naive and essentially innocent. This morning she was acting like a siren from a 1940s film noir, extending her body on the bench seat facing me, raising her face and looking down her nose … I almost expected her to lift a cigarette holder to her lips and take a sucking drag on a long white cylinder, blowing out the smoke in a pale cloud of disdain.

I said, 'This is your meeting. What did you want to tell me?'

'Oh, yes, right, get down to business. Time is money and we don't waste money so why should we waste time? That's one of my dad's. He used to tell me that when I was six years old. Imagine.'

'Perhaps he had good reason …'

'Oh ha ha. You bloody men are so practical, aren't you. Okay …' She sighed and sat up straight on the seat. 'When we were talking the other night I gave the impression that Alistair was probably upset by all the politics in the household and had gone into hiding because of it.'

'And I said you weren't the only one who thought that.'

'You did. But now I think I was wrong. I started wondering about it after you left and I couldn't see it like that. Everyone's saying it's politics and I think I believed them, but to be honest I don't think Alistair gave a shit about what Dad was doing.'

'So if it wasn't that, what was it? Have you got an alternative theory?'

'That's not the point, is it? If Dad hired you to find Alistair, that's your job, not mine. I'm just telling you he's not in hiding because he didn't like all the talk of politics. If he *is* hiding, it'll be because of something else. I don't know what.'

'So you don't want me to have any wrong impressions of your brother, even though it sounds like you barely knew him?'

She shrugged. 'He's not here to defend himself, is he? Not that he'd do that anyway.'

'Did your parents tell you I've already spoken to Alistair?'

This surprised her. 'You're kidding. You let me ramble on like that when you've already talked to him. Thanks a bunch. What did he say?'

'You're right, it wasn't the politics … he talked about hypocrisy. He says your mum and dad are trying to pass themselves off as something they're not.'

'Like what?'

'More socially liberal, perhaps.'

She giggled, lifting a hand to her mouth. 'Now you *are* kidding. Mr and Mrs Banker, socially liberal? You haven't heard the conversations I've heard.'

'What does that mean?'

'Guess. I told you once to look around the place, at the money. Do you really expect people living that life-style to have liberal leanings?'

'Having money isn't the only deciding factor in your politics. Look at you.'

'What about me?'

'You're not a right-winger, are you, despite your upbringing?'

'I can't bear politics. Lots of people shouting about things that are not interesting to me.'

'Do you have any reservations about what your dad's doing—standing for Parliament?'

'It's not up to me to have any reservations, is it? I'm Princess Minton.'

It felt as though we'd arrived somewhere, though I didn't know exactly where. I remembered what the journalist had said to me after Giles' speech and wondered whether I could raise the subject.

Instead of tackling it directly I went on a roundabout tour.

I said, 'Do you have a boyfriend?'

She grinned as though I'd given her the opening to a punch-line. 'You want to apply for the position?'

'Just wondering.'

'I'm off men for a while.'

'Why's that?'

'They're trouble, aren't they? Say one thing and do another. Do one thing and say another.'

'Are we still talking about your dad?'

Now she frowned, her blue nose-stud moving and catching the light briefly. 'Why drag him back into it? I'm talking about real men. Other men.'

I leaned over the table. 'I heard you had some trouble a year or so ago. What was that about?'

Her expression didn't change. 'Who told you that?'

'It doesn't matter. Is it true?'

'What do you think?'

'I think it could be. I think you're daring enough to try anything, and trying anything can get you in trouble. What kind of trouble was it?'

Now her lips moved slowly into a small smile. 'I hate to be obvious.'

'I heard it was man trouble.'

'You see, I have all these hormones …'

'Which man? I heard it wasn't another student.'

She looked shocked. 'What would be the fun in that?'

'So … a tutor. Who was it?'

'That doesn't really matter, does it?' she said.

'You know I'll find out eventually.'

'I expect nothing less. It's your job. Though it has nothing to do with the job you've been hired to do.'

'I'll be the judge of that.'

She was about to reply when my mobile phone rang. I found it in my jacket pocket and answered. It was Carol Minton.

I said, 'What can I do for you this morning?'

'Where are you?'

'In Nantwich.'

'Good. I'd like to see you—would that be possible?'

'Certainly, give me a time. I can be there within half an hour if you're at home now.'

'That would be fine. Giles has gone to the office but I'm at home. Come when you can.'

We hung up and I found Deborah Minton watching me closely.

'That was my mum, wasn't it?' she said. 'I recognised the desperation in her voice. Go gentle with her.'

I was working on a reply when her own phone rang and she held a finger up to me and answered, saying, 'Hi, Sweetie,' and then waved me away with an imperious hand.

CAROL OPENED THE door distractedly when I rang the bell and turned away, heading back into the depths of the house. She'd changed from her official Candidate's Wife's dress into a loose top and black pants. They couldn't disguise her figure as I followed her through to the sitting room. By night the room looked cosy and rather sophisticated; in daylight it looked drab and worn out, as though the furniture had been bussed in from a failing antique shop.

The central heating was set to stun and I took off my jacket when we arrived. She pointed to one of the upright chairs at the table where she'd been sitting the previous night and I draped the jacket over it. She sat on the blue sofa.

'Please, sit,' she said, with the formality of an ambassador's wife greeting a local tradesman. Which, in a way, I was. I wondered why the formality had returned after the cosiness of the night before, but she broke it almost immediately by smiling. The Minton mood switches were dazzling.

I sat facing her and she leaned forward earnestly.

'What did you make of Giles' speech this morning? He's very sincere, isn't he? Were you persuaded?'

'He seemed to believe what he was saying, which is a form of sincerity I suppose.'

'Sincerity can be faked. Not that I'm saying he was — faking, I mean. But he's a politician now and you can't always believe what they say, can you?'

'Do you?'

'Do I what?'

'Believe what he says.'

The smile had seemed to have settled on her face … but now it was switched off and she became morose.

'Of course I do,' she said. 'The foundation of our marriage is that I always believe what Giles says.'

'That sounds to me like you're not allowed an opinion of your own.'

She glanced over at me sharply. 'Just because you don't share our political convictions doesn't make us Neanderthals, Mr Dyke. Giles and I are a team. We speak as one. It's no hardship for me to align myself with him on a vast range of subjects.'

'I'm not interviewing you for the Daily Mail, Mrs Minton.'

She caught herself and leaned back and a flush reddened her throat and cheeks.

'Of course not.' She laughed unconvincingly. 'I'm doing a good impression of a Stepford Wife, aren't I?'

'It's none of my business how you two run your election campaign.'

She seemed to take this as a cue and pointed a wagging finger at me.

'Exactly. That's it. What *is* your business, Mr Dyke? Why did you come to the meeting this morning after Giles asked you to stay away?'

So neither her husband nor Wolfe had told her I'd been attacked—perhaps to prevent her worrying about the same thing happening to Alistair.

I said, 'I was just finalising the business arrangements with them.'

She narrowed her eyes. 'You're lying to me. You're a very bad liar. I expect you've got a code or something, haven't you, about lying to clients … and you just broke it. You're hiding something from me. Everybody hides things from me. I must be such a gentle flower. What is it?'

'Ask your husband.'

Now she did an extraordinary thing. She lifted her legs on to the sofa and laid back on it, staring at the ceiling and allowing me to look at the length of her body, one leg slightly raised, her breasts full, her profile sculpted. Her pale blue eyes were almost transparent from a side view. She knew I couldn't avoid looking at her. Nor did I want to.

She said, 'We've talked enough about my husband. It's time we talked about you.'

'Probably not a good idea.'

'Is there a Mrs Dyke? Mother to your child?'

'She's not with us any more.'

'Oh, I'm sorry to hear that.' She glanced at me, shifting her head slightly. 'Does it bother you if we talk about your past?'

'Not particularly. I could send you my clippings to speed up the process.'

'I've already read them. Why do you think I called you the other day to offer you this job? Do you call it a "case"?'

'I call it a closed case. I've been paid my expenses and

an invoice is in the works for completion of the initial contract. My staff are working on it as we speak.'

'You have staff?'

'My son owns a printer.'

She smiled again, at the ceiling, her lips pulling back minimally across the line of her teeth, her eyelids wrinkling. But it wasn't real. It was as though she was animated by some inner puppeteer manipulating gears and levers. I wondered what mental compartments were being opened up to her by the absence of her son and whether she could be held responsible for her subsequent actions.

'Ah yes,' she said. 'Your son. Is he a good son? Does he talk to you? Does he check on you from time to time to see that you're okay, that you haven't been shot in some wild shoot-out, like Wyatt Earp?'

'Mrs Minton, why did you ask me to come over today?'

Her expression changed again and she sat up, brushing down the top of her pants and pulling at the creases. It was as though she were returning from a long journey—and perhaps she was, in her mind.

'I wanted to ask you,' she said, 'whether you're certain that Alistair's safe. You mentioned two men the other night, and the more I've thought about them the more concerned I've become.'

'Why do you think that is?' I said.

'No, why do *you* think that is? I've heard nothing but platitudes and obfuscations from Giles and Tony—I was hoping you would be honest with me. Do you think Alistair is in any danger? And if so, from whom?'

I waited a while before answering because I thought she might say more. Eventually I added, 'I can't answer that. I don't have enough information yet. When I met him he didn't seem overly worried and he had no idea himself who the men were. He doesn't seem to have made any enemies—he didn't confess to owing anyone money, or stealing someone's girlfriend, or bullying anyone … So, do you know something that I should know?'

She had pushed herself back into one corner of the sofa while I was speaking and her eyes were moving back and forth as if searching an inner database.

While she was still thinking, I said, 'In fact, you can tell me something, if you will.'

'What's that?'

'Why does Giles seem reluctant to pursue this? Yes, he's allowed you to call me in, but he wants me to keep my distance now. I have to say, he doesn't seem to share your concern for your son's safety.'

She blew out a long breath and all of a sudden I could see the source of her daughter's body language and general attitude. Deborah was a younger version of her mother. And they both had a sexuality they didn't care to disguise.

'If you must know—and I suppose you must—Alistair and Giles haven't seen eye to eye on things for a while. Pretty typical, isn't it? With me, the mother, cast as peace-keeper. What a cliché we are. Even Deborah is following the script.'

'The affair with an older man?'

Her eyes settled on mine briefly then moved away, as if she'd seen something she didn't like—or couldn't face.

'Yes, that. Thank god she seems to be over it now. She's a lot more … calm. I suppose we've spoiled her.' She shifted her position again, arching her back and pushing her breasts out as a result. She didn't look at me, but said, 'Do you think I'm a bad mother?'

'I've no idea what that might mean.'

'Don't be obtuse, Mr Dyke. Do you think I've been lax with my children? I find it hard to … accept that I've got grown children. That's hard for a woman to do. Getting older is difficult, especially when men don't look at you the same way they did only ten years before.'

I knew she was fishing for a compliment but I was in no mood to respond to the bait. I said, 'Everyone gets older, Mrs Minton. Better that than the alternative.'

She sighed again and withdrew into herself, drawing up her knees and hugging them tighter.

'We get older but we don't really learn, do we? Our characters keep ploughing on as they've always done. Getting us into trouble. I see that in my husband, incidentally. The poor thing is so introverted he can't express himself adequately.'

The conversation had come round again to a topic I could deal with. I said, 'So Giles and Alistair were not getting on?'

'I'm afraid it's the politics. That's what Giles says, anyway. Even though Giles has taken this line on immigration and the EU, Alistair still can't see it. Can't see us clearly, what we're trying to achieve.'

'He said you were hypocrites and you didn't believe what Giles was saying.'

'Did he?' she said, almost dreamily. 'Maybe he's right— who knows?'

'Could it be that Alistair is more to the right politically than you two claim to be? Is he over-compensating?

Children do that sometimes—like the children of atheists who become avid church-goers.'

'No, he's always been to the left of Gandhi … it's not that.'

'Then what is it?'

Still avoiding my eyes, and attempting to appear more business-like and practical by sitting up again, she said, 'I'm sorry, I don't want to go into it.'

'Is there something else?'

'Like what?'

I was exasperated now. 'You tell me. You're the one who asked me to drive over here for a little chat.'

'I don't pay you to badger me.'

'You're not paying me at all. This is a free consultation. But if you did, you'd pay me to find out the truth, because that's what I do. And at the moment I don't think you have a very good grasp of what that might look like.'

———

I DROVE HOME and had a late lunch—tuna sandwich, on toast. I sat in my living room looking out of my window at the fields falling away behind the house and wondered what had just happened. It was as though Deborah and her mother had been working in tandem on their seduction routines, while at the same time trying their best to irritate me.

Or maybe the daughter had just learned so much from her mother, she didn't realise when she was using the same tactics.

But Carol was the one who intrigued me the most. She was old enough to know exactly what she was doing: she was using her sexuality to find an advantage of some kind. She was trying to throw me off my stroke ... so why? What did she hope to get from confusing me? Did she really intend to seduce me, there on the compliant blue sofa? Was I supposed to react in a purely masculine way and take up her offer ... if it was truly an offer?

No, of course not. She would have screamed blue murder on the blue sofa.

The point was to make a point—to tell me she was still a woman with a sexual appetite, to say something covert that might later become overt, when she'd further explored the lie of the land.

What had begun as a simple case of tracking down a missing student was morphing in front of my eyes into something more convoluted.

I didn't know where it would end, but I'd soon receive an indication of a possible terminus.

CHAPTER TWELVE

AFTER LUNCH I drove to my office in central Crewe to check my post and use the desktop computer. I still kept an office for the sake of professional appearances, though nowadays I did most of my work from home.

The post was nothing but junk, so I treated it as such, but there was a message from my occasional partner, Belinda McFee. She wanted me to ring her back, so I did.

'I'm staring into space,' she said, 'wondering if a rich client is ever going to walk through my door.'

'Do you advertise?'

'No.'

'Do you network?'

'No.'

'Do you have a box in the Yellow Pages proclaiming your services?'

'I'm beginning to get the gist of this conversation, and I promise I'll get a website soon. How do you get *your* clients, Sam. You never seem to be short of work.'

'It helps having a reputation as a bad-ass. Perhaps that's something you should work on.'

'I'm not selling my pink Volvo.'

'I never said you should,' I said. 'But perhaps you could have it sprayed a more … aggressive colour.'

'Hot pink is very favourable to my aura …'

'You win some, you lose some.'

Belinda was one of the toughest people I knew. Every time she worked with me she seemed to suffer an injury of some kind but she didn't blame me and kept in touch. She was living in South Manchester and I don't think she had many friends: she didn't do small talk.

She said, 'So what are you working on now? Can you tell me?'

I said I could and outlined the Minton case. It was breaking client confidentiality but I treated Belinda as part of my extended team, working under contract from time to time, so she was effectively bound by the same rules and she knew it.

'Sounds like you didn't do anything they couldn't have done for themselves,' she said. 'What's the family like?'

'The usual middle-class dysfunctional mess. Both the mother and the daughter are sexually frustrated, if I can still say that. Mind you, so am I, so I'm not throwing any stones.'

'The love of a good woman would only screw you up, Sam. You couldn't take the attention.'

'You make me sound like a sad case.'

'And your point is what?'

'Anyway, the men of the household are not much to write home about. The father is introverted and self-centred and seems to be a politician in name only. He gave a rousing speech about immigration this morning but I didn't believe a word of it. And Alistair, the son, is still going through teenage angst even though he's at university.'

'Any idea who the men were, the ones who tried to beat you up?'

'Nobody knows—or if they do, they're not saying.'

Belinda was quiet for a moment. Then she said, 'When they hired you, did they only want you to find the son? Or was there something else?'

'That was the job, allegedly. Then Minton and his election agent, Wolfe, wanted me out of the way as quickly as possible.'

'So they got you in to do a job a child could have done, then sidelined you immediately. Sounds to me like they were covering their backsides.'

'It looks that way to me, too. They were keeping the little woman happy but don't really care whether Alistair comes home or not.'

'So it was the wife who wanted to hire you?'

'Yes, and she's still worried about the boy, despite the fact I've spoken to him and he seems fine.'

There was silence as we both chewed over Carol Minton's state of mind.

Then Belinda said, 'What's the husband's attitude now?'

'Hard to say. Either he didn't care one way or the other about Alistair—which I find hard to believe—or he already knew the boy was safe and thought hiring me might somehow bring that to light, making all the worry he'd put his wife through seem cruel.'

'And if he already knew the boy was safe, why didn't he tell his wife?' she said. 'It would have made things easier all round.'

'Because he didn't want *her* to know …? But that makes no sense.'

Belinda thought for a moment. 'Or for some reason he didn't really want Alistair spoken to or contacted. He was happy for the boy to be off in the wilds somewhere.'

'Which suggests he didn't want Alistair under foot, back home in the limelight, taking part in the campaign, the dutiful son … Well none of that was going to happen anyway because he doesn't care and he's supposed to be a student.'

Belinda sighed. 'It all sounds messed up. You should just get out and leave them to it.'

'I intend to,' I said. 'But thanks for the advice, and the commentary. If I need a spare pair of hands I'll let you know, okay?'

'Don't leave it too long. I believe I see a stretch limo pulling up outside my place right now … my luck's turning. Speak to you later.'

WHILE I'D BEEN talking to Belinda another call had come in and gone to message. I retrieved it and recognised Tony Wolfe's voice.

'Yeah, Dyke, I know we asked you to stay away and everything, but could you call in tonight at the Mintons'? About seven o'clock would be good.'

I made a mental note and hung up the phone—which rang again immediately. It was Sally Collins, Wolfe's young assistant. She spoke quietly and I thought I heard a tremor in her voice.

After she introduced herself I said, 'Sally, are you all right? You sound stressed.'

'I stole the number from Mrs Minton's phone book. I didn't know whether you'd answer.'

'I'm here now, answering. What's the matter?'

'I want to talk to you, in private.'

'We can talk now if you like.'

'Not on the phone. Face to face.'

'Okay,' I said, 'when would be good for you?'

'Tonight,' she said quickly. 'When it's dark. I can come to you. I can drive to Crewe.'

'Where do you live? I can meet you there if you prefer.'

'No! No … it's all right. What about that big hotel on the roundabout near the station? In the bar, there?'

'I have a meeting at seven. Can we make it eight-thirty?'

'Who are you meeting?'

Something told me to play it carefully. I said, 'I'm sorry, I can't say.'

'Oh, all right. Eight-thirty in the bar. Don't tell anyone.'

'Of course not,' I said.

I hung up, feeling deflated. There was something in her behaviour that led me to believe other layers were being peeled back from this case. I hated when that happened.

CHAPTER THIRTEEN

I ARRIVED AT the Mintons' house early and sat in my car in their driveway, watching the shadows play inside the lighted rooms. I'd only known them a few days but my view of them had changed dramatically. I'd once thought they were gilded and the inhabitants of a world where everything was dealt to them: riches, health, looks. Now it seemed to me they were like circus freaks, burdened and unhappy and unable to support themselves without a huge hinterland of helpers and hidden resources.

Of which I had been one, at least for a short period.

Wolfe answered the door and stood back, saying nothing. He pointed me to the room where I'd first interviewed him and Sally, a small room off the entrance hall. There was no sign of Carol and no sounds from the rest of the house.

Giles Minton was already inside the room, sitting in the leather chair and staring into space. His face was pale and his skin dry, and even his grey hair had lost some of its lustre.

He stood up and shook my hand and then we all

remained on our feet. He seemed to find my closeness disturbing and edged away until he was standing in front of the TV screen. Wolfe stayed behind me, almost as if he were guarding the entrance—or preventing my exit.

I said, 'I brought an invoice, in case you want to keep your accounts up to date,' and handed over an envelope. Minton took it and dropped it on a small drinks table.

'We'll pay it within seven days,' he said, clearing his throat. He added, 'We just wanted to tell you that you can't continue to come to my events or talk to the members of my family. We asked you to keep your distance but we want to take it a step further. As far as we're concerned you've done your job and there's an end to it. Do you understand?'

'You could have said all that over the phone.'

'Some things are better said in person,' Wolfe said, behind my back. 'Look, we don't have any hard feelings but you were seen talking to a journalist this morning, then we've had other people asking what you were doing there. I didn't realise you were so well-known to the running-dog press.'

'You'd better smile when you say that.'

Minton said, 'I've talked to Carol and she agrees with me that Alistair must be fine. She's been getting overly-anxious about something quite ordinary.'

'You didn't tell her about the attack on me, though, did you?'

'How do you know that?'

'I saw her this morning, here, after your speech. Didn't she tell you?'

I realised my question was abrasive and challenging but

I was getting tired of being the punching-bag for their superiority.

'No,' Minton said, his eyes registering the unexpected information. 'She didn't. What did you talk about?'

'We talked about you, and whether you're trustworthy or not.' His eyes flicked towards me. 'Don't worry, she said you and she were a team. Then we talked about Alistair and Deborah.'

'Anything else?'

'She's worried about those men—the ones who seemed to be after Alistair and who, though she doesn't know it, tried to beat me up.'

'What did you tell her?'

'Does it matter? Your voice is far stronger and persistent than mine. She'll believe what you want her to believe, in the end.'

'I suppose so.'

He appeared to drift off again and Wolfe pushed past me to gain his attention. He said to me, 'If you keep talking to the family, or turning up at events, we'll have to report you for harassment. We wouldn't want to do that, because you've been very helpful, but we have to focus on the campaign now all this is behind us.'

'Is Carol comfortable with this decision? Or is it something else you haven't mentioned to her?'

'I told you,' Minton said, 'I've spoken to her.'

'You told me she's agreed to stop worrying about Alistair. You don't appear to have told her anything about me being canned.'

I suppose the expression Wolfe adopted at that point was a sneer. I'm not sure I've ever seen one before, except on TV. He said, 'So that's why you talked to her this morning, was it? Trying to get more work out of us? A bigger pay-day?'

'Nah,' I said. 'You're on my shit-list now. I wouldn't work for you if you paid double, upfront. You're not worth the hassle or the cost to my self-esteem.'

'Brave words from someone who's just handed over an invoice and expects it to be paid.'

'An honest day's pay for an honest day's work. Do you begrudge that?'

'Stop it!' Giles said suddenly. 'Tony, please leave us alone for a moment.'

Wolfe hesitated, then said, 'Fuck it,' and pushed past me again to leave. The space in the room seemed to expand. Minton said, 'Please, sit down.'

I watched him sit in the grand leather chair and I took a seat on a small stool that was pushed into a corner.

He said, 'I'm going to tell you something now that you can't repeat to anyone. Is that understood? I want you to know what the cause of all this … business … is.'

The pallor of his skin had gradually disappeared during the meeting and now his cheeks were full and pink, as though he'd slowly been growing more embarrassed—or perhaps ashamed—as time had passed. He looked down at his hands, then at the blank television screen.

He said, 'Seven or eight years ago Carol started having anxiety attacks. She would get anxious about inconsequential things—like crossing a street she didn't know—and she'd have heart palpitations. Then she would have long periods of depression followed by emotional outbursts where she'd cry and scream at me—and at the children. At first we thought it was the early onset of the menopause but the incidents were believed, in the end, to be too serious for that diagnosis. Finally, after a particularly difficult outburst, she went into a … a unit, where she was treated for several weeks.'

He looked up at me with hollow eyes.

'We all thought that she was cured,' he went on. 'Over it. The pills and medication had done their job, we thought.'

'Is she relapsing?'

'I don't know, and I don't care to find out. I love my wife, Mr Dyke, and I couldn't bear to see her go through all that again.'

'Then pull out of the election. Let them find someone else.'

He became almost wistful. 'I wish I could. You don't understand the pressure the party association puts on you. Having gone through the selection process, you're the focus of their emotional investment. They can't switch horses, as it were, mid-stream.'

'Even when your wife's mental health is endangered?'

'We have four weeks to get through. If I lose, it all goes away. If I win, at least the pressure is released somewhat and our situation changes. Either I go away to London and stay there during the week, meaning she doesn't have to see all the political stuff. Or we find somewhere together down there and I can look after her while I'm working. We just have to get through these weeks.'

'So why are you telling me this now?'

He took out a handkerchief and blew his nose. 'I'm afraid Tony saw this as a simple transaction and has treated you like a tradesman, which wasn't very nice of him. Of us. I'm appealing to you now to consider the human cost of all this. I'd rather you didn't feed my wife's fantasies, or anxieties. So please stay away. I'll see if I can use alternate means to get in touch with Alistair to ask him to contact his mother.'

I stood up, feeling a little soiled.

'I take it the children knew about their mother's condition at the time?'

'Yes, of course they knew. It was inescapable. Perhaps typically we all tried to smooth it over. And then she went away for a month and I took them to visit once a week. We came home afterwards and didn't talk about it again.'

'Perhaps you should,' I said. 'It might save you some misery later on.'

I DROVE AWAY from the Mintons' thinking I'd probably never see any of them again, except on TV. It was possible that Giles would win his election and it would be all over the local media, and then he'd pop up from time to time on the national news. The election had been called in the first place because the sitting Member had resigned in disgrace after a financial scandal—he'd been found taking gifts from a local businessman and not declaring them in the MPs' register of interests. The limit above which MPs were supposed to register any gifts or benefits was £300 in any given year—this nincompoop had accepted a brand new Mercedes from a local car dealer and had then gone to bat for him when the dealer wanted to knock down a listed building to create a new forecourt for his cars.

The corruption had rubbed off on his party, so it was a probability that Minton would win the seat.

Despite ridding myself of the Mintons, I'd promised Sally I'd meet her so I drove back to Crewe and parked in the Best Western car park, then walked through into the bar. I had half an hour to spare so I chose a seat and found a newspaper someone had left on a table. I read about Europe and I read about politicians and given what I knew about Giles Minton and his domestic situation, I started to think about things differently. A few years ago I'd handled a case involving a man who was on the cusp of becoming a Secretary of State—except his ambition and lack of conscience had done him in. I'd got to know him but I knew nothing about his family background, his wife, his children ... with Minton it was different. They were all vulnerable, including Giles, but the threat to them came from within, not from me or from anyone else.

I began to wonder whether it was the same for all politicians—their greatest weakness was perhaps their lack of understanding of the environment that created them.

SALLY COLLINS APPEARED on the threshold of the bar looking completely out of place. Despite her jeans and short jacket, she actually belonged in a movie from the 1950s, clutching a handbag and wearing a two-piece suit and pearls, her hair intricately coiffed. I shifted in my seat to catch her eye and she smiled tightly and came across, sliding into a chair and starting to wriggle out of her jacket.

'I was early,' I said. 'I've been catching up on your game.'

'What's that?' she said.

'Telling lies for fun and profit. Politics.'

Her smile was replaced by a pouting frown and she settled herself further into her seat. I looked at her properly for almost the first time. Her blonde hair was also evidenced in her pale eyebrows and lashes, and she had a country-girl ruddiness in her cheeks despite her white skin. She didn't appear to wear make-up but she was pretty enough without it and didn't need any more decoration.

She settled herself down and placed her hands on her thighs. Then she glanced up at me with a look that suggested she was carrying a burden larger than she wanted to bear.

'I'm not going to work for Tony Wolfe any more,' she said. The thought seemed to brighten her momentarily. 'I've discovered that I don't like politics and I certainly don't like working for people who are negligent with the truth.'

'Negligent?'

Her face now suggested a struggle to pin down exactly what she meant. 'I've worked for Mr Wolfe for a few weeks and I have to say, there's something odd going on.'

'Odd in what way, Sally?'

She sighed. 'You have to understand this is the first job I've had in politics. I've got a degree in languages, specialising in French and Spanish, and I've been trying to get work in government. I even went down and lived in London for six months, in Twickenham, going for interviews and so on …'

'But you're back here now.'

'It seems I can't do interviews,' she said. 'I freeze. My

personality doesn't come through—that's what one person told me in the feedback. They all give feedback, now, as if I'm terribly interested in why they didn't want me. It's so bloody condescending—excuse me, I shouldn't swear.'

'That's okay, I've been known to let the odd swear word pass my lips.'

Her smile acknowledged that I was probably more street-wise than she was. She said, 'I'm sure. Anyway, I thought you ought to know that there's something going on between Tony and Giles Minton.'

'What kind of something?'

'Tony meets people from time to time, people he doesn't want *me* to meet because he keeps me away from them. And he won't let me near the accounts. I know he was a trained accountant and everything, but I'm pretty good with a spreadsheet myself and I'm sure I could have helped him. But no, he won't let me near them.'

'Do you think he's fiddling Giles Minton's election expenses ... or something like that?'

She sat back in her chair. 'I wouldn't think so. He knows Giles was a banker—why would he take the risk?'

'There are all sorts of bankers,' I said. 'I doubt Giles saw an actual bank account from one week to the next. He might have been involved in security. Or strategic planning. Or customer management. Or selling products. They don't all stand behind a counter and count money.'

'You may be right,' she said. 'Whatever—I'm going to leave them to it.'

Her eyes flicked away and I had the sense there was something else pressing on her, something she'd come here to say but was now finding difficult. I sat for a moment and said nothing while she thought it through.

After a moment I said, 'Do you want a drink?'

'No—no, thanks.'

'There must be something else you want to say. A reason you wanted to see me.'

'I'm worried about Alistair,' she said quickly.

'Why? I thought you didn't know him.'

'That's mostly true,' she said. 'But I heard Tony talking to Giles earlier today.'

'About what? What did you hear?'

She bit her lip. 'That's the thing: I'm not sure. They were talking quietly and I wasn't concentrating to begin with.'

'But you heard something.'

'Tony was saying something about bringing Alistair in. And he said Giles was up to his neck in it.'

'In what?'

'I don't know!' she said with exasperation. 'I've been playing it over in my head and I can't put it all together. I don't even think it was so much the words … it was the air of, well, menace between them. As if Tony was threatening Giles or vice versa. I can't be any clearer than that.'

'Were you threatened yourself? Did they know you overheard them?'

'I told Tony I'd heard something, just to see what he'd do.'

'That was very brave. What did he say?'

'He just told me to keep my mouth shut and suggested I hadn't heard what I thought I'd heard.'

'But you're pretty sure of it.'

'I heard something, even if I don't know the details.'

I looked around the bar at the salesmen and businessmen sitting in pairs and threes, discussing their day's affairs. Everything that Sally had mentioned had taken place in an ordinary world, even while it made that world seem less ordinary. The extraordinary world was one I was familiar with but it still surprised me from time to time.

I said, 'Do you think Giles Minton is genuine? Is he really pro-immigration, for example?'

'Why are you asking me?'

'I'm interested in your opinion. You worked closely with him, with the campaign.'

'Do you think he's making it all up, his position?'

'Do you?'

She didn't answer. Perhaps I'd been too blunt. Perhaps she was still marginally invested in seeing the campaign succeed, despite leaving it.

She looked down at the table in silence, and I thought we were moving past the subject of the Mintons and their politics, when she added, 'You should talk to Deborah.'

'About what?'

'Just talk to her. She might surprise you with what she knows.'

'That sounds mysterious. I don't think she likes me.'

Now Sally turned her full gaze on me and I thought I saw a toughness and a vengeance there that I hadn't seen until now. She suddenly looked ten years older. She said, 'Talk to her about her mother and Tony Wolfe. See what she says about the two of them.'

I took that in, then countered it by asking, 'What can you tell me about Deborah and the man she had an affair with, at college?'

Her gaze was still cool. 'You'll have to talk to her about that, too, won't you?'

'Do you know who it was?'

'You'll have to ask someone else. Now, about that drink.'

———

AFTERWARDS I WALKED her out to her car, a red Mini, and asked what she was going to do now.

'I don't know,' she said. 'Sit at home and think about things for a while. I'm not sure politics is for me. Everyone's so angry all the time.'

'I've noticed that,' I said.

'Perhaps I'll retrain as a vet. Animals are nicer than people.'

'Sleep well and don't worry. Go home.'

She was in the car now and had slid down the window. She said, 'I'll be in touch, one way or the other.'

The car drove away and I walked to my own. I sat inside and hunted in my pocket for the card the journalist, Forster, had given me that morning. It seemed like a lifetime away. I called him and when he answered I asked him a question and he said he'd get back to me.

Ten minutes later, he did.

CHAPTER FOURTEEN

BEN PRESCOTT LIVED in a 1960s detached house in a row of similar-but-different executive homes in Betley, one of the swankier villages on the back road from Stoke to Nantwich.

Each of the houses had a separate drive leading to an up-and-over garage or car-port, and they each had a patch of untended council grass in front of them, like a reminder of the wilderness the village might revert to if the inhabitants didn't watch their step. Betley was the kind of village that supported an olde-worlde pub, an antiques showroom and a garden centre and not much else. You had to drive twenty minutes in either direction to get a pint of milk or a packet of cigarettes.

I rang Prescott's bell and after a moment a tidy-looking man in his early forties opened the door, his face smiling pleasantly. 'Yes?'

I introduced myself and added, 'I'd like to talk to you about Deborah Minton.'

Now he stood up straight and the smile vanished from his even features. He was tall and slim and had dark hair that curled on to his collar. He wore a Lacoste jumper that emphasized the breadth of his chest and at his full height he was maybe an inch taller than me. He was like an advert for middle-aged masculinity at its finest, though I detected a weakness in the downturn of the corners of his mouth. I couldn't have stood it if he were perfect.

He said, rather aggressively, 'Who are you? Are you from the press?'

'No, I'm a private detective and I'm doing some background checking on behalf of the Minton family.'

He stared at me for a moment, then stood back and let me in. 'Go to the back,' he said. 'I'm sitting in the veranda.'

I followed his instructions and walked down the hallway, through a modern black-and-white kitchen, and then turned half-right into a warm and light room filled with bamboo furniture. The view through the curved glass wall at the back presented a view of a square garden bordered by trees, but the closest item was the side aspect of a full-length outdoor swimming-pool, so close you could almost touch it. A hard plastic winter cover was pulled over the chilly water beneath. It looked to be as tough as double-glazed glass and was sectioned like the shell of an armadillo so that it could fold in on itself.

He pointed me to a round chair with a soft cushion and I sat but he remained standing. Having got this far I wasn't sure what I was going to say. I didn't have a client and I didn't really have a direction for the interview: I'd just wanted to see the man who'd seduced Deborah Minton and take it from there.

He said, 'How did you find me?'

'It wasn't difficult. I'm a detective, I know people.'

'It was that newspaper, wasn't it? They had it in for me

from the beginning.'

'Can you blame them? Forty-year-old tutor and seventeen-year-old girl?'

'Have you seen her? Do you know her?'

I closed my eyes. I hoped he wasn't going to use the Lolita defence. Thankfully he didn't, though perhaps it was a variation.

He sat down and leaned forward, resting his handsome head in his hands.

'She's a manipulative little … gorgon,' he said to the floorboards.

'How did it happen?'

He stared at the floor a while longer, then took a deep breath and raised his head.

'I can't talk about this … I really can't.' A thought occurred to him and made him frown. 'What did you mean, you're doing some background checking for the Mintons? They told me to keep well away from Deborah, which I was happy to do. So why are they sending you to talk to me? What do you want me to say?'

'You know what Giles Minton is doing now …'

'Who doesn't? He's all over the bloody place, it's like he's sticking pins in me.'

'Naturally they're worried that what happened between you and Deborah might resurface.'

'Thankfully they kept our names out of it, not that it helped. Everyone who mattered knew or could work it out. Nothing went to court so they didn't have an excuse to print our names, just used innuendo and heavy hints. I don't suppose it would take much digging to find the old reports and dredge it all up again, now Minton's developing a reputation. And I wouldn't put it past the press to do just that. The articles are probably still on the Crewe Chronicle's website …'

'Well I suppose that's why I'm here … to find out how you feel about the Mintons, and what you're up to.'

'Up to? I'm up to my neck in debt, trying to keep this place going. My wife left me and I had to buy out her half of the house, giving me a bigger mortgage than I thought was humanly feasible.'

'You could sell it.'

'In this market? If we'd sold ten years ago, maybe, but we're still in negative equity. I am, I should say. Lorna's out of it. Gone back to Scotland with a few thousand in her pocket and an abiding hatred of me.'

He was starting to feel sorry for himself, lowering his head into his hands once more.

I said, 'So tell me what happened. What's your side of the story?'

He looked up abruptly. '*Now* somebody wants to listen? Brilliant. Too bloody late.'

'Just tell me. I've only had one side of it so far.'

A shadow passed over his features and then it was gone, leaving him transformed with irony.

'She wanted to be an actress, at least to begin with. I was teaching a theatre studies course at the university in Chester. She couldn't stand it—too much reading. She wanted to get on stage and perform. She got a part in one of the college productions the students put on and then came to me for private tuition in the verse speaking—Shakespeare was hard.'

'It wasn't Othello, was it?'

'How did you know?'

'Wild guess.'

'She wasn't Desdemona. She played Emilia, Iago's wife and Desdemona's maid.'

'She ends up denouncing Iago because she's developed a loyalty to Desdemona.' Now he was staring at me. 'I saw it on TV a few weeks ago, the Branagh film.'

He nodded, glad to have his astonishment clarified.

'Of course she was far too young and, I have to say, not particularly good. But I suppose I was flattered she'd come to me for extra-curricular tutelage.'

'Then one thing led to another.'

'Yes,' he said. 'It's exactly as sordid as you think. I consoled myself with the knowledge that she was about to turn eighteen—that's what she said, anyway—and I was forty-two. How noble was I?'

'Where did you meet?'

He sighed again and I watched the whole catalogue of his self-deception unwinding as he spoke.

'At first it was on campus, a spare room. But she complained it was too noisy, we'd get interruptions and she'd lose her concentration. She had a flat in Tarporley—staying clear of her parents because she could—but that was busy, too. There were other people around all the time and when we started … the affair, she felt it was too risky. Imagine—risky, for her! I was a married man with a career and she was worried about the risk to her.'

'Awful. So what did you do?'

'Hotels, usually. Tragic one-night stands. Or that's what it felt like. She loved the excitement, the naughtiness.'

'Love makes us do crazy things.'

Now he snorted. 'Love! Don't be stupid. It was a kind of infatuation, at least for me. Lorna and I had drifted apart, largely because of our different interests and schedules, and of course I felt rejuvenated.'

I looked around at the room: there was a nice rosewood bureau against one wall and an oak bookcase against another, filled with biographies of actors and directors. There was a tastefulness in the choice of the furniture, the rugs, the brass light fittings … Prescott and his wife had probably enjoyed a peaceful, satisfying life until Deborah had come into the midst of it. Then she had destroyed it with the insouciance of youth, not realising the consequences of anything she did.

I said, 'How did it end?'

His eyes had got darker and more haunted. He said in a quiet voice, 'There was a fortnight where Lorna was going off to Rome in pursuit of some rare bug or other, so Deborah and I went down to London for a couple of nights. Took an Air b'n'b flat. Disaster. The place was too small and dirty. Of course we argued dramatically. And bad news travels fast. Giles Minton turned up on my doorstep here a week later, leaving his wife in the car outside. I saw her through the front window, staring at me, while her husband poured vitriol in my ear. He showered me with all sorts of dire threats about my career and marriage. Bad luck had it that Lorna came home from work, wondering who was parked on our driveway, and caught the tail-end of my conversation with Minton. I don't think she'd been aware of anything until that moment, though I'm probably deluding myself. Then she took one look at my guilty face, went upstairs, packed a bag and was gone in thirty minutes. Two days later a reporter knocked on my door and asked whether it was true I was having an affair with one of my students. I denied it and threw him out on his ear, but a suggestive story appeared in his newspaper the next day and although my name wasn't mentioned, my teaching hours were suddenly reduced—I wasn't on staff, I was on a short-term contract whose hours they could alter at will. So they did.'

'And now?'

'Thankfully there are always pupils needing private tuition, especially in this part of leafy Cheshire, where the parents can afford it. I scrape by with a loan from my mother. Imagine the embarrassment.'

'It seems to me you got off quite lightly, considering.'

He looked at me coldly.

'Do I seem bitter? I suppose I am. Though I have no right, do I, because the narrative is that I seduced a vulnerable young woman. Maybe I did. But it certainly didn't seem like that as she was peeling my belt from my trousers.'

'You don't shock me, Mr Prescott.'

'Perhaps not,' he said. 'But I shock myself sometimes. This wasn't what I intended to become twenty years ago. Living hand-to-mouth in a house I can't afford in a place I can't stand doing a job which gives me no satisfaction. So yes, I suppose I'm bitter.'

I stood up to leave, saying, 'Don't expect any sympathy from me. You may think Deborah was the instigator but you should have known better, don't you think?'

'Perhaps you're right. If you have an unbendable moral code, congratulations, not all of us are able to be quite so self-righteous.'

He walked me to the door. 'What will be the outcome of this?'

'Nothing, as far as you're concerned,' I said. 'Background is background. Information only.'

'If you need anything else, don't bother calling. I'm going away this afternoon. I won't tell you where, except to say it's considerably warmer than here.'

'Isn't everywhere?' I said as he closed the door on me.

———

BEFORE I DROVE away I called the reporter, Forster, again. He'd given me Prescott's name and address and I wanted him to think I'd give him something in return, eventually.

But first I needed more information.

'So did you speak to Prescott?' were his first words when he answered. 'What did he have to say for himself?'

'Nothing you don't already know. He was a fool, she was a temptress, his life is ruined.'

'You sound like a cynical newspaperman.'

'Maybe we have the same job—hounding people for information we can use to our own advantage.'

'The difference being, my client is the public good. Yours is a paying customer.'

'I give in—you're morally superior to me. Tell me, what happened to this story? I know Prescott suffered for it in his marriage and to some extent in his career … but he's still living in the same place, still teaching. Was there no follow-up?'

'After you called I talked to the guy who wrote this up. He said there was no appetite for it. To be honest, I don't think it was interesting enough to keep digging at. The girl was turning eighteen, not a child as such. It was scuzzy but not illegal and my man said he got nothing from the university and nothing from the Mintons, so he just packed it in. Everyone lives happily ever after. Except Prescott's wife, of course. Poor love.'

'How did he find out about them in the first place?'

'Anonymous call. Some woman, he said. She gave him the names and the location but wouldn't say anything else. He did some digging and found out he was married, she was his student ... but, you know, these days, how far could you push it? People don't get outraged so easily.'

'Did anyone talk to Deborah? Did she get any counselling or help?'

I could hear Forster's open-mouthed grin when he spoke: 'You'd have to talk to the Mintons about that, wouldn't you? We're not social workers.'

'So nobody gave a damn what happened to her?'

'In so many words.'

CHAPTER FIFTEEN

IT WAS CLOSE to lunch when I got back to my office, and as I approached the street door I saw Carol Minton leaning against the glass of the abandoned furniture store next door. She was wearing a white wraparound mackintosh like an actress from a 1960s French film, its belt tied at the waist. Her hair was pulled back in a bun, revealing more of her face than I'd seen to date. The cold air had given a rose-coloured edge to her cheeks and tightened her skin. She looked fifteen years younger than I knew she must be.

'Mrs Minton, I'm not supposed to talk to you.'

'You must call me Carol. Is your office upstairs? I looked you up in the Yellow Pages but this was as far as I could get without breaking in the door.'

'You should have phoned me first.'

'Stupidly, I left my phone at home. Stress does terrible things to one's performance, doesn't it? Are you going up? Or can I take you to lunch?'

I hesitated, caught between irritation and politeness, then unlocked the entrance door and ushered her inside.

I followed her up the narrow stairs, careful to keep my

gaze low. I didn't want to embarrass her, but the way she sashayed up each step made me think she was enjoying it.

Inside my office I directed her to a client chair and sat facing her. She'd undone the mackintosh and revealed a tight black polo-neck jumper beneath it. Her eyes were clear and her expression pleasant, as though I were a headmaster and we were settling down to talk about young Johnny's prospects next year.

'Let me apologise again, Mr Dyke, for—what do they call it?—doorstepping you. But I was coming into Crewe anyway and after our conversation yesterday I thought I should follow up with you. I don't think we left on particularly good terms and anyway, I'm still worried about these two men who seem to have appeared out of nowhere and we don't know who they are or what they want with my son.'

'I don't think they'll bother him again.'

'Oh, and why do you think that? Do you have more information, or is it just detective's hunch?'

'I'm a naturally optimistic person.'

She moved her head and looked at me sideways. She was right to be sceptical of me: I had no real idea what the intentions of Scarface and his friend were. I'd put them out of my mind. They'd mumbled some fake political commentary at me during the attack, but I had no illusions they were working for Minton's political opposition. It was too clumsy ... and pointless. Perhaps I should have investigated the opposition, found out what kind of dirty tricks they might have used before ... but my heart wasn't in it.

Which didn't answer the question of who the men were

or what they wanted.

Or who they were working for.

———

SHE'D BEEN WATCHING me think but now she was bored with it. She said, 'I can't say I'm very impressed with your office. I'm the kind of shallow person who places great store on appearances, as you've probably noticed. If I were you I'd invest in some better furniture and at least dust your blinds. Do you have a cleaning woman? I can recommend one if you wish.'

'Why are you here, Mrs Minton?' I was deliberately ignoring the fact she'd told me to call her Carol.

'I want to hire you, on a personal basis.'

'I'm not sure your husband will approve of that.'

'Oh, I'm certain he won't. Don't you think that adds to the excitement?'

'He's threatened to drag me into the courts, claiming harassment.'

'Really? Do you think he'll do that a month before the election? He'd die of shame if it were known his wife had gone behind his back to hire someone like yourself—no offence.'

'None taken. I know my place.'

'Don't be like that—I like you. I find you ... direct. Living with a politician—even if he's not officially recruited yet—can make diplomacy the basic currency in a household.'

'And you don't like diplomacy?'

She smiled slowly, as though recognising that she might have said something humorous.

'It's not terribly exciting,' she said, emphasising the last word.

I felt the conversation might be heading somewhere I didn't want it to go, so I turned business-like.

'What is it you want to hire me to do? Perhaps we can come to some arrangement, though I have to say I'm not going to be involved in deceiving your husband. I won't tell him anything because you'll be the client, but if he asks me directly about you I won't lie.'

'See, I knew you could be flexible. You might have guessed what I want you to do: I want you to find Alistair again and do your best to persuade him to come home. He can carry on with his studies, of course, but I'd like him to at least come home every night. It's not too much to ask, is it?' She aimed a worried frown at me, willing me to understand. 'You can tell him his mother is worried. You can tell him she needs to feel all of the family around her while his father is off saving the world from socialism.'

I noticed that despite her apparent confidence, her hands were shaking. I supposed all of her energy was going into presenting the appearance of rational concern, rather than screaming at me at the top of her lungs. I said, 'He didn't strike me as the kind of person to succumb to emotional requests. He seemed quite cool.'

This upset her. 'I don't want to hear talk like that, Mr Dyke.' I noticed for the first time that she was carrying a small handbag, which had been tucked under her arm. Now she reached it around to the front and opened it, taking out a small packet of tissues. She used one to dab the corner of one eye. 'Alistair is a sensitive boy who, I'm sure, is going through a difficult period. That can be the only explanation for the way he's treated me. And us, as a family. I'm not happy that he's moved out of the house he shared with Jack, especially as we're still paying for it—dear me, I sound like Giles now, don't I?—but if I'm perfectly honest I also worry about his mental health.'

She caught my eye briefly but looked away before I could read anything into it. I suspected the mention of mental health troubled her, given her own history.

'Do you have any reason to be worried about that?' I asked.

She hesitated, then said, 'One reads a lot these days about students having problems, that's all I meant. I wouldn't want us to have missed anything … later, if you know what I mean.'

'You mean if he self-harms?'

She looked down and said nothing. I had the sense there was an echo of something from her own past, something she might be unwilling to pursue.

In the event she found a smile and lifted it towards me, as if trying to persuade me that life was good despite any temporary problems one might experience. She said, 'What I'd actually like is for you to act as a kind of … coach, or personal trainer in this regard. Someone who could act as a positive role model to help him see that life at home can be, well, healthy.'

'You talk as though he might not already believe that.'

'Of course not. I'm probably giving the wrong impression of him. I know you've already met him and formed your own opinion, but you haven't seen the real Alistair, have you? You've met an Alistair under pressure. Possibly frightened by these men who seemed to want to talk to him. Worried by the studies he's undertaking.'

'I think you may be making too much of all of that.'

'Please don't talk down to me, Mr Dyke. I'm very sensitive to that mode of discourse.'

Her tone had hardened and I realised I'd made a mis-step. I shouldn't have downplayed her fears—even if I didn't want the job, it wasn't polite.

I said, 'I'll email you a standard contract. There's enough money from the first check your husband gave me to pay for a few days' expenses. I'll invoice you later for any extras.'

She stood up and smoothed down her skirt, though she seemed reluctant to leave. She said, 'Is there anything else you need from me?'

I busied myself with my desk-drawer for a moment, avoiding her eyes. Then I looked up at her and said, 'I came across some information about Deborah.'

She stiffened. 'Yes?'

'You and I both know she got into trouble when she went to college in Chester.'

She looked down. 'Yes.'

'It may or may not be connected, but what do you know about her relationship with Prescott?'

It was as though a cold wind had run through the room. She visibly shivered.

'I knew—and know—very little. Deborah wouldn't talk to us about it. We had some calls from reporters but I had the idea they were fishing for information. It was hard to know exactly how much they'd learned, after the first tittle-tattle was published. Neither Deborah's nor his name were mentioned in the initial article.'

'So how did you find out?'

'We had an anonymous email.'

'You can't guess who?'

'Giles tried to reply to the email to get more information but it kept bouncing back. In the end we thought it might be someone who knew Prescott personally … perhaps even his wife, trying to get some sort of revenge on him. It didn't seem that important once we found out what it said was true.'

'Prescott's wife didn't find out about it till you and your husband went to visit him. By chance. Don't you remember her arriving while Giles was talking to him?'

She looked away, ignoring my question, as if unwilling to be reminded of her own complicity that night. She turned back, her eyes now shining with some kind of righteousness. She said, 'And how do you know all this? … I suppose you've talked to Prescott yourself, have you? I fail to understand how any of it has any bearing on Alistair.'

'I don't know either,' I said. 'But I can't ignore the fact that the story has cropped up again.'

She seemed to have made a decision about how much longer she could talk about Deborah and her affair with Prescott. She turned to leave, but when she reached the door she hesitated and looked back at me, and for once the look of concern on her face seemed real and not the product of hyper-anxiety or some other kind of mental fixity. She said, 'Seeing as you brought it up, I should tell you I believe she's seeing him again. She goes out from time to time and won't tell me where she's been. I know she's older now, just old enough, and I believe he's divorced and single. But still …'

Then she hesitated as if waiting for me to open the door for her, so I rose wearily from my own chair and reached for the handle. As I opened the door she stepped closer to me, letting me feel her sensuality, looking down at her feet before raising her face to look into my eyes.

'I hadn't realised how tall you were,' she said.

'Goodbye, Mrs Minton.'

I placed a gentle hand on her back and she walked away rather grandly, as if I'd launched her.

I SAT BEHIND my desk and breathed in the last of Carol Minton's perfume, which lingered like an open promise. This led me to think about her daughter again. There was something about Deborah Minton that was beginning to intrigue me. I had no brief to concern myself with her, and her parents were substantial members of the community who didn't need my help bringing her up.

That's what I told myself.

The problem was, I didn't believe me. She'd already made one bad decision in throwing herself at Prescott. I wondered just how adult she was and whether her current decisions were any better.

Besides, Sally Collins had suggested I talk to Deborah about her parents and their politics, and also about Carol Minton's relationship with Tony Wolfe.

After a few minutes' consideration I persuaded myself that if I were to find Alistair again, it would be necessary and helpful to talk to Deborah first.

I had her number on my phone but she didn't reply. No

one replied at the Minton house, either, so I was stumped. Where would an adventurous nineteen-year-old girl go if she were bored?

CHAPTER SIXTEEN

I GAVE MYSELF the afternoon to think about it by filling the time with paperwork. I had a VAT form to complete, and a new contract to draw up for Carol Minton. The time flew by.

By the time I'd finished it was gone four o'clock and it was dark outside. I phoned Deborah again and got no response. The Mintons' phone went straight through to an answerphone this time. Had I been more paranoid I might have thought people were avoiding me.

Something wasn't feeling right, though I couldn't have explained in simple words what it was. Carol had said her daughter was seeing Prescott again. I didn't know whether this was true or simply Carol's fears kicking in. But I didn't trust Deborah to make any good decisions, and if Prescott was leaving the country I wouldn't put it past Deborah to go with him. In anyone's book, this wasn't a good idea.

IT WAS A pleasant drive through the countryside, even at night, but when I got there I saw that Prescott's house was dark. There were no cars in the driveway.

But still I parked and got out of my car and stood leaning against it. There was little traffic through the village and I could hear a television playing somewhere, and further away, perhaps at the end of the village, a car door slammed and a dog barked. Country life. I looked again at Prescott's house, and now that I was in a more elevated position than my driver's seat I could see a dim glow coming through Prescott's frosted glass front door.

I walked up the path and peered through the glass, seeing nothing but a vague illumination, then stepped sideways and looked through the front window. The room into which I could see was sombre and empty—a flat-screen TV faced me, switched off, and a glass-topped coffee-table piled with hardback books squatted next to a comfortable leather chair.

I went to the front door and rang the bell. There was no reply, though I could hear it sounding somewhere in the house. Then I glanced behind me into the street and, seeing no one, passed in front of the house again and turned down the driveway that led to a white-painted garage.

A tall wooden fence with a gate prevented entrance to the back of the house. The handle was a simple old-fashioned thumb-lever type and when I pressed down, the door opened. Now I was looking at the swimming-pool cover I'd seen earlier in the day, marching away from me in sections and illuminated from beneath by the pool's solar-powered inner lights.

And inside, face down, floated the body of a young woman, arms spread out, hair swirling lazily in a slight ripple, her face staring at the pool's floor tiles as if they were asking her a question she could never answer.

———

THE POLICE CAME quickly and swarmed the street with an ambulance, half a dozen striped Volvos and a couple of unmarked cars.

The first policeman to arrive put me in his car and told me to wait until someone came to talk to me. That was half an hour, during which I saw the uniforms start to spread out to canvass the neighbours, all of whom were on their doorsteps, willing to talk.

The man who finally opened the car door and sat next to me was a squat Detective Inspector in his forties, who was efficient and reasonable. I explained who I was and what I was doing there and why I'd let myself in the back way.

'Do you know the girl?' he asked.

'Her name's Sally Collins,' I said. 'She's been working for Giles Minton's election campaign, though I think she just quit. I mean, yesterday.'

'When did you talk to her last?'

'Yesterday evening.'

'What was her connection to Mr Prescott?'

'None, so far as I know. I should tell you I was here myself this morning. I talked to him for about fifteen or twenty minutes. He told me he was going away this afternoon, but he didn't say where. We didn't talk about Miss Collins. I don't see any reason why he'd know her.'

'Why were you talking to him?'

'In connection with some work I'm doing.'

'What work?'

'I can't tell you. It's actually not connected to Miss Collins directly.'

The man, whose name was Sawyer, had been making notes. Now he looked up at me with curiosity in his eyes and I knew what was coming next.

'I know you, don't I? You're the man who keeps getting in the way.'

'Not everyone sees it like that,' I said.

'Well you can't fool all of the people all of the time. I'll want you to keep out of my way on this one. And you'll have to come in and be interviewed formally.'

'I'm shocked.'

'I can tell. Where's your car?' I pointed it out to him. 'I'll send someone to go with you. Anything else you want to tell me right now?'

'She had a red Mini. I don't see it on the street.'

'Okay, we'll look out for it.'

'I'd like to know how she died, when you find out.'

'It'll be in the pathologist's report. Whether you'll get to see it depends on the coroner.'

'Never mind. It'll be too late then.'

Sawyer nodded back towards the house. 'It's too late for her already.'

I silently agreed. I'd liked Sally—whether it was in spite of or because of her naivety, I didn't know. And now I never would.

I WAS RELEASED in the early hours of the morning. Despite what Sawyer had said, my connections and reputation had worked in my favour for once and I was released earlier than I might have been. It also helped that I'd only met Sally twice and had no obvious motive to harm her.

When I was questioned by Sawyer and another detective, I left out what Sally had told me about the conversation between Wolfe and Giles Minton. And the threat Wolfe had made to her. It was probably a bad decision on my part, but to begin with I couldn't be certain that what she'd heard as a threat was really actionable and not just bluster. And secondly, if he *had* followed through on it I wanted to be the one to find out. I thought I owed her that much.

I'd appeased my conscience by telling them who she'd been working for, though I didn't have Wolfe's address. I also gave up the Mintons.

In fact the Mintons and Wolfe were likely to come under far more suspicion than I was. They'd known her for longer and had more interaction with her recently … who knew what might have passed between them all?

Which left Sawyer and his colleagues with quite a lot to do and hassling me wasn't part of it.

I went home and microwaved something and slept, dreaming staccato dreams that featured blonde hair getting trapped in my mouth and eyes. I woke brushing my hand across my face and breathing heavily, my eyes tense and focused a few inches in front of my face, as if I'd been reading my own obituary. I felt heavy and unrested but with a sense of purpose roiling in my gut.

By 8.45 I was ringing Minton's doorbell. If I'd known where Wolfe lived I would have gone there first, catching him alone, but I didn't so I thought I'd talk to both of them at the same time.

Surprisingly, Wolfe opened the door. He looked as though he'd had as little sleep as I had, his round face pink and his eyes squinty.

As an opening statement he said, 'Well you can fuck off, can't you? Nobody's here and nobody wants to talk to you anyway.'

'It's you I want to see.'

This set him back on his heels momentarily and I saw the calculation in his eyes. But then he turned and walked back into the house, leaving the door open. I followed him in.

'You've heard about Sally,' I said to his waddling rear.

He raised the back of his hand. He said, 'Her parents rang me at four o'clock this morning wanting to know what happened. What could I tell them? Fuck all is what I could tell them. The police wouldn't explain how she died but her mum and dad expected me to know.' We'd reached a kitchen where he had an Italian coffee-maker on the go and papers spread over a broad wooden table. He turned back to me. 'That was the first I'd heard of it. That's a great phone call to get. Barely twenty-two years of age and some bastard killed her.'

'Did the police tell her parents where she'd been found?'

'Of course. They wanted to know if Sally even knew this man Prescott.'

'Did she?'

He let his round shoulders sag expressively. 'I wasn't her keeper. I didn't know who she did or didn't fraternise with.'

'Okay … so do you have any idea why she was there, at Prescott's house?'

'Course I don't. I know of this Prescott man because of the business with Deborah, but that's as far as I stretch. What about you?'

'I talked to him yesterday morning. He never mentioned her. And she never mentioned him. I don't think they knew each another.'

'You talked to her then?'

'She talked to me.'

'They'll want to talk to Deborah.'

'If they make the connection. I didn't tell them.'

He nodded. 'Someone will. Fucking busy-bodies everywhere.'

He poured himself a coffee without offering me one. Then he stared at me over the top of his mug as he took the first sip, almost as if it were a dare. I didn't think I'd get any further down this road. Wolfe was too cunning to let anything slip. I said, 'So where have the Mintons gone this early in the morning?'

'I sent them out for the day. The press will find out Sally's connection to me, and the fact she's working for Giles, and then they'll be around like wasps on a sugar lump. It's better for them to deal with me than him, and I'm going to ignore them. Problem solved.'

Although he'd let me in I knew he wanted me to leave as soon as possible. So I walked further into the kitchen and sat at one of the round-back oak chairs at the table. He put down his coffee and stepped to the table quickly, tidying up the papers and stuffing them into a tan leather briefcase. I caught a glimpse of columns of figures.

I said, 'You don't seem too cut up about Sally.'

'Don't I?'

'You said the parents were friends of yours—I thought you'd be acting out a bit more grief.'

'Look at me, can't you tell I'm heartbroken?'

'She came to see me a couple of days ago. Do you want to know why?'

'Is it anything to do with the election?'

'She said, in so many words, that you threatened her because she overheard something you and Giles were talking about.'

'That's not true. Repeat it to anyone and you'll find yourself in court.'

'Are you denying the conversation or the threats?'

'Both,' he said. He'd picked an apple from a bowl and had begun paring it with a short knife. 'So first—what was this conversation about? You don't know, because it didn't take place and you have no records that prove otherwise. Therefore second—there couldn't have been any threats because the conversation didn't exist and I had no reason to threaten her. Why would I threaten her? And what with?'

I let a pause hang in the air for a moment, then said, 'Did you know that Carol Minton has asked me to stay on? She wants me to find Alistair again and bring him home. What will Giles say about that?'

He opened a cupboard door and dropped his parings into a bin attached inside it, shaking his head as though troubled by a persistent fly. I heard the nine o'clock pips sounding on a radio somewhere in the house, then the low rumble of a male newsreader's voice.

As if he'd found a better answer to one of my previous

questions, Wolfe said, 'Hear that, the news? The world's waking up with absolutely no interest in poor Sally's death. I feel for her. She was too young to die a lonely death in a swimming pool.' He cut off a section of his apple and fed it into his mouth with his knife, then pointed it at me. 'I'm a very pragmatic soul, Dyke, and I have no emotions to spare at the moment. I'm using every ounce of my limited emotional intelligence dealing with Giles and Carol. She's cut up about it something terrible. We had to give her some sleeping tablets to get her back to sleep and I think they're still in her system.'

I said sharply, 'So you stayed here last night?'

'I often do. Giles and I work late on tactics. Strategies. We're both night-owls.'

'So you can support each other's alibis.'

Now he frowned. 'If you're thinking I could do this to Sally, you're seriously mistaken. She was naive and a pain in the backside sometimes, but she was a nice kid and very willing and, worse, I'll have to do all the running around myself now, won't I?'

'Your troubles never end.'

'As for Carol hiring you … go for it. She'll run you ragged. You know, when I first met the Mintons all those years ago I was a slim young thing. My wife and I used to play tennis with Giles and Carol. Can you believe that? I'll dig out one of my old photos. I did bits and pieces of work for her—she ran a landscape gardening business when she married Giles and I looked after the books—but even though she had a small turnover and few customers, she still cost me more days' work than my regular clients. A worry-wart, my mother would have said.'

I was on the point of asking him about Carol's psychiatric problems when I thought better of it. He'd already admitted to having a low level of emotional intelligence. He didn't need to demonstrate it to me again by minimising any mental health problems she might have had. I was getting tired of his cynicism … and my complicity in drawing it out from him.

I stood up and replaced the oak chair under the table. He was leaning against the work-surface and looking at me as though the kitchen was his rightful domain and I was an unwelcome visitor. He'd finished his apple but still held the short kitchen knife carelessly in his right hand. One of the front flaps of his shirt was hanging over the top of his trousers like a bookmark.

I said, 'As for Sally, do you have any idea who would want to see her dead?'

'I'll keep my speculations for the police, if that's all right with you. I expect they'll be on their way, don't you?'

'Yes,' I said. 'Especially as I told them who you were and where you were likely to be at least some of the time today.'

His expression soured and he dropped the knife in the sink with a clatter.

He said, 'Don't let the door hit your behind on the way out.'

CHAPTER SEVENTEEN

When he was sure Dyke had gone, Wolfe laced up his shoes, put on his waistcoat and jacket, then reversed his BMW in a semi-circle in the driveway and headed towards his own house. As far as he was aware, Dyke didn't know where he lived so probably wouldn't have gone there. And why would he? There was no reason unless he wanted to break in and snoop around ...

He felt his heart quicken a little at that thought, and sped up.

He left Nantwich the back way, by-passing Crewe, and headed out on the old road towards Weston. Ten minutes later he turned right at the White Lion Hotel and a few minutes after that was pulling into his own driveway. The Mintons' Mercedes was parked by the side of the house and he parked behind it to help conceal their car from nosy neighbours. He stood for a moment, looking around for signs of observers or people who didn't belong. Then he thought he might be going mad and instead looked up at the sky, currently a blue bowl without a single cloud. *Get some perspective*, he told himself. *It's only an election.*

Inside the house it was quiet. He found Giles reading a newspaper in the living-room but there was no sign of Carol.

'She's upstairs, lying down,' Minton said, answering Wolfe's unasked question without looking up. He had the air of a child being compelled to enjoy himself but not wanting to. Wolfe knew it was Minton's version of contrariness, trying to prove that Wolfe was paranoid if he thought the press would hound them out here ...

'Feet off my sofa, if you don't mind,' Wolfe said, tapping Minton's heavily polished black shoes. Minton swung himself upright, folding the newspaper as he did so.

He said, 'Anything from the police?'

'Worse. Fucking Dyke turned up on the doorstep, asking awkward questions.'

'That was the idea, wasn't it? You were the point man to answer awkward questions during this difficult time ...'

'The idea was to distract the press and keep them away from you. They'll swallow any old shit. We've cancelled all your visits for the next two days, out of respect. I didn't anticipate Dyke turning up like a fucking moth to a candle.'

'What did you tell him?'

Wolfe realised they were both keeping their voices down so Carol wouldn't hear. *When did that start?* he wondered. From time to time he caught sight of himself in dishonest or spurious behaviour and it disgusted him, like a drunk looking at his own vomit on the street and wondering where did *that* come from ...?

'I told him nothing, what do you think? Except what he already knew. Poor Sally, didn't deserve it, so on and so forth.'

'Be honest,' Minton said, 'she didn't. I thought you were telling your wonder boys to put a scare in her, not to leave her floating face-down in a swimming pool.'

'You got me there,' Wolfe said. 'That's exactly what I thought I told them. I'm beginning to think you're right—I've got to cut them loose. Danger is, of course, they flap their lips and it all comes back to us anyway.'

Minton stood up and looked out at Wolfe's back garden. He seemed to be fascinated by gardens, always looking at them, walking in them, sniffing a rose. Wolfe never looked at the garden himself—he had people come to deal with it once a fortnight in the summer. It was green and he had the sense there were coloured bushes in it from time to time.

Minton said, 'Have you heard from them? I mean, since ...'

'No, and I don't expect to.'

'We were right, weren't we?'

Wolfe looked to the doorway, anticipating Carol. 'What, to send a message? I promised her I would. I didn't reckon on it being terminal, poor kid.'

'You liked her.'

'Didn't you? What wasn't to like? Except for her ability to be in the wrong place at the wrong time.'

'You sure she heard?'

'She told me she'd heard something. She said she was going to quit. Did you want her running around three and a half weeks before the election with that weird memory in her head, the one she'd worry about till it all came clear and then she just had to tell someone ...?'

'You're extrapolating. You don't know that would

have happened.'

Wolfe knew Minton was right but still found he was justifying his behaviour to himself. Christ, perhaps this was hitting him harder than he thought. Perhaps he was making bad decisions now. He said, 'Well it's the mother of all fuck-ups but what's done is done. We've got to keep a calm head and deny everything. Fuck knows why Laurel and Hardy thought to dump her body in that man Prescott's pool. It's either a weird coincidence or an act of genius, and I don't know which.'

'What will you do with that pair—Laurel and Hardy?'

'I can't do anything, can I? They just have to keep clear of us—you especially.'

Minton lowered his head a moment and Wolfe saw the strain in the slack lines around his jaw, as though his skull were contracting and leaving his flesh to hang loosely from it. When *he* was stressed, he ate and got fatter—Minton was obviously at the other end of the spectrum: stress squeezed the fat out of him.

He said, 'Dyke told me something else.'

Minton glanced at him. 'The winning Lottery numbers for next week? We could do with some good news.'

'Carol's been to see him and hired him again.'

Wolfe might have expected an outburst of anger, but Minton just lifted his jaw, as if clearing his Adam's apple from a tight tie-knot. He said, 'Let me guess: she wants him to find Alistair … and what? Smother him with kisses?'

'He said she wants him to bring Alistair home. Make what you will of that.'

Minton turned away from the garden and abruptly lashed out with his foot, kicking a soft leather pouffe that

Wolfe used to rest his sciatic leg on. It skittered two feet.

He said, 'I'll talk to her.'

'Don't get mad. You don't want to make things worse.'

'How can things possibly get worse? I could drop dead, I suppose, but at the moment I think I'd count that as a blessèd release.'

'Eyes on the prize, Giles, eyes on the prize.'

Minton looked sideways at him, his gaze miserable, his cheeks pink. 'And what exactly *is* the prize?' he asked. 'I'm not sure I ever knew and now I don't think I ever will.'

Wolfe couldn't bear to look at him, so turned and walked through into the kitchen.

HE WAS STANDING waiting for the kettle to boil when Minton came in and grabbed him by the arm, as if he were continuing a fight they'd been having in the other room. Wolfe noticed a strange glint in the other man's eyes, like the gleam of a hard mineral. He'd known Minton nearly twenty years and had never seen him this consumed by an emotion—any emotion.

He said, 'What are you thinking?'

Minton looked at his own hand and realised it was gripping Wolfe's arm tighter than necessary. He gave it one last shake then let go. He said, 'We can't let Dyke loose on Carol's say-so. There's too much … too much that could go wrong.'

'And whose fault is that?'

Minton continued to stare at him. 'Don't start that again. The job's done. Apologies were made.'

'I'm not the one you needed to apologise to.'

Minton laughed, once. 'I should have apologised to Carol? For what she did? Did to me? I don't think so.'

Wolfe wondered if the Mintons had been playing that scene over and over during the last fifteen years. Perhaps it was their version of a bedroom farce.

He said, 'What can we do about it now? She seems determined to have Alistair back home, for some reason. And obviously she's taken a liking to Dyke.'

The kettle boiled and Wolfe used it as an excuse to move away from Minton, whose personal space was becoming rancid. He poured water over a tea-bag and watched it infuse. For the first time he was beginning to think he needed to get out of this … the problem being, he was as implicated as Minton was. Carol, too. It was a terrifying dance of death they were all engaged in, holding hands round a hole in the ground that led straight to hell.

Minton seemed to have calmed down. He said, 'I can handle Carol. The Sally thing has nothing to do with us. It's Dyke. I've read about him. He's a terrier. We might think we fired him but we didn't. I can persuade Carol to sack him, but he won't finish up until he's finished. You can see it in his face. Looking down his nose at everyone like a … a vengeful priest. If such a thing exists.'

Wolfe smiled to himself. He hated to admit it, but Minton was right. Dyke was the problem, wasn't he? Everything else could be handled but Dyke was that fucking moth drawn to the flame, casting bizarre shadows everywhere.

He said, 'You shouldn't be thinking about this stuff. Let it go. Do some yoga, watch morning television or something. Phone the office and see what's happening there.'

'What are you going to do?'

'I'm not sure,' Wolfe said, knowing full well what he was going to do.

Minton waited a moment, as if a new suggestion might occur to him, then he turned and went back to the sitting room. As soon as he left the kitchen, Wolfe stepped through his back door into the square of concreted yard next to the garage and phoned someone who would look after his problem with the efficiency of a steam-roller.

CHAPTER EIGHTEEN

AFTER LEAVING WOLFE I drove to my office to have a think. I should have been working out how to track down Alistair again but my head was filled with images of Sally Collins floating face-down in Ben Prescott's swimming-pool. The one thing I had done earlier that morning was ring back the number Alistair had left on my phone when he contacted me. It was now dead. If he was trying to stay hidden, he really meant it.

I let myself into the office and put on the kettle in the small kitchen next door, then slumped in front of the computer and watched it boot up. I opened Microsoft Outlook to see what spam mail had been delivered today.

Amongst a number of uninteresting emails, there was one from Sally Collins, with an attachment. I sat upright and opened the email.

The attachment was a Word document containing scanned and pasted newspaper articles, including photos. There were three sentences in the email: 'I just found this on Tony's computer. I don't know what it is. Perhaps it will help.'

They might have been the last sentences she ever wrote.

THE WORD DOCUMENT was six pages long and contained ten labelled clippings from the Crewe Chronicle and Stoke Sentinel. The post-it labels identified the source and the date, and had been fixed to the clipping before being scanned. All the clippings covered one story: the disappearance of a local man, a part-time gardener, Aditya Dhawan, of Indian extraction but living in the UK for twenty years. Apparently he was very popular with his customers and lived a quiet life with his wife and young daughter. He'd gone to work one morning fifteen years ago and simply never returned. All the customers on his route had been questioned and all of them disavowed any knowledge of his whereabouts. The bicycle he used to get to his clients was never found.

The photos showed a good-looking man with a wry smile, smooth skin and regular features. The articles said he was thirty-four years old.

This was all very interesting, but why was the document on Tony Wolfe's computer? And did it have anything to do with the Mintons? Or with Sally's death?

The time-stamp on her email was 10.00 on the same night we'd met. She must have gone home and somehow found a way to get into Wolfe's computer … or perhaps she already had the document but hadn't known what it meant, or what to do with it. Why had she been poking around in Wolfe's computer anyway? And why would he have given her access to it if it contained sensitive information? Perhaps she was given access so she could her fulfil her role as Wolfe's assistant, and Wolfe had forgotten about the file … or thought it was inaccessible, or invisible in some way. Perhaps he'd uploaded it to the Cloud and she had access to his account. Sally had said she knew her way around a spreadsheet: perhaps she had more computer competence than I was giving her credit for.

I read the articles again and found the story tragic. He'd left behind a young wife and a daughter aged ten, neither of whom had any financial support except for the kindness of family and neighbours. Life would have been a struggle for them, I suspected, during the last fifteen years.

———

I RANG WOLFE to ask him about the articles but he didn't pick up and I didn't leave a message. I realised I wanted to surprise him with the information, wanted to see his soft round face take in the questions and then watch how he handled himself. Asking him directly gave him the opportunity to deny any knowledge of the file or what had happened to Dhawan, but it would also be a prod to see if he took any subsequent action—action that might incriminate him.

It was also true I would enjoy seeing Wolfe blind-sided.

By now it was lunch-time, so I rang the Mintons' house to see whether they'd returned from wherever they'd been. I wanted to speak to Carol.

It was Deborah who replied.

'Mr Detective,' she said. 'I gather you were the one who found Sally. Do you know who did it yet?'

There was something cool in her voice that made me pause. Then I wanted to shock her. I said, 'I thought it was you in the pool at first.'

'Me? We're completely different types. Why would you think that?'

'I don't know,' I said, regretting my anger immediately. I softened my tone. 'You knew her, didn't you ... had you talked to her much lately?'

'No,' she said. 'I knew her from school. She was a few years ahead of me. Alistair probably knew her better than me. They were in some kind of computer club together. They were both a bit nerdy about that.'

So my hunch about Sally's computer competence was right—she might have found a way into one of Wolfe's accounts online without even needing to be in front of his physical computer.

'I'd like to come and talk to you. Would you be up to it?'

'Why wouldn't I be?' Before I could answer, she added: 'Do you think I'm upset about her dying?'

'It crossed my mind.'

'I keep telling you, I'm made of tougher stuff. I was upset when I heard about it because she was a sweetie, but, you know, life goes on.'

'Are your mother and father back home yet?'

'No, I'm as free as a bird. Eating mustard from the pot and drinking vodka like it was water. Usual adolescent stuff.'

'Have the police spoken to you?'

'No, why should they?' Her scorn nearly burned my ear. 'Not everyone you talk to is a criminal, you know.'

'I'm sorry, I didn't mean it that way. But they'll want to talk to everyone who knew her, especially as she was working for your father, indirectly. And she was found in Ben Prescott's swimming-pool. That's a direct link to you.'

'You people really don't understand us, do you?' The signal from her phone had gone sibilant, and then it surged louder and I had the sense she'd walked outside, into the garden I'd seen her father looking at so intently.

I said, 'What kind of people do you mean?'

'You people who don't live here, like we do ... like I do.'

'What don't we understand?'

The energy went from her voice suddenly. 'Oh, I don't know. Don't listen to me. I get worked up over things and then poof! they're gone. I've been like that since I was a child. I sometimes wonder if I saw something nasty in a woodshed, you know, like in that book. Something I can't remember but maybe somebody told me a story and I think the story I heard is what I experienced. Do you ever have that? You're convinced you've got a memory of something but when you think about it really hard, you realise you can't possibly remember it because it's impossible. I was convinced when I was fifteen that I'd walked around the world. I had memories of walking through wheat fields and forests and crossing rivers ... but of course it was rubbish. But the memory was real, and I could call it up whenever I wanted and it was always the same, always the same sensations, the same temperature, the same smells. It makes you doubt your sanity sometimes.'

I had no medical or psychiatric experience to offer any meaningful comment, and I didn't want to antagonise her by offering platitudes. I wondered whether Sally's death bothered her more than she was aware. I pictured Deborah in her father's garden staring at the autumnal plant life, dying in front of her eyes.

I said, 'I've got to go but I'd still like to talk to you. Face to face.'

'What about?'

'I'm not entirely sure.'

She laughed, an unpleasant and harsh sound. 'That's exactly my kind of conversation.'

We arranged a time and a place to meet and then I hung up.

The more I talked to the Mintons, the more I believed they were not actual human beings but aliens wrapped in human flesh. Their range of responses to any situation stretched my credulity, and I'm the sort of person who'll believe almost anything.

MY FINAL PHONE call that lunch was to my son, Dan. He also lived in Crewe, in a small house out near the hospital. This was fortunate because he'd recently been stabbed in the chest by a megalomaniac I was hunting down, so he needed to go in for occasional check-ups. Thankfully, his physical recovery was going well. I wasn't so sure yet about the mental aspect.

After he'd answered and we'd exchanged news, I said, 'I'm going to email you a file for you to look at. It's a Word document.'

'Great,' Dan said, 'Legacy software.'

'Don't be like that. I'd like you to have a read of the content and see what you can find out on the back of it. Plus, tell me something about the document itself—where it originated, if you can.'

'You mean, like who created the document?'

'Yes.'

'That's easy, all you do—'

'No, don't tell me how to do it. I don't need to know now. Just find out and let me know afterwards.'

'Okay, will do. Is this the current case, the politician?'

'In a manner of speaking.'

'And is it connected to the death of that girl, the one who's working on his campaign?'

I shook my head. 'Nothing much escapes you, does it?'

'Not when it's headline news in all the local press and a small box on the Guardian Online.'

'Oh,' I said. 'Shit.'

CHAPTER NINETEEN

HE WONDERED HOW it was possible to be both tired and furious at the same time.

Ever since Wolfe had told him Carol had re-hired Dyke, he'd wanted to punch something. He was surprised and rather pleased with himself for harbouring such a naked emotion. He'd heard himself described as placid and even-tempered, and in a work environment it had served him well because it seemed like he was taking a rational approach to problem-solving.

In fact, he was calm most of the time because he couldn't bring himself to care about anything. For a few years now, life had been nothing more than a sensation of boredom from which he couldn't rouse himself.

That had been the idea behind running as a Member of Parliament. He'd known an MP when he was younger—they'd gone to the same college at Oxford and she'd moved north the same time as him—and had always been impressed by her sense of commitment, her willingness to push at barriers to get things done. He thought perhaps that when he became the local Member, he'd also find a commitment. It was true he could drum up something approaching passion when he talked about the immigration issue, but there were special circumstances behind that, weren't there? It was understandable. It was also a useful tool to have in his armoury, given the party to which he'd committed himself. It made him less of an ideologue — someone more interesting to an electorate used to seeing people cut from the same cloth, whether it was self-interested, greedy nincompoops or ineffectual, mild-mannered wimps.

He hadn't realised how tiring it was to go on hustings, though — to be always 'on', answering questions, smiling at potential constituents, looking serious when occasion demanded it, standing around, walking down streets, listening to other people discuss things they knew nothing about …

HE WALKED INTO the bedroom where Carol was lying down. He didn't believe she was sleeping, just lying on her side staring at Wolfe's disgusting wallpaper and flimsy IKEA furniture. The whole of Wolfe's house had a temporary air about it, despite being over a hundred years old. It was as if he'd moved in and stripped out any last shred of its personality. When his wife, Georgia, had died he'd moved out of Crewe and found this place and Minton had thought he'd spend time renovating, using his hands, get into a rhythm again after the agonies of dealing with Georgia's death.

Instead, he'd hired some people to cover the oak floorboards with carpet, repaint the walls, replace the old windows with plastic ones and generally ruin the feel of the cottage entirely. Then he'd looked at an IKEA catalogue, chosen the furniture he wanted, phoned them up to make the order and paid to have it delivered.

Now it was functional but hurt the eyes to walk around the place.

Still facing away from him, Carol said, 'Stop staring at me and say something.'

Minton walked further into the room and sat on the edge of the bed, which was almost too wide for the space. He said, 'You hired Dyke again. Why?'

She sat up and turned towards him, pushing her hair back from her face, which was creased on one side from the pillow. 'You mean, why did I do it without consulting you?'

'That as well. We look like fools. I sacked him, politely, and you've taken him on again. He's going to think we don't talk to each other … or that we've got secrets we can't talk to each other about. Surely you see that Alistair is fine? He doesn't need us to mollycoddle him.'

'Shouldn't you be away addressing a meeting somewhere? Talking about the marvellous advantages of immigration? Persuading the people how thoroughly modern and progressive you are?'

As she had begun to talk, Minton had recognised she was close to one of her moods. Her voice became reckless and loud and her features somehow unfocused, as though turned inwards on the rage that seemed to burn constantly inside her these days. He wondered whether he'd become more calm over time to help cope with her growing internal anger—or was it the other way around?

As if reading his mind, she said, 'How did we come to this? We made one mistake—no, I made the mistake. And it still clings to us like a bad smell.'

'We can't go back in time, Carol.'

'I know,' she said sourly. 'Don't I know it. I can't undo anything. But I don't like who we are now, and you being an MP isn't going to change that.'

She put her hands to her face and he wondered if she was going to cry. He realised he didn't want to comfort her.

He said, 'I want you to contact Dyke and tell him you've changed your mind, it was a bad idea, you've seen the light now. Something like that. Blame it on me, if you like. Tell him I bullied you, or told you we couldn't afford it. I don't care.'

'Of course you do,' she said snappishly, dropping her hands to reveal dry eyes. 'You care more than you can admit to yourself. Whatever I do seems like a dagger in your chest. I can barely breathe without you getting a wounded look—'

'Carol …'

'There you go, the hangdog expression, the what-have-I-done-to-deserve-this look. You know damn well what you've done.'

He kept his voice low: 'Not now. Not here.'

'No,' she said. 'Never. And nowhere. Pretend it didn't happen. Well it did, and it's tearing this family apart. *That's* why I want Dyke to find Alistair and, if possible, persuade him to come back, at least during the election. You need the semblance of a stable family, don't you, for your election profile? Well what if it were real instead of constructed out of *papier mâché*? Don't you want your son to be here and to be safe?'

'He's not a child, Carol. He was away all last year and it didn't seem to bother you. What's changed?'

Her eyes darkened. 'What do you think?'

He felt himself starting to feel angry again, as though the blood in his chest and arms was heating up before moving into his neck and jaw. He said, 'You agreed to this. You thought it was a good idea. You said you thought it would help me … overcome the problems I was having. And you just said you can't go back in time.'

'I'm allowed to change my mind,' she said. 'I've come to see that yours aren't the only feelings that are important in this relationship, Giles. How I ever persuaded myself of that fact I'll never know. I've gone along all these years—and listen to me, I'm still going along. Here we are, hiding out from who knows what, when I could be having a life.'

'We're in this together.'

This set her back and her eyes went flat. 'It wasn't my choice. Or Tony's. You took that away from us, remember?'

Once more she'd tricked him by seeming on the verge of moving into an episode, then pulling back so that he tumbled into the abyss instead. She was so practised in it and he was like a child running towards the edge of a cliff, over and over again, and never learning that there was fresh air just beyond the place where the grass ended.

He turned towards her, his anger now directing his movements, and gripped her leg as he'd gripped Wolfe's arm downstairs.

'Listen, you cow, I want this. You're not the only one who feels trapped. Is that what it is? A feeling you can't escape? You're locked in a box with the rest of us, so you need darling Alistair here as comfort? Don't think I don't know what that feels like. Every day I cry for the life I lost. Every day I want to tear out my eyes. It's murderous just getting dressed and shaving this lying, treacherous face, the one that stares back at me from the mirror and says, What are you doing? Go out and be happy! So this is my belief: if I do this, and if I win, it will prove to anyone who looks that I'm not what they think I am. That's what I want. I want to prove people wrong. And that includes me. I don't want to be the person I think I am. This is a massive hall of mirrors stunt, and it's intended to trick me as well as everyone else. No, I'm wrong—it's more than a trick. It's proof. Proof that my life hasn't been the waste I think it's been.'

Carol had turned away, unable to face his anger, but now she turned back and looked down at his hand on her thigh. She said, 'You're hurting me.'

He let go and she rose from the bed as though weightless and walked into the en suite bathroom, closing the door behind her.

DOWNSTAIRS AGAIN HE saw Wolfe talking on his phone outside. He used gestures as punctuation. Wolfe had been useful in many ways, but Minton thought he was losing his direction. Wolfe had started as a young man working for Carol's family for a while, before he, Giles, even knew her. When Giles had married into the family it was understood that Wolfe would continue to work for her, at least initially, given her independent income from her share in the farm business her parents ran. Notwithstanding Giles worked for one of the major British banks, both he and Carol wanted to keep Wolfe on the books.

It was only later that he discovered Wolfe's creativity, which was why Carol's father, in particular, liked him. Her father had managed to run up debts and was in danger of losing two of the five farms he ran. Wolfe applied for two sets of European Union subsidies for land that, if you looked closely at the grid references, were off the Greenland coast—literally under water. At the same time, he applied successfully for a grant to build a barn. He managed to squeeze nearly £100k from the Government and the EU without being caught. Two years later, a farmer in Devon was gaoled for almost the exact same crime.

Carol's father, a tall, pink-faced loudmouth, had taken Minton aside not long after he'd married Carol and told him about the whole thing. Minton wondered whether it was a kind of blackmail, intended to keep him quiet, especially given his increasing role in the bank in Manchester. Or whether he was genuinely proud of the fraud, putting one over on the foreigners.

'Got a young whizkid working on stuff for me,' Carol's father had said. 'I think he's set his sights on Carol, even though he's married himself. Keep an eye on him for me, would you? I'll arrange a meeting for you.'

So the meeting had been organized at a Rotary Club dinner and in fact he'd got on well with Wolfe and Georgia, his wife: he had a rakish sense of humour he liked—since descended into sarcasm—and he was full of ideas for managing their money. Giles had even tried out some of his own ideas on Wolfe before taking them up the chain in the bank ... now he hated to think that some of his own success might have depended on Wolfe's contributions.

He knocked on the glass panel of the back door and Wolfe hung up and came in. He was no longer the young tennis-player he'd been all those years ago, but in his eyes Minton could see the creative glint he'd often witnessed before.

He said, 'Who was that? The office?'

Wolfe grinned humorlessly. 'Never you mind.'

Minton thought about arguing but gave it up. He imagined Carol upstairs, perhaps in the room above them, lying on the bed and hearing their male voices going back and forth beneath her.

He said, 'I spoke to Carol but there's no dealing with her. She wants what she wants and she's daddy's girl so gets what she wants.'

'Fuck's sake, Giles, she's about to be the wife of an MP. Won't she see sense?'

Minton felt the memory of his relationship with Carol swelling in his chest like indigestion. But it was nothing more than a reminder, the nourishment long gone.

He said, 'What's the word? Intractable. She can't be moved.'

'I'll put a fucking tractor on her …'

'What do you think we should do, if we were being sensible and not overly aggressive?'

Wolfe put his hands in his pockets. Given his girth it looked a difficult pose, but he kept them there through an act of will. He said, 'You agree that Dyke is the problem, then?'

'As Carol won't listen to reason and just leave Alistair alone, then yes. The same as before.'

'Then Dyke is what we'll deal with.'

Minton felt the weariness descend on him again. There seemed to be a purposefulness in the direction events took around him. He wasn't a religious man, but sometimes he just felt he was a small cog in a larger wheel. His politics proclaimed the virtue—and the possibility—of self-direction and accountability. But lately things just seemed to happen for which he could find no cause in himself, nor blame.

Like Sally Collins, for example. He didn't remember directly sanctioning that she should be scared so hard she wound up floating in a swimming-pool.

He realised Wolfe was still looking at him, his round face and small eyes as coarse as a farmyard animal's. 'What?'

'Nothing. I'm just checking you're still here, with us. I've made a phone call—you don't need to know any details whatsoever. But it should clear everything up for us.'

'I'm not going to like this, am I?'

'I have no idea, Giles. I lost touch years ago with what you like or dislike.'

'I thought you said we were still friends.'

'Is that what you want? Or do you want someone who can get stuff done? No questions. Minimum of fuss. Think of me as a chief of staff, running the business while you … well, I don't know what you'll be doing, frankly.'

'While you're doing what?'

Now Wolfe opened his mouth wide in yet another grin. 'Why, running the country, of course.'

CHAPTER TWENTY

THE WEATHER WAS turning sunny as I parked around the corner from Alistair and Jack's house in Stafford. Signs had directed me to a designated parking area, provided, I suppose, to prevent strangers like me from taking the residents' parking slots.

Nothing had changed since the last time I'd visited, and probably nothing would before the next. It was a quiet suburban street where young married couples might both be at work, waiting for their circumstances to change so they could afford a child.

Jack answered the door and I knew from the flicker in his eyes that he recognised me straight away. He glanced in both directions up the street, then stood back to let me in. As we walked through to a small sitting room, he said plaintively, 'He's still not in, and I don't know where he is.'

'You don't have to cover for him,' I said. 'I don't care where he is right now, so long as you can get a message to him.'

His eyes were still doubtful, but some primitive social graces kicked in and he said, 'Do you want a coffee?'

'Okay.'

On the back of his tee-shirt was a fake touring schedule, with dates and locations. The headline read: 'Adolf Hitler, European Tour, 1939-45.' I hoped it was meant ironically.

In the kitchen he put on the kettle and organised mugs with instant coffee and tubes of sugar stolen from a variety of local cafés.

His voice made sharp with seriousness, he said, 'I don't want anything to do with this. I've told him. I don't want strange men knocking on the door and asking for him. Including you.'

'I'm hurt.'

'And I've told him I'm looking for someone else to rent his room. I can't keep paying for everything by myself.'

'If he's not here, do you know where he is?'

'No, and I don't want to.'

I leaned against the kitchen counter, stained with circles of coffee mugs long dead. A Zanussi washing machine rumbled truculently beneath it.

I said, 'How long have you known him?'

'Since school.'

'What's he like?'

'What does that mean? "What's he like?" He's a pain in the arse.'

'But you got on well enough to want to share a house with him.'

'Yeah, well, it was more our parents' idea than ours. Particularly his mum. He could have gone to Oxford but decided he didn't want to, said he wanted to slum it with me instead. He couldn't give a toss about economics. Which really pissed off his dad. Originally he wanted him to study law but Ali wasn't interested in that, either.'

He was an awkward boy, and when he handed me my coffee it spilled over the edge and on to my hand. I flinched and he muttered a half-hearted apology. We went back into the sitting room and sat on the worn furniture. He carried on as if I'd asked him another question. I realised I'd given him the opportunity to unload.

'I think he thought he was a disappointment to them, particularly his dad. His mum's a bit nuts—I suppose you've noticed.' I sipped my coffee and said nothing. He went on, 'Thing is, they were always richer than us, so I don't know why he stayed friends with me. My mum and dad had to get another mortgage to pay the deposit on this place, whereas *they* just took it out of their savings or something. No sweat.'

'So Alistair didn't want to go to Oxford and he didn't want to come to Stafford … what is it he *does* want?'

'Fuck knows. He sits around watching telly, reading novels. He's big into horror. He scrapes by with his essays but he wouldn't really care if he failed them. I have to help him out.'

'Why do you do that?'

Jack shrugged. 'He's a mate, isn't he? He lends me money from time to time.'

The room we sat in could have been a student room anywhere: an iPod nestled on a speaker, piles of books on the table, posters for Pulp Fiction and van Gogh's Sunflowers on the wall, mugs and tea-cups standing on the carpet—which looked as though, like nature, it abhorred a vacuum …

I said, 'When I met him he seemed jumpy, a bit

paranoid. What do you make of it?'

'You didn't see the men who came to talk to him.'

'No, I didn't.'

Jack held his mug in both hands, like a survivor of some terrifying event. He said, 'His family made a big show of being the perfect family, you know? But to be honest I think they all got on his nerves. He never talked to his sister and he only phoned his mother because she complained if he didn't.'

'They'd put up the money for the house. Perhaps he felt like he owed them something.'

'Alistair acted like he didn't owe anyone anything.'

I let that hang for a moment, then said, 'Did you actually like him?'

He glanced at me, his freckled face dark in the gloomy room. 'Hard to say. I just called him a mate but he stretches that. He was generous with money, probably because it wasn't his. He could be a bit serious. He acted … lonely. Spent a lot of time in his room. That's not me, but hey, he could do what he wanted, couldn't he?'

'Does he know Sally Collins is dead?'

He closed his eyes and leaned back in his chair. A tragedy of memories played behind his eyelids before he opened them and looked at me again. He still didn't trust me.

'That's Sally from school, right?'

'Did you know her too?'

'Of course … she fancied herself as the little beauty queen. She was pretty but naive. Always with the hair and the make-up. She's dead?'

'Drowned. Could have been an accident but I don't think so.'

'What then? Someone killed her?'

I said nothing. He'd lost his passivity but I wasn't going to feed any thirst for salacious details.

'Jesus,' he said. 'Who'd want to do that?'

'You tell me.'

He was startled. 'Me? Why should I know? I haven't seen her in years.'

'Was she a friend of Alistair's?'

'She'd never been here, if that means anything. He never talked about her. I reckon he was like me, hadn't seen her since school.'

I didn't know how far I could trust this assessment, especially as Sally had been working for Wolfe on Giles Minton's campaign. Alistair must have come across her when he'd been home.

I changed tack. 'What do you think of his family?'

He looked at me through eyes that were still dark with contemplation of Sally's death.

He said, 'Do you want me to tell you they were weird?'

'Is that what you think?'

'Not weird,' he said. 'Inward-looking. Like the rest of the world barely existed. Maybe that's why his mum wants him back home. She can't imagine him having a life without her being involved.'

'That's harsh.'

'How well do you know them?'

I shrugged. 'Probably not as well as you.'

'Yeah, right. So don't try to persuade me you know them better. And even I didn't know them like I thought I did.'

'Why do you say that?'

'Just one thing I keep going back to. Deborah came on to me one night. We'd known each other since we were ten, for Christ's sake. We were at a party and she kept brushing up against me and sticking her tongue in my ear. Now *that* was weird.'

'Did she like you?'

He stirred uncomfortably, then stood up and took his empty mug back into the kitchen. When he came back he looked as if he'd had an argument with himself and lost. He said, 'She had a reputation at school. She was a bit nuts. Wild. Everyone said she'd try anything. Course, lots of boys took her up on that.'

'Not just boys,' I said.

I meant to imply older men as well. But Jack said, 'No, not just boys. Girls, too.'

I ASKED TO see Alistair's room and Jack led me upstairs while the Zanussi roared its final spin in the kitchen. There was a corridor containing what I presumed were two closed bedroom doors, with a bathroom visible through an open door at the end. Jack pushed one of the closed doors and it swung open easily. I noted where the lock had been kicked in by Alistair's visitors. The room contained an unmade bed under a mountainous duvet, a scarred desk, an upright chair and several piles of books on the floor. More Tarantino posters were taped to the walls. I crossed to the window, raised it and looked out. Beneath me a wooden ladder lay flat on the ground.

I said, 'What does Alistair say about the day he left?'

Jack had put his hands in his pockets and retreated into

the corridor, as if trying to withdraw from whatever had taken place here. He said, 'He told me he heard them come in downstairs so he locked the door—we've put privacy locks on all the bedrooms. Then he went out that window. He'd put a ladder against it a few days beforehand.'

'So not really paranoid, then,' I said.

'It freaked him out when I told him about the men who asked about him.'

'They did sound pretty scary. It would be good to find out who they are.'

'I don't understand it. He's never hurt anyone, so far as I know. Why would anyone come after him?'

'Gambling debts? Run off with someone's girlfriend? Could be any reason. There are lots of people out there these days who don't need much of an excuse to go full vigilante.'

He was shaking his head before I finished. 'None of those things are him. I can't work it out.'

'Have you told anyone else he's moved? Anyone at the university?'

'No, he doesn't want anyone to know. You can see why.'

'But he's still coming to lectures?'

Jack nodded. 'As much as he ever did, which wasn't much. I think he only comes in to eat in the canteen.'

We went downstairs and I told him to let Alistair know about Sally Collins, which was the message I'd come to deliver in the first place.

'Are you trying to frighten him?' Jack asked.

'Of course not.' I didn't know whether I believed myself. 'Tell him to ring me again and we can talk about it.

We don't even have to meet if he doesn't want to. Tell him he can carry on playing these childish games if it makes him happy.'

Jack sighed. 'I probably won't say that bit.'

HE LET ME out the front door and it closed quickly behind me. I couldn't blame him wanting to get rid of me: I was throwing his life into turmoil and he'd done nothing to deserve it.

I walked around the corner to my car and unlocked it.

Climbing into the driver's seat, I realised at once I was in trouble. A strong arm came from behind the seat and pinned me around the throat. At the same time a hooded figure appeared in the doorway and the next thing I felt was a needle point entering my neck behind the ear.

I felt myself fighting the constraint but I was being held in place and had no room to manoeuvre.

Besides, I told myself as the blackness approached, why struggle …?

CHAPTER TWENTY-ONE

WHEN WOLFE WENT into the sitting room carrying the three mugs he was glad to see they were all behaving themselves. Jordan and Stevie were sitting next to each other on the sofa, as prim as aunts, while Smith had taken one of the wooden upright chairs to give himself a bit more height. As a man below average height he was always looking for ways to advantage himself.

Smith seemed to have two expressions: neutral and pissed off. It was five years since Wolfe had met him at a Military Vehicles Show and the first time he'd hired his expertise. He hoped he wasn't going to be disappointed. Smith had arrived early that morning by cab—'I don't drive'—and spent most of his time in the room Wolfe had set aside for him upstairs. Wolfe had the impression he'd been polishing his weapons, whatever they were.

'So,' he said, when they all had their drinks. 'Jordan, Stevie, this is Mr Smith.'

'No names,' Smith said peremptorily.

Wolfe shrugged. 'Too late. Besides, we'll never know whether that's your real name or not, will we? As for

Jordan and Stevie, they don't care, do you, lads?'

'Bit fucking late,' Jordan said.

Wolfe ignored him. He felt exhausted. He'd spent most of yesterday afternoon holed up in a police interview room explaining his relationship to Sally Collins and he'd had to work at containing his anger and remembering to act polite. He'd slept about two hours last night and his patience was wearing thin.

When he was released he'd seen the Mintons being walked in to undergo the same fate. Thankfully there'd been no reporters around, that he could see. In a day or two it would all disappear in the miasma of current events.

NOW HE HAD to show he was in charge of this meeting, despite the fact Smith frightened him a little and he suspected he was losing control of Jordan. He and Stevie had turned up that morning looking dishevelled and, Wolfe thought, a little nervous, their eyes watery and unfocused. Stevie had a broad tape across his nose and stuck to his cheeks while the bags under his eyes were turning blue. Wolfe suspected they'd been ingesting something the night before—something stronger than alcohol. He didn't care so long as they could concentrate for the duration of this meeting with Smith. He hadn't had time to talk to them yet about Sally Collins, but he needed to find out how it had gone down ...

Smith was in his mid-thirties and had a tight, small-featured face whose major distinction was startling blue eyes with black pupils barely the size of pin-heads. The eyes gave him a slightly otherworldly air because you couldn't read anything in them. He'd been staring at the two younger men blankly, as if they'd barely registered on his retinas. Now he said to Wolfe, 'You said this was a quick job, in and out. Who are these jokers and are they going to get in my way?'

'Who the fuck you calling a joker?' Jordan said, leaning forward and sticking out his chin as if daring Smith to hit it.

'I heard about your first attempt,' Smith said. 'He fought you off with a toothpick, didn't he? Two of you? Jesus.'

Stevie said, 'Id wadn't thad eady.'

'I wouldn't talk, bandage-boy, if I was you. You sound like a moron.'

'He broke my fuddin node.'

'Then you should have kept out of his way, shouldn't you? I'll show you how to do it.'

Wolfe had been enjoying watching them taunt each other like jackals, but now he said, 'Jordan, Stevie—I want you to help Mr Smith here. Be spotters for him. Point out Dyke and anyone else you know that he talks to. You've got the easy part now—let him do what I'm paying him for.'

'What's he going to do, bore Dyke to death?'

Smith smiled to himself and looked down at his hands. At this point Wolfe couldn't tell whether Smith was supremely confident in his abilities, or just trying to create an aura of competence. He'd always believed when you were dealing with crooks and villains you had to reduce your IQ by a good thirty points to appear on the same radar screen. Even when he'd been working deals for Carol's father he'd known that the man was an arrogant fool who believed himself to be clever simply because he could hire smart people.

But that was all behind him now. He was working on a bigger canvas and he had to gather up his courage and put down his marker.

He said, 'Smith, how do you want to do this? And what can I or the boys do to help?'

The man seemed to like being addressed as the expert in the room. He adjusted his seating position and looked at a list written on his phone's screen.

'Obviously, we've got to find this man Dyke first. I suggest we keep a look-out at his home address till he comes home, then follow him, see where he goes, whether he's got any kind of routine. Next we'll see if there's a likely spot where I can pick him off. I'll need a clear line of sight, up to three hundred yards. Transport readily available to take me straight to the station … What is it, scar-boy?'

Jordan had been holding his hand up from the end of Smith's first sentence. Now he had a wide grin on his lined face. He said, 'We don't need to look for him, Tony.'

'Why's that?'

'Because we've already got him. Stevie and me followed him and picked him up.'

<hr>

'What in buggery does that mean? Where is he? Did he know it was you?'

'Nah, I broke in his car when he was out and we got an anaesthetic in a syringe. I've had it years. Used to use it in London, one of the Chinese lads got hold of them. He went out like a light.'

Wolfe found himself doing rapid calculations in his head. If that were true, then he could dispense with Smith quickly, pay him expenses and maybe half of the fee, just for turning up. Then he'd get Jordan and Stevie to deal with Dyke so they could wash their hands of him.

Smith said, 'So what the fuck's this, then? Does the right hand not know what the left-handed tossers are doing?'

'We showed initiative,' Jordan said. 'We didn't need any fancy planning or spreadsheets to get the job done.'

'So is he still alive?'

'Pending further instructions, yes.'

'Where is he?' Wolfe asked.

'He won't get out,' Jordan said. 'Stevie and I took care of that.'

———

As if the sound of his name had woken him, Stevie said to Jordan, 'Perhaps you'd bedder dell him aboud dat udder ding dow.'

Jordan's nervousness returned as he glanced from Stevie to Wolfe. 'Yeah, right.' He tipped his head towards Smith and said to Wolfe. 'He'd better not hear this bit.'

Smith stood up. 'Knock yourselves out. I'm going for a walk round the village.' To Wolfe: 'Let me know when and where.' Then he walked out.

Jordan waited until he heard the front door close, then said to Wolfe, 'You know that other thing …'

'For Christ's sake, you can say her name. Sally Collins, my assistant.'

'Yeah.'

'The one you were supposed to throw a scare into but

ended up throwing her into a swimming pool. Very well done. I spent an afternoon in the cop-shop because of that.'

Jordan was licking his lips. 'The thing is … it wasn't us.'

'What the fuck …'

'We couldn't find her, to talk to her. We went to the address you gave us, her flat, but her car wasn't there. We hung around outside for a couple of hours but she didn't turn up so we packed it in, ready to come back the next day. Bloody freezing in my car. Couldn't sit there with the engine on for the heating—people would notice …'

'So you're telling me you didn't find her, you didn't talk to her or do anything else.'

'We had the hood ready and everything. We were going to take her into Delamere Forest and warn her about telling anyone anything, then let her loose, find her own way home. She would have been shit-scared.'

'But you didn't find her in the first place.'

Jordan raised his shoulders in a shrug. Wolfe could have punched him.

Instead he muttered, 'So who the hell *did* kill her?'

CHAPTER TWENTY-TWO

THE JOURNEY BACK to consciousness was painful and took a long time. I dreamed of young nurses in white dresses turning into yellow-skinned harridans, baring their brown teeth to mock me. For a while I thought I was a small, scuttling sea-creature moving between rocks to hide from the sun and the poisoned darts of predators. Then I seemed to wake into a room lined entirely in leather, so that no matter how hard I threw myself against it, I couldn't hurt myself.

And then finally I knew I was waking up properly because I didn't want to open my eyes to discover where I was. I must have moved, because a voice said, 'He's waking up.'

'Then put him out again.'

'There's no more stuff left.'

'So?'

That's when they started to kick me.

WAKING UP AGAIN was harder.

This time I kept my eyes closed and lay still. My sides were sore and a migraine had set up its hammer-testing facility at the rear of my skull. If I'd had anything to eat I would have vomited.

I breathed deeply through my nose, letting my senses take in details as best they could.

I knew I was lying on my side on a hard floor that felt like wood, but wood that had been polished so that when I moved my legs they slithered easily over the surface.

I was aware that my face was covered, as if by a bag, and that I had to breathe through my nose—my mouth was sealed. Then I realised it wasn't a bag ... my head was wrapped in thick tape, like duct tape, with holes cut in it for my nostrils.

So when I tried to open my eyes, I couldn't.

I felt the beginning of panic set in and tried to move my arms.

No luck. They were tied behind my back.

Likewise, my ankles were also bound.

I made a gurgling noise to learn whether anyone else was in the room with me ... then realised that somehow I knew it was a room.

The acoustics resonated as I moaned and gurgled and gave me a sense of the size of the place. I wasn't in a theatre or a hall or anywhere else where there might be wooden floorboards.

Of course not. Too chilled and echoing to be a basement. Too spacious, perhaps, to be an attic. I guessed I was in a location the size of a bedroom.

THERE WAS NO sound of anyone else breathing or shuffling, so I didn't think I was being observed. I gathered my strength and, still lying on my side, used my bound feet to propel me in a circle, segment by segment.

On the last turn my knees hit what felt like an upright wooden chair. It skittered across the floor loudly.

I waited a few minutes but the noise had drawn no one's attention.

My breath was laboured, now, and I realised also that my neck was stinging where I'd been stuck by the needle. Without use of my hands I couldn't rub the spot so I just moved my neck back and forth, then rested again. My face was sweating inside the duct tape mask but the sweat was going nowhere.

Trying to get upright when I had nothing to balance myself with—no outstretched arms—was proving difficult, so I lay quiet for a while and listened, sending my attention beyond the room, searching for sounds that might give a clue as to where I was.

From somewhere distant came the faint noise of traffic moving on a street.

So I was in a town or city, not in a cabin in the woods … that was good news.

Then I began to consider who had done this to me, and the obvious answer was the man with the scarred face and his yellow-haired colleague. I hadn't seen them when they attacked me but I guessed they would have been wearing balaclavas and masks again, as before. When I'd gone to my car it was already dark and the attackers could have been hiding behind other cars … wait, one of them was already inside. He must have jimmied the lock and then ducked down in the well behind my seat. It was dark, I hadn't looked, he'd been agile enough to surprise me and hold me down while the other one had yanked open the door and injected me.

It was a much more effective method of incapacitation than chloroform, which takes minutes to put you under, not the seconds you see on TV. The injection had put me down before I'd taken a dozen breaths.

SO THEN THEY'D driven me here ... how? In my own car? Did I have my own keys?

I wriggled around on the floor for a while to see whether I could feel them in my trouser pocket. No, the keys weren't there. So they might have driven my car or brought the keys with them.

Nor was I wearing my leather jacket so my phone and wallet weren't in reach.

Of course, that's why I was cold. I was in a cold room in an empty house, wearing my shirt and trousers but no shoes and no jacket.

I pulled my legs up as far as I could to my chest, then rocked myself upright till I was kneeling, my arms still bound behind me.

If I was in a room, there would be walls. I shuffled on my knees, moving about three inches at a time, until I felt the presence of a wall coming near through a shift in acoustics and air pressure. I slowly leaned forward, head first, in darkness ... and then the top of my head butted against a wall.

Progress.

I stayed like that for a few minutes, catching my breath, trying to breathe deeply through my nose and not inhale the gummy odour of the tape against my mouth.

The only way I was going to stand was by separating my legs enough to get one foot flat on the floor and lever myself up. I squatted back on my heels and with my hands behind me felt for the binding around my ankles.

It was a chain, wrapped around several times and then both ends brought together on the loop of a padlock, pulled tight.

It seemed I wasn't going anywhere just yet.

CHAPTER TWENTY-THREE

WOLFE HAD HIS own key to the Mintons' house and he let himself in quietly. He'd cancelled Minton's events for the day so expected to find him at home, if he wasn't in the office.

In fact he was in the kitchen surrounded by pots and pans and listening to classical music on an Alexa speaker. In the moments before he realised Wolfe was watching him, he seemed younger, more alert, as if he were doing something he enjoyed. Wolfe hadn't seen that kind of behaviour in him for months. Politics was a hard master.

Then Giles sensed he was being watched and turned, his eyes losing their spark as soon as he saw Wolfe observing him.

'Carol's out,' Minton said. 'Friday afternoon—my turn to cook.'

'Smells good.'

'Just a simple chicken basquaise. My fingers will smell of garlic for a week.'

'I need to talk to you.'

'Can you do it here? I need to watch this …'

'I'll be in the sitting room. You can bring us a sherry, if you like.' He added, 'And Alexa, shut the fuck up.'

Minton turned back to the cooker and Wolfe left the kitchen, wondering how he was going to phrase the conversation.

⸺

TEN MINUTES LATER Minton came through carrying two small glasses of mud-coloured sherry. Wolfe took his glass and downed half of it while Minton sat opposite him, his politician's face once more in situ—blank, unresponsive, giving nothing away that might later be a hostage to fortune. Wolfe noticed as so often the regularity of Minton's features: he had all the accoutrements of a handsome man and yet somehow wasn't. There was something weak in his eyes and soft around his mouth, and when he spoke his voice was lighter than you expected. He looked good on a poster, but not when animated. He needed to grow his hair out longer and achieve the full leonine look that might get him somewhere in the party.

Minton spoke first: 'Whatever this is, it's got you worried, hasn't it? I can almost see the pee in your pants.'

'Shut up and listen.'

'Now look—'

'My men had nothing to do with Sally's death.'

He watched Minton take in the implications of this, his eyes—formerly bereft of expression—darkening and moving inward, sifting and sorting the various outcomes resulting from the new information. Finally he said the obvious thing: 'So who did?'

'I don't know and I'd rather not care, but I have to—you

180

have to. If it was an accident, all well and good. If it's someone we don't know, fine, we've got no connection other than the employment situation between me and her.'

'But if it's someone we know ...'

'Exactly. But who do we know who'd do something like that, would even have the opportunity?'

'Could it be that man, Prescott? It was his house.'

'I had a word with someone I know, someone in the cop shop ... he says that's the operating thesis at the moment for the cops. They can't find Prescott, but apparently he told Dyke he was going away. Maybe he did it then scarpered. Or maybe he's totally innocent and it was someone else using his place.'

'Who else do we know that might—hold on, you don't think ...'

Wolfe measured his words. 'Why not? Carol knew where he lived. She's not feeling herself these days, is she? Is another episode on the way?'

He realised he was being cruel but it had to be done. Minton had to face consequences some time.

The darkness returned to Minton's eyes. 'Don't be ridiculous. She's been with me all the time. And besides, do you really think she could do it? Carol?'

'Why not? We're all capable of something, aren't we?'

He was being cruel again but he was past caring. He added, 'You've not heard the half of it yet.'

'What now?'

'My men—'

'Laurel and Hardy?'

'—they found Dyke, knocked him out and they've got him in safe keeping.'

A silence as deep as the grave fell in the room. Then Minton said, 'You're not joking, are you?'

'No, I'm—'

'You're trying to tell me that your two cretins kidnapped someone and are currently holding him prisoner.'

'Yes, but—'

'Do you have any fucking idea how serious that is? *Kidnapping*?' Minton's face was turning sunset red. '*That* man? Are you out of your fucking mind?'

'We've done worse.'

'We've done worse because we had to, because we had no choice. This time we had a choice, didn't we? We didn't have to prod a bear with a stick. We didn't have to find a big can of fucking worms, open it and look inside, then say, "Hmm, tasty!" We could have left him alone, couldn't we?'

Wolfe let him go on. He'd been here before. Minton was two-toned when it came to his temperament—he could be quiet and mild; and he could be rip-roaringly vicious. It made no difference: he saw reason eventually. You just had to weather the storm when it started and not take it personally. It was like a switch flipped in Minton's head and a million volts of energy suddenly ran through him.

Minton stood up and paced. The electricity seemed to be vibrating through his hands now. He clasped them together, wringing them as if cleaning them of recent events. Wolfe couldn't blame him.

Minton said, 'You know what this means, don't you? You know what situation this leaves us in? Three weeks before the fucking election and we're on the verge of some kind of conspiracy charges, kidnapping, all that shit you see on TV. And that's going to be us, handcuffed and walking into the back of a police van with the Daily Mail paying a cop for photos inside the gaol. I hope you've got clean fucking underwear, because you're going to go through it at a rate of knots in the next few weeks.'

'Finish your thought,' Wolfe said calmly.

Minton stopped walking. 'What thought?' His eyes were wide and had the clarity of spring water. 'Oh, Christ, you mean this situation ... Yes. That thought. I'll finish that thought for you—we've got to get rid of him, haven't we?'

Wolfe said nothing but let his expression show his agreement.

—————

MINTON SAT DOWN again, apparently exhausted. He rubbed his eyes as if trying to rid them of the view in front of his face.

He said, 'Why can't you ever be the bearer of good news? Why is it always shit?'

'It is what it is. What do we do?'

'You're asking *me*?'

'Two things are going on here: first, there's someone out there who knocked off Sally, and we don't know who it is. The danger there, of course, is that this person knows what Sally knew. Sally told him or her and then was killed for her trouble. That could be bad news for us.'

Minton blew air out of his lips and Wolfe frowned at him.

'Second, we've got to clean up Dyke in a way that doesn't implicate us. We've already had one body associated with us in the last few days. We can't have another. That means he has to disappear completely.'

'No argument from me. But can we trust Laurel and Hardy to do it without falling down the well themselves?'

'I've got them some help,' Wolfe said. 'He'll sort it out. And them, eventually.'

Minton looked at him but didn't seem inclined to ask what he meant. He didn't want to know.

Wolfe said, 'How did it go with the cops? Anything tricky, anything I should know about?'

'No,' Minton said. 'But I'm used to telling lies, aren't I? That's what will make me a great politician.'

OUTSIDE, HE SAT in his car and stared through the windscreen at the Mintons' house. All that money, all that class … and they were relying on him to wipe their backsides for them. A terrible lack of judgement, he thought.

He took out the phone he'd bought that morning and called Jordan, who answered after two rings.

Wolfe said, 'Take Smith with you and do it. No fuck-ups. I don't want to know anything, but get rid of, you know, the body. I'll get you another five grand on top of what we owe you.'

He heard Jordan grunt at the other end of the line and he cut the connection. He looked at his watch: just gone two o'clock on a Friday afternoon. How banal.

Dealing death was that easy.

CHAPTER TWENTY-FOUR

IT TOOK ME an hour, but by flexing my calf muscles and releasing them, and alternately lifting my right and left legs, I managed to slacken the chain around my ankles. It wasn't loose, but I could at least move the legs independently of each other, just a little.

This eventually gave me sufficient latitude to raise my left leg and plant the front sole of my left foot on the floor, while leaning forward into the wall with my forehead. My right foot was still pointed down and back, beneath my haunches.

I gave myself a two-minute rest, snorting through the nose holes cut into the tape, then pushed up with all the force I could muster into my left leg.

Nothing happened.

I realised my weight distribution was wrong. I was trying to lift my whole body weight just by flexing my left ankle joint—it was never going to work. The design of the human body was a wonderful thing: you couldn't stand upright unless you could put your feet flat on the floor and then use your big leg muscles to lift your weight.

I sat back again and rested.

I needed some help. Trying to stand upright *and* maintain my balance was placing too great a strain on a single ankle.

I leaned forward again till my head touched the wall, then started shuffling on my knees to the right. After a couple of minutes I hit the corner of the room and I leaned sideways against the other wall.

The movement across the room also had the advantage of loosening the chain further. I set myself and found I was now able to get my right toe underneath my weight as well as the sole of my left foot.

This time I pushed up with help from both ankles and leaned both forwards and sideways. I heard myself grunting and thought I still wasn't going to make it—but some neanderthal anger kicked in and I forced myself to straighten my legs …

And then I was upright, leaning into the corner, every muscle in my legs throbbing while my nose sucked in air through the mask.

———

SO NOW WHAT? My migraine had settled into its regular throbbing pattern, I'd practically lost the feeling in my hands, and I desperately needed to go to the toilet. When I had a migraine I usually wanted to do nothing but lie down, but I couldn't afford that luxury today. I wanted to be prepared for when the bad guys came back.

First, I had to see what I was doing, so I had to get the duct tape off my face.

I leaned into the wall again and rubbed my face against

it. Nothing happened. The tape had been put on in overlapping loops so all I did was smooth down the overlaps further.

I began a tour of the room, crabbing sideways with my head against the wall so I kept a sense of where I was. I'd gone along one wall without feeling anything and had begun on the second when my nose hit something that swung away slightly, then returned.

It was a picture.

There were pictures hanging on the walls.

I felt with my nose and got a sense of the picture's proportions. It was small, about the size of an A4 piece of paper in landscape format. And it was light. I had the sense it was a tapestry or something made from fabric, without glass in the frame.

But the fact it had swung back and forth gave me hope: it was hung on a nail.

I bent down and placed the top of my head beneath the bottom edge of the frame and lifted upwards. The picture moved up, but when I dropped it, it fell back on its hanging nail.

After the third try, it fell at my feet.

I leaned gently forward again, trying to find the nail with my forehead.

I did … but as soon as I touched it, the tackiness of my tape mask pulled it from the wall and I heard it fall to the floor.

I REPEATED THE manoeuvre around the wall and found a second picture, one that was slightly heavier. I lifted it with my head again and let it fall to the floor.

This time when I found it, the nail stayed put. The heavier picture had required a firmer placing of its support. When I moved my forehead up and down against the nail, it seemed solidly entrenched.

I rotated my head against the nail until I felt it snag, then I moved my skull up and down slowly until the tape began to come away from my hair.

Ten minutes later I'd managed to scrape the mask from the top of my head, my forehead and, at last, my eyes. By standing on my tiptoes I ran the nail against the tape covering my mouth and then it too peeled away.

I took in great sucking breaths and turned to look at my cell.

———

IT WAS A bare room containing the wooden upright chair I'd kicked with my knees, an old radiator, two woven samplers in wooden frames, now on the floor, and a double-glazed window.

Looking outside I saw I was in a town of some kind, and I was looking from a back window over small walled gardens. The room was cold but there was a low sun, so I guessed it was the middle of the afternoon, perhaps a little later.

Now I had to work on the binding of my wrists. As my arms were behind me I couldn't see the binding but I could tell it was cord, not chain. I looked around the room for a sharp edge of some kind. The nail in the wall that I'd used on my mask was too high, but I found the one I'd pulled out. The problem was, it was on the floor, and I didn't want to risk getting down on the floorboards again and not being able to stand upright afterwards. Besides, it wasn't a real nail … it was a panel pin, about an inch long and with no real heft.

The only other possibility was the radiator. It was painted white and was old and rusty around the fittings and there was a single large nut at one end, near the top edge. It might once have held an adjustable thermostat.

I hopped towards it and turned my back on it, then found the nut with my fingers and positioned myself. As I passed the rope back and forth across the jagged edges of the nut, I began to think about what I was going to do to Scarface and Yellow Hair … at that moment, the thought of revenge was an ache in the centre of my chest. It wasn't noble, and it wasn't client-focused, but it gave me some calm as I worked on the knots.

IT TOOK FIFTEEN minutes but eventually the cord frayed enough that I could snap it and my hands came apart. I tore the remains from my wrists and rubbed them to encourage the circulation. Then I hopped to the chair, righted it and sat down to begin work on the chain around my ankle.

All the movement I'd been performing had been working the links looser and looser, but it still took me ten minutes to wriggle my feet out of the chain's loops and finally stand free. Outside the light had begun to fail and I started to wonder whether my captors would return— either to feed me or to kill me. I didn't want to be around to find out.

First, I needed the toilet.

The door to my cell was locked, of course, but wasn't particularly strong. Certainly not strong enough to withstand the angry weight of a six foot one inch male throwing himself against it repeatedly. Eventually the frame split against the tongue of the lock and I was able to pull it open.

I'd realised long ago that the house was empty, otherwise someone would have come up to investigate. They undoubtedly thought I was so well wrapped-up I couldn't get away.

I stepped outside. The room was in a short corridor with a green Lloyd loom chair at its far end. My jacket lay on top of it and my shoes on the floor beneath. I put on the shoes, then the jacket, checking my keys, phone and wallet were inside. Thankfully they were.

Opposite my cell was the bathroom.

I was inside relieving myself, shivering with cold, when the downstairs front door was unlocked, sounding loud in the empty house, and admitting the roar of city traffic and the unmistakable rumble of male voices in argument.

CHAPTER TWENTY-FIVE

He already wanted to smash Smith's face in. All the way
to the house there'd been a string of snide comments—
about his skin, about his driving, about the state of his car
… Smith criticised everything.

Jordan had worked with a lot of pricks in his time—in
the army and in London, with the triads. He considered
himself easy to get along with, slow to get angry and
perhaps not the quickest to make decisions. But there was
something about Smith's smugness, the way he had of
looking sideways at you, and then coming out with some
criticism phrased as a question: 'So doesn't this car go any
quicker?' or 'Did you get the bastards who did that to your
face?' or 'Why do you work for that knobhead Wolfe? Has
he got your balls?'

He'd hear Stevie sniggering through his nose-bandage
on the back-seat and want to turn around and hit him
again, give him something to snigger about.

The house they were using belonged to his landlord but

was empty, for sale. Jordan had persuaded him to give him the key by saying he knew someone who was interested in buying it. The house was around the corner from his own rented flat, on the edge of the Hoole area, so he knew the streets well.

He parked and they locked the car and went up the path, Smith looking around at the other houses in a way that Jordan knew would provoke another comment.

'This the shithole you live in?' Smith said. 'I thought Chester was all olde worlde and posh.'

Jordan silently agreed with Smith's judgement but he wasn't going to let him see it.

Putting the key in the lock, he said, 'I don't live here, do I? It's just a safe house.'

'Not safe for Dyke, though, eh?'

'Keep your fucking voice down, don't let anyone hear you—'

'Are you telling me my job?'

'You're fucking great at telling everyone else theirs.'

Jordan suddenly noticed Smith was pulling a grey pistol from inside his jacket pocket and his eyes had gone flat—even more expressionless than before.

'What the fuck are you doing, man? Wait till we're inside.'

He'd pushed open the door and now he held it while Smith and Stevie came through. He said, 'Go in the kitchen, let's talk it through. Stevie, why don't you go upstairs and look in on the man? Don't go near him, just look.'

Stevie nodded and started up the wooden staircase. Jordan considered what he was going to say to Smith, what he wanted to get off his chest, though he was worried that

Smith had his weapon in easy reach.

He led Smith, who had pocketed his weapon, along the downstairs corridor and turned right into a dim back room that was set up as a rudimentary dining room, with a small wooden table in the centre and three upright chairs ranged around it. It was his landlord's attempt to dress the place to impress prospects. Pointless, Jordan, thought. It was only going to get bought by some Paki who'd rent it out to uncles and cousins at an exorbitant rate …

They had to pass through another door to get to the kitchen and as soon as they were through, Jordan closed it behind Smith and then jammed his finger in the other man's face.

'Look, you prick, Wolfe's put us on this together but I don't take shit from superior arseholes like you. You don't come in—'

He got no further because Smith had reached up lightning quick and seized Jordan's pointing finger, bending it down so Jordan had to collapse sideways or it would have broken. He heard a guttural noise emerge from his own throat as pain shot up his arm.

Smith had stayed calm, and now he said, 'What was that? Were you trying to say something to me?'

Jordan was wondering whether he could pivot and take the man down at the knees when there was a yell from upstairs and moments later thunderous footsteps on the staircase.

Smith let go of his finger and reached for his gun once more. 'Now what?' he said quietly, taking a deep breath.

———

JORDAN STOOD UPRIGHT and opened the kitchen door in time to be confronted by Stevie, holding a handkerchief to his nose, his eyes wide.

'Fucker's god,' he said, breathing heavily.

'Dyke? What do you mean, gone?'

'The door was busted oped, bud before I could do anyding he durned me round and hid me on de node agaid. I dink I passed oud. De front door's oped ...'

Smith had been passive while Stevie spoke, now he seemed to come awake. He said, 'He's on foot, right? We've got the car. You, bandage-boy, you got a phone?' Stevie nodded. 'You're on foot, tracking behind us. You phone your man here if you see anything, *any*thing, right? You, scarface, you're with me. Now he's seen this oik he knows for certain who you are so we've got to get to him pronto.'

———

IT WAS ALREADY growing dark outside as they ran to the car, Jordan tossing the house key to Stevie and saying, 'Lock it!' He didn't like leaving Stevie in charge of anything but he had no choice—Smith looked like he took no prisoners. He wouldn't want to get on his bad side. He watched Stevie run back to the door and lock it, then followed Smith.

Once inside the car, Smith said, 'Which direction will he go?'

'How the fuck do I know?'

'Okay, he probably won't even know where he is, will he? But he's got no transport so he'll look for a bus or a train to get home. Head for the train station.'

Jordan swung the car around so it was facing the right

direction and headed south. The train station was only a couple of minutes away by car and they could be there before Dyke … if that's where he was going.

He slowed so they could look in gardens and down the occasional side road they passed. The houses were all the same—red-brick, semi-detached, dull and lifeless. Kids were still in school, adults at work. Lots of traffic on the road but they hadn't passed a bus or a taxi. The middle of Chester was dripping with medieval architecture and half-timbered houses and old churches and shit … out here, literally over the railway tracks, the suburbs looked exactly the same as the suburbs in Manchester, Leeds, Stoke … all places Jordan had visited and which had depressed him. He was beginning to feel the same way again: time to get out.

'Fuck,' Smith said, 'I don't even know what he looks like.'

'Six foot, black leather jacket, black hair. Fit-looking.'

'He could have knocked on someone's door, gone in a shop, anything.'

'Do I carry on?'

'Pull up here, wait for bandage-boy.'

'Then what?'

Smith turned sideways in the passenger seat and looked at him, his expressionless eyes reflecting the sunset. 'Well first you come up with a good story as to how Dyke escaped your foolproof prison. I'm sure your man Wolfe is going to be very entertained by it. Then we have a think about how we're going to pick him up again.'

Jordan thought about coming back with a reply but knew he'd be letting himself in for more abuse.

What he'd do was, he'd blame Stevie.
Anyone could see he was useless, anyway.

CHAPTER TWENTY-SIX

I'D HEARD ONE of them coming up the stairs and stepped back into the toilet, closing the door quietly. Through the crack I saw the man with the yellow hair slow his pace and approach the door. He must have seen the frame was splintered but he came on anyway. He stood in front of the partly-opened door and pushed it with a finger ... which is when I stepped out of the toilet, turned him by the shoulder and hit him on the nose.

It must have been painful. His eyes rolled up in his head and he collapsed, but he didn't hit the floor because I caught him. Close-up he looked to be in his mid-twenties, unshaven for a day and with greasy skin. He wore an old-fashioned blue duffel-coat with wooden pegs for buttons.

I lowered him to the ground and listened for anything from below. No ruckus. I knew the man on the floor wouldn't be out for long so I had to hurry.

I went to the head of the stairs and heard two other men talking, but muffled, perhaps coming from behind a closed door further back in the house.

No point in waiting—I ran as quietly down the steps as

I could, opened the front door and went out into the cold November evening.

———

THE HOUSE WAS on a main road with traffic passing back and forth. It could have been Manchester or Leeds or any other large town or small city. I couldn't see any landmarks against the darkening sky, but I couldn't wait—I turned right and ran, pounding on the pavement and looking behind me occasionally. I thought I probably had a minute or two before Yellow Hair came round and started squawking.

I soon came to a junction and I was in luck: roadsigns. And one directing traffic towards Hoole Lane—I recognised the name: Hoole was a district of Chester. That made sense. The men were probably local to Cheshire but maybe not known in Crewe—or Stafford. I didn't recognise the street itself, but ahead, on the other side of the road, I spotted a narrow path that rose to cross a railway line. I ran across the road and up the path and saw a round brick gasometer to my left. Now I had a better idea of where I was: fairly close to the city centre.

Then I practically smacked myself on the head—I had a phone with Google Maps on it. I pulled it out of my pocket and pulled up the app. It found my location and I told it to search for the train station. When the route came up I had to backtrack thirty yards, then take a sloping path down to the canal-side. The path ran parallel for several hundred yards with the canal, and I stared at the tranquil water as I walked to calm my breathing. The three men, if they were in a car, couldn't follow me along here.

Less than ten minutes later I walked into the wide concourse of Chester Station, bought a ticket from one of the vending machines, then found the open-air café and sat facing outwards with a sandwich and a coffee to watch for my pursuers.

WHILE WAITING FOR my train I rang Belinda. When she answered I asked where she was and what she was doing. She was on the alert instantly.

'What's the matter, Sam?'

'How did you know?'

'It's in your voice, you dummy. What's happened?'

I told her where I'd been for the last twenty-four hours, and why, and told her I was safe but asked whether she could pick me up at Crewe Station.

'Of course. Are you hurt?'

'In these circumstances I think I'm supposed to say, "Only my pride." But actually I don't give a damn about that. I'm tired and hungry and need a shave but otherwise all right.'

I told her what time my train arrived and she said she'd be there.

'Then I'm taking you to the police station to report it,' she said. 'Right?'

'Maybe.'

'Good god, Sam, give it up. Have a rest.'

'Gotta go—got another phone call to make.'

SHE WAS STANDING in the small entrance foyer of Crewe

Station when I arrived alongside thirty or forty others. I'd inspected as many as I could but none of them looked likely to be Scarface or the third man they'd recruited.

Belinda came forward and gave me a hug, inspecting my face closely.

'You've got bits of something sticking to your face. And a piece of duct tape on your collar. What the hell did they do to you?'

'I told you, I was kept prisoner in a house in Chester. The stuff of dreams.'

'You didn't tell me they'd trussed you up like a parcel for the Royal Mail. Why don't you go to the toilet and wipe some of that stuff off your face.'

I did as I was told, then joined her outside and we walked across the road to the car park. It was now fully dark and I felt sheltered and safe in a location I knew.

We buckled into her Volvo and she said, 'So where now? I suppose the police station is out of the question?'

I showed her a location on my phone's Google Maps and she pulled a face like I'd shown her an obscene picture. But she put the car in gear and set off.

———

SALLY'S PARENTS LIVED halfway between Crewe and Nantwich, but the easiest way to get there from our start point was to drive almost into Nantwich then drive out again past Alvaston.

I didn't know what to expect from the address that Dan had found for me when I rang, but the GPS directed us to a large house set back from the road and barely visible until we turned in between two worn concrete pillars. The house name was listed on a plinth on one of them: The Rose House. Belinda said, 'So who is this and why are we here?'

'It's the parents of a girl who died a few days ago. Be respectful.'

Belinda's face became serious and she nodded, her focus still on the tarmac drive ahead, lit only by her headlights.

We arrived and climbed out. The house looked as though it had once been a farm-house, though there were no barns or farm machinery standing around now. The whole plot had been gentrified. There was a light over the front door but I could see nothing coming from the windows.

However, it wasn't long after my knock that the door was opened and a man a little older and stouter than me stood four-square in the opening.

'Mr Collins?'

He nodded. I saw the grief even in this short gesture and thought about driving away and leaving them in peace. But Sally's memory wouldn't be served by my giving up at the first sign of emotional difficulty.

I gave him my name, and Belinda's, and told him I'd met Sally briefly and would like to talk to him about her.

'And who are you, exactly?'

'I've been working for Giles Minton and Tony Wolfe … on security. Miss McFee is my associate.'

I hated using the Mintons as the way into the house but I thought the more official I sounded, the more likely I was to get a hearing.

For a man his age, Collins' hair was very grey and his movements stiff. Perhaps the tragedy of his daughter's death had prematurely aged him. He said, 'We've had a woman from the police with us already, support services or something. You're not with them, are you? I'm sick of being sympathised with.'

'No, we're not. We're a bit more proactive.'

He looked at us a moment longer, then stepped back. 'Come in. I'll tell Sarah you're here.'

He showed us into a sitting room full of well-stuffed furniture and flower-wreathes then disappeared for a couple of minutes. Belinda and I looked at the flowers and the well-wishing cards ranged on the mantelpiece, then glanced at each other. I shook my head. I knew she was feeling as uncomfortable as I was but I didn't want her to leave right now.

Collins came back in with his wife, who looked as though she'd been crying for a month. She was slender and blonde and carried herself like a debutante from the fifties, her slim wrists emerging from a dark-blue knitted pullover and showing perfectly manicured hands.

I told her what I'd told her husband and they both sat down and faced us.

Sarah Collins began talking before I'd asked a question, taking as her cue the mention of the Mintons' name.

'Of course she'd known the Minton children for ever,' she said, 'before Giles began this politics nonsense. They were all at school together in Nantwich, though Deborah and Alistair were a little younger. In small schools you get to know everyone, I suppose.'

I said, 'Have the police said anything to you yet about the cause of death?'

'No, of course not,' Collins said. 'It's barely been two

days ... why, is there some suspicion of something? We just assumed she drowned while swimming. She was never a very strong swimmer. And maybe the cold ...'

'I was just wondering if the police had said anything to you, as the parents.'

'No. Tell me, what exactly is it you want?'

I cleared my throat, which had become clogged. 'I feel some responsibility for finding out what happened to Sally,' I said. 'I didn't know her well but I thought she was very nice and I want to ... well, offer my services, if you like.'

'What, you want us to pay you for something?'

'No, no, nothing like that—'

Belinda cut in. 'What Mr Dyke is trying to say is that if we can discover anything that can help the police, we'd like to help. We can't do anything that might interfere with their investigations, of course, but Sally was a colleague so we'd like to do whatever we can.'

'Which includes knocking on our door out of the blue within two days of her dying?'

'I'm sorry,' I said, sensing this conversation going downhill. 'That's my fault. We were travelling in this direction and I remembered you lived out here.'

Collins looked unimpressed, but Sarah Collins touched his hand, saying, 'Let them help, James, if they can.' She turned to us. 'So what do you want to know that we haven't already told the police?'

ALTHOUGH THEY HAD no idea what had happened to Sally, they did at least know the Mintons and Tony Wolfe. In fact

Collins had done charity work with Wolfe in the past, which is how Sally had got the job with him.

'I can't say I particularly like Wolfe,' Collins said. 'But at least he gets involved, gets things done. We thought working with him might toughen Sally up, make her less of a dreamer.'

'What do you know about Wolfe?'

'You tell me. You work for him.'

I smiled. 'Temporarily. On contract.'

'Well to be honest he's got a bit of a reputation as a shyster. He helped Sebastian Roberts—Carol's father—get more than his fair share of European Union money, if you know what I mean. And there's a rumour it's not always been done honestly.'

'I didn't know that,' I said.

'I was surprised, frankly, that Sebastian took him on. I understand he came out of nowhere, a college down south, and talked his way into Sebastian's employ. He's normally so cautious. Very full of himself but more bluster than anything else.'

'So nobody knew Wolfe before then?'

'Nobody knew his family, no. I suppose he must have had some paper qualifications but Sebastian doesn't normally worry about that. As this was a case in point.'

'And then he set about making money for Carol and her family. First for her father, then for her.'

'It seemed like that,' Sarah Collins said. 'Of course Sally didn't care about what Wolfe might have done in the past—or perhaps it's better to say she didn't know. In fact I'm sure she would have cared if she thought anything untoward was going on. But on the other hand she realised this was a good opportunity for her. And it meant she could get back in touch with Deborah.'

'Had they been friends?'

'Oh, very much so. Up to about a year or eighteen months ago. There were three or four years' difference between them but they seemed to get on very well.'

'What happened?'

Mrs Collins looked down at her beautifully-presented hands. I felt she was about to crack open and reveal something she'd been harbouring for a long time.

'Oh, you know: girls. They had a big bust-up. Probably about a boy. And then there were all those rumours about Deborah and that married teacher. Nothing was ever said officially, but everyone knew. I believe it just added tension into their relationship. So they stopped talking for a while. But recently they seemed to have made up, especially with Sally working for Deborah's father.' She raised her head and looked at us almost with defiance, as if she expected to be challenged. I saw no reason to do so.

Belinda said, 'Was she named after you? Sarah and Sally?'

Sally's mother smiled for the first time. 'Actually, no. It was my grandmother who was known as Sally. I've always been Sarah. My daughter was always Sally. And now she always will be.'

Tears sprang to her eyes and she stared at us as the water ran down her cheeks.

It was time to go.

CHAPTER TWENTY-SEVEN

I HAD ONE more favour to ask Belinda: to drive me back to Stafford to pick up my car. She raised her eyebrows but set her GPS and we headed back along the Nantwich bypass and then on the A500 till we hit the motorway, heading south. The sky was still lighter than the countryside because of a bright moon, and the silhouetted trees lining the motorway had the shallow aspect of stage cut-outs. The journey took about three quarters of an hour and Belinda didn't say much on the way. I think Sarah Collins' plight had affected her—as it had me. The girl was probably blameless in whatever had happened to her and yet everyone was suffering. Worse was to come, because I was certain Sally had been murdered while her parents entertained the conviction she'd drowned accidentally.

I'd tried to finesse that in the conversation but it was likely the parents were suspicious—why else would two people from 'security' be visiting?

THERE WAS NO one home at Jack's house but my car was

still in the private car park, its door closed but unlocked. I suppose Scarface and Yellow-hair had kept me in the driver's seat while they brought their own car next to mine and transferred me. Were there three of them? My scattered memory said no—there'd been one to hold me and one to administer the sedative. But maybe the third had been driving the other car …

But if there were three of them they'd have brought my car with them: one to drive it, the other two in their own vehicle—one driving, one watching me in case I woke up, sedatives being notoriously variable in their effects. If there were only two of them, as I thought, they'd have left my car where it was and bundled me in the back of their own.

I thanked Belinda and we drove back up the motorway in convoy; she carried on up to Manchester while I turned off at Junction 16 for Crewe.

WHEN HE OPENED his front door Dan looked tired, which made two of us. He'd thickened across the chest in the years since I'd first met him, and had taken to wearing polo shirts and designer jeans, giving him the air of a junior advertising sales manager on his day off. He was still in his early twenties but was probably eating better than he had in his life, and I had the sense he'd been going to the gym for more than physiotherapy. I half-expected a hipster beard to sprout soon.

'You got my text, then,' he said.

'No, I've been driving. Amongst other things. What did it say?'

'Come in and read. Incidentally, you look like shit.'

'I'll tell you about it later.'

We went through into his lounge, where he'd set up a table for his laptop so he didn't have to keep going upstairs to his office. His wound still bothered him, I knew. But when someone forces the first two inches of a knife into your chest it's going to leave a mark.

He gestured for me to sit at his chair and read the screen, which was a large, curved item that sat on a small plinth. I saw immediately that he'd found the online pages of the newspaper stories that Sally Collins had sent me in the post. What was on the screen was no different to what I'd already read.

As if knowing I'd be disappointed, or confused, he said, 'There's more,' and reached over to click another tab on the browser.

This showed a different document. It looked like a printed flyer: there was the same photo of Aditya Dhawan, the gardener who'd gone missing, but there were a couple of paragraphs of text to the right of it asking anyone who'd seen him to ring a phone number or write to an address listed below.

'The family had these printed up and plastered all over the area, so a few weeks after Dhawan went missing the paper did a follow-up story and reprinted the flyer while they were at it.'

'There's an address and a phone number.'

'That phone number's dead now—I wouldn't be surprised if they got a lot of crank calls and changed it. But I think the address is still right.'

I leaned back in the chair and felt the weight of my bones sinking into the seat. It was possible the sedative was still in my system and I hadn't done enough yet to disperse it. My head felt as if it were filled with iron filings.

I said, 'Did you find out anything about the Word document I sent you?'

'I'm hurt,' he said. 'I'm not an amateur, you know. The original author of the document—that is, the person who opened it and pasted in all the newspaper clips—was Carol Minton. That's the wife of your MP, isn't it?'

'Unfortunately, yes.'

'But it's since been modified by a computer owned by Tony Wolfe. Would that make sense?'

'As much as anything does,' I said.

—————

DAN HAD SUBSEQUENTLY researched Carol and Wolfe to satisfy his own curiosity. He'd found information that backed up what Sally Collins' father had told me earlier that evening: before she married Giles Minton, Carol had been known as Carol Roberts, whose father, Sebastian, had been a big-wheel in local politics, working as a kind of facilitator or sponsor, as well as being one of the biggest farmers in the area. Wolfe had started working for Sebastian in his twenties, but soon started managing Carol's finances, too.

'From what I can work out,' Dan said, 'not long after she married Giles, Wolfe went to work for Minton. Like he was part of the wedding settlement from her father.'

I told him what Sally's parents had said about Wolfe, but Dan already knew most of it. 'Whatever old man Sebastian felt about handing over Wolfe to his daughter, I know the other farmers were glad to see the back of him.

You'd be amazed how many farmers write blogs, and how bitchy they are. Even sixteen or seventeen years ago they were at it. They got it all off their chest, especially when they thought someone had been gaming the system. These days they're all trying to suggest they're organic and sustainable and the only good guys in town, but they still go for the jugular when they feel slighted or cheated. Those who were writing stuff when Wolfe was still working for Roberts really didn't like him, and it showed.'

'Perhaps you should dig into him a little.'

'Already on my to-do list.'

He was grinning at me because he'd outsmarted his old man. Not for the first time.

I said, 'So Carol's a farm girl. She's probably stronger than she looks, I mean physically, all that baling hay and mucking out stalls.'

'I've no idea.' He added, 'Going back to Wolfe, I should warn you he's not very visible online. No Twitter, no Facebook, no LinkedIn.'

'Sounds like me.'

'At least you've got a web page now.'

'Have I?'

'You're obviously tired. You should go home and sleep.'

'One more thing,' I said. 'Tony Wolfe—I want you to concentrate on finding any connections he might have to anyone operating illegally. Individually or company-wise. I want to know if he might be in contact with criminals. Through charity work, perhaps. Or as a prison visitor. If not that, then look for ex-military types who might be in his circle. People with a chip on their shoulder or a resentment against society.'

'Jesus, Dad, are you turning into a social worker now?'

I sighed. 'I always have been.'

CHAPTER TWENTY-EIGHT

There was one more conversation to have that night.

I drove into Crewe again and turned into the Best Western car park. Inside, the bar's laminated floor clicked out my footsteps as I crossed to the table where Deborah was sitting, nursing a Perrier water. She'd made an effort tonight with her make-up and looked both older and more vulnerable as a result. She wore several layers of blouses and shirts beneath a thin velvet jacket, as though the effort to keep warm had confused her. Or perhaps it was just a fashion trend I'd missed.

I'd bought a beer from the bar on the way through and I put it on the table, realising immediately that I didn't want it. I wanted to eat something and then sleep and then perhaps sleep some more.

She said, 'I didn't think you were coming. You're late.'

'Blame my social secretary. Can I ask you a question?'

She rolled her head from side to side in consideration. 'I suppose so.'

'When we met the other day, you took a phone call from Sally just before I left.'

She widened her eyes. 'Wow, you are a detective after all. How did you know it was her?'

'An educated guess.'

In fact I'd remembered she'd answered the phone using the name 'Sweetie' and then later called Sally a sweetie … it hadn't been much to go on, but it seemed to have been correct.

'Impressive,' Deborah said, though she didn't look impressed. 'So you found me out. Now what do you want to know?'

'What did you talk about?'

'Oh my god, I don't remember. Nothing important. I think she was fed up with the politics stuff and wanted to let it out. But she was more fed up with all the hours she was working than anything else.'

'Her parents told me you and Sally were close once but you'd had a bust-up. Then recently you'd made friends again.'

'All of that is true.'

'Can you tell me why?'

'Why what?'

'Stop playing games, Deborah. Why the bust-up.'

Her skin beneath the sheen of her make-up glowed slightly with youth and energy, but her eyes had turned dark and furtive. She said, 'Well it's no bloody business of yours, is it?'

'Was it to do with Ben Prescott?'

Now the skin beneath the make-up bloomed a little redder and her features became hard.

'No, it was nothing to do with Ben Prescott. As far as I know she'd never met him.'

'Even though she was found dead in his swimming pool? Don't you think that's a hell of a coincidence?'

She put down her coffee mug and stood up, looking around as though someone might come to her rescue if she looked helpless enough. Tonight she was wearing a green stud in her nose, and as she turned her head from one side to the other it caught the light with an emerald flash.

I said, 'Sit down, Deborah. We're not finished yet.'

'Well I am.'

'I spoke to Sally the night before she died.'

She looked down at me wildly. 'What?'

'We met here, in this bar. She told me something had happened between your mother and Tony Wolfe. Do you know anything about it?'

'Why should I? I'm still young and innocent.'

'Sally gave me the impression you knew a lot. Was she right, about your mother and Wolfe? Or are you accusing a dead girl of lying?'

This stung her and she sat down again, hard, leaning over the table towards me.

'You bastard. Don't say things like that to me. Sally was my best friend when things were tough.'

'When your mother was sent away?'

Her eyes blazed again. 'Yes. She was four years older than me. I was fourteen and she was in her last year at school. She was always a goody two-shoes and she kind of took me under her wing.' The memories had taken the heat from her. She leaned back, spent. 'Then term ended and a couple of months later she went away to university, so we broke up. When she finished her degree and came back we met at a party and made friends again.'

'So how did Wolfe fit into this?'

'He didn't, you moron. Mother talked to him because she couldn't talk to Dad. Dad couldn't deal with all the moody stuff, all that emotional neediness. We all went to see her in the unit and he sat stiffly in a chair while she cried and Alistair and me cried with her. Then we came home and Dad went into the kitchen to cook our dinner. His favourite thing.'

I watched the shadows pass across her face as the memories played out. I lowered my voice.

'So for your mother, perhaps Wolfe was just a grown-up shoulder to cry on.'

She seemed to hesitate, lifting her head to look at me through eyes that were misty.

'I found some letters.'

'From your mother?'

'You can't tell her I know all this.'

'She won't hear it from me.'

'They were all bundled up in a shoe-box upstairs. He must have returned them and she couldn't bring herself to throw them away. She knew Dad would never find them amongst all her shoes but I was trying some of them on for a party and I came across the letters in a box.'

'And you read them.'

She was defiant. 'Yes, I did.'

———

WHILE WE'D BEEN talking the bar had grown busier and people had started to occupy the nearby tables. Deborah glanced across at them angrily and leaned closer to me rather than raise her voice. Something had been shaken loose in her and I could tell she wanted to talk. I let her.

'I'm not proud I read them,' she said. 'I feel like a cow, if you want to know the truth.' She glanced up at me as if expecting a validation of her feelings; I kept my features neutral. 'There were about a dozen of them, all dated in that period she was away. Hand-written. All self-pitying.'

'How long was she away?'

'About a month.'

'Was she actually sectioned?'

'I don't know what that means.'

'It's when someone is examined by psychologists to decide whether you should be kept somewhere secure for a while, usually for their own safety. Sometimes for the safety of others, too.'

She was uninterested in the details and waved them away. 'I don't know. Whatever. I was fourteen years old and my mum was being treated like a nutcase, when she's not.'

'If she wasn't placed in there through the legal process, she must have been persuaded to commit herself. Presumably by your father.'

This was painful, and the hurt ran across her face like a stain. 'She was just so bloody depressed all the time. Nothing we did could bring her out of it. Then she'd have crying fits and was inconsolable. You can imagine how Dad handled that.'

'Badly?'

'He started drinking even more. Took all his yearly holiday in one go so he could be at home with us and go visit Mum during the day. He went every day while we went to school. Then once a week he put us in the car and drove us out to this place in Macclesfield. Big white Victorian building like something out of Dickens. God, I remember acting up during that time, and I know Alistair did.'

'And now here you are, the perfect politician's family.'

'Yep, here we are.'

I waited a moment, then said, 'What was in the letters from your mother to Wolfe? I mean what kind of thing? Did she talk about her illness, why she was in hospital?'

Her eyes moved away. She'd lost the aggression she'd shown earlier but I had the sense she was still presenting me with the front she wanted me to see: she changed her moods too quickly to be genuine.

She said, 'Mostly she was apologising for things she'd said and done. To him, Wolfe, and to others.'

'Mostly?'

'Yes, there was some other stuff, too. I got the impression something had happened years before, something they both knew about. She would hint at it but not describe it directly. She'd say things like, "I can't get over what we did. It haunts me. I still dream about it ..." Things like that.'

'What do you think she was talking about?'

'Isn't it obvious?'

'Try me.'

'Obviously they'd had an affair and she was feeling guilty about it. I hate that bastard Wolfe, but he's got more liveliness in him than my dad, hasn't he? I'm not going to blame her for trying to find happiness somewhere else, even if it is with a fat, crooked gangster.'

CHAPTER TWENTY-NINE

MY BED FELT like one huge pillow when I finally collapsed
on to it. I didn't set an alarm so I didn't wake till almost ten
o'clock the next morning, Saturday. I could have just lazed
around all day nursing my bruises, but at least I had a
client again now Carol Minton had re-hired me.

Finding Alistair for her, however, was the least
interesting part of this job. And as I'd left a message via
Jack for Alistair to contact me, I told myself I'd done my
duty by the case so I was free to dig elsewhere.

I phoned Belinda.

'I'm going to start billing you for petrol,' she said, when
I opened the door to her knock. 'I don't mind doing the
favours, especially as no one seems willing to pay for my
services right now, but I can't afford to keep driving
around for free.'

'I'll fill the car up for you.'

'And buy me lunch.'

'And buy you lunch. So long as a Tesco's sandwich is okay.'

She narrowed her eyes. 'Okay. Where are we going?'

'You'll see.'

'Why am I coming with you?'

'You'll see.'

I closed the front door behind me and led her to my car.

———

THE DHAWANS' HOUSE was in a row of small redbrick cottages less than a mile from the Mintons' imposing lodge in Nantwich. The news reports of the missing gardener's disappearance had said his bicycle hadn't been found. If his other clients were as close together as the Mintons then evidently a bike was perfectly adequate to move between them. Apparently he'd also had a little two-wheeled trailer he attached to the back of the bike and which contained the few simple implements he used.

I parked on the street and we got out and I rang the bell. Opposite the row of houses and across the road was a large park where people were walking their dogs and a Saturday morning football match was taking place, watched by half a dozen men in overcoats who appeared to be playing the game by proxy, judging by their body language.

I told Belinda who I hoped to see and she raised her eyebrows.

'And you think you might have more success talking to the widow if I'm here. You might have told me earlier.'

'So you could prepare?'

'So I could say no. I don't like being used as a ... a sweetener, for want of a better word.'

'I don't think of it like that. You have good instincts and

you might prevent me dropping myself in it.'

We were prevented from further argument by the door opening. I was expecting to see Aditya Dhawan's widow—a sad woman approaching fifty, perhaps. Instead it was a woman in her mid-twenties with long black hair, wearing a tee-shirt and jeans and with a dozen coloured plastic bracelets on her left wrist. Her eyes were large and bright and her skin deep gold. I guessed she was the daughter who had been ten when her father went missing.

I said, 'Miss Dhawan?'

'Yes—what can I do for you?'

I introduced myself and Belinda, then said, 'I'm a private detective and while I've been working on something I came across the name of your father and the fact of his disappearance.'

'What about it? Have you found him?'

'No, I'm sorry. I didn't mean to get your hopes up. In fact I was hoping to talk to your mother.'

Her attitude and tone changed. 'You can talk to me. Where are you from, again?'

'I'm based local—'

'No, who's paying you?'

'I have a client but I can't actually tell you the name.'

'Well I can't actually tell you anything either, so we're even.' She moved to close the door when Belinda stepped forward.

She said, 'Miss Dhawan, can I ask … were you angry when they couldn't find your father?'

The daughter halted her movement but seemed to vibrate with tension. 'I was furious. No one would tell us anything. He went out one day on his bike and we never saw him again. How does that happen?'

'Did the police have any ideas?'

'Don't talk to me about the police. Worse than useless. I don't know what they thought was going on—they acted as if my dad was a serial adulterer so he deserved everything he got.'

I glanced at Belinda.

'Can we come in and talk about this rather than do it on the doorstep? We'd like to help if we can.'

She hesitated and I regretted I hadn't called to prepare her or her mother for raising all these memories again. My idea had been to make it difficult for them to say no if they were confronted by someone on the doorstep. Now it just felt cruel.

She said, 'You ought to talk to my mum, really. I was only ten.'

I nodded. 'But it sounds like you remember it all quite well.'

She dropped her head and opened the door. 'Come in, then. Though I don't know what good it'll do now.'

———

BELINDA AND I walked through the front door and straight into a sitting room furnished in a comfortable style, with an old sofa and chair, a television screen in the corner and various brightly-coloured watercolours on the wall. There was a shelf in the corner above the television holding photos of the girl's father, Aditya, one of them being the same one reproduced in the press cuttings I'd seen. She waved us to sit down and Belinda and I took the sofa while the daughter flopped into the chair.

I said, 'What did you mean about him being treated as an adulterer?'

'See, you're doing it too. Mention sex and everything else vanishes. That's what the police said. Someone tipped them off that Dad visited lots of lonely women at home … well of course he did! He was the bloody gardener! After that they didn't take him seriously.'

'Was there any proof he'd been involved with customers? Sexually?'

She turned her hands palm up. 'I was ten. I don't know. I only found out about all this stuff later, when I asked Mum about it. You can imagine how she felt. Angry, betrayed—by the police, I mean. At the time, what I remember is the police coming in and asking a few questions and then leaving. I wouldn't say they were thorough.'

'Do you think your mother will talk to us?'

'I don't know. It hurts when she has to talk about it. We keep off the subject, which I don't always think is the right thing to do. We've never really sat down and talked about Dad because I think part of her still thinks he'll come back one day. She can't face it.'

Belinda said, 'It's a horrible thing to have happened.'

The woman's eyes turned inward and their brightness dimmed.

'She kept us going—the pair of us. She didn't let me see what she was going through until much later, and then only in bits and pieces. She kept me in school. She carried on working. It was like nothing had changed. We just had no idea where Dad was. We still don't. He went out one morning and never came back. We don't know whether he's still alive or something happened to him. They didn't even find his bike or trailer.'

'What does your mother do?' I asked. 'Is she still working?'

'Of course—she has to. She works in a shop in Crewe. That's where she is today.'

'And you still live here?'

'No, I've come back for the weekend. I live in Manchester.'

The fierceness came back into her eyes and she sat up with a stiffer spine, as if expecting me to challenge her. Perhaps she thought I was accusing her of not taking care of her mother.

But she cooled down and said, 'You didn't tell me how you came across Dad's name. How did it happen?'

I wanted to tell her the whole story about the Mintons and Wolfe and Sally Collins, and how the reports of her father's disappearance had come to me … I wanted to include her, to show her that her father was important to someone, even this long after he'd disappeared.

But I couldn't tell her about my clients and I certainly couldn't link her and her mother to Sally Collins' death. What good would that do? How would it help them recover from a defining event in their lives? It might briefly make me feel useful, doing something for someone's benefit, but it would be a cheap victory and I'd end up feeling bad about the whole thing.

Eventually I said, 'I can't tell you anything at the moment because other people are involved and I don't have the right to break their confidence. Perhaps when it's over I can come and explain what I'm doing. I promise, it's not anything that's going to hurt you any more than you've already been hurt.'

That was a promise I should never have made.

—·—

BELINDA ASKED HER a few more questions and we learned her name was Nishi and she worked for a firm of accountants in the centre of Manchester. There were no other children. She was successful and independent and seemed to have made a good life.

But after five minutes of this kind of chit-chat I sensed we were beginning to outstay our welcome and I stood up.

'Can you tell your mother that we called?' I gave her one of my cards. 'She can call me if she wants to but tell her I'll try to contact her again anyway. Does she have a mobile phone?'

'I'll get you the number.'

She left the room and a few minutes later came back with a Post-It note that she gave to me. I folded it inside my wallet and thanked her. She saw us to the door. Her body language had softened but I sensed the anger we'd aroused in her was still there. As we stood on the pavement waiting to cross the road, she stepped outside and let her anger have the final word.

'My dad had lots of clients around here,' she said. 'And do you know, not one of them came to visit or say anything to us after he went missing. Not a letter or a phone call.'

'What would they have said?'

'They would have said, "Hello, your dad worked for me. He was a lovely man and I hope he comes back. I'm sorry you're having to suffer like this." But we didn't get anything. So please don't ask why I went and got a job in Manchester.'

She turned and went back inside, and I became aware again that the people I met on a daily basis were suffering in ways I could never fully understand, or relieve.

CHAPTER THIRTY

'So who's the Paki?' Smith asked.

'No idea,' Jordan said. 'She's probably nothing to do with us.'

They watched Dyke and the blonde woman cross the road towards Dyke's car. The Asian woman closed her front door behind them. She was nice, Jordan thought. He liked that thick black hair and the dark skin/white eyes combination.

Then he found that despite his attraction to this woman, his mood was still grim. He was irritated because Smith had refused to let them take Dyke the previous night, after they'd watched him go home. But at least he was pleased they'd managed to pick him up again after the disaster the previous day: once they'd seen Dyke walk into the train station in Chester, Smith had run after him and bought a ticket to Crewe, assuming that's where he was headed. He was wearing an anorak and wore a cap so he looked like a normal person. Meanwhile, Jordan and Stevie had driven back to Crewe, keeping out of Dyke's sight in case he recognised them. Why wouldn't he?

They were waiting outside Crewe station when Dyke came out, followed by Smith, and walked with this same blonde woman to the car park. He found a position where they could see Dyke get into the woman's pink Volvo and then followed them all night—over to Nantwich, down to Stafford where he picked up his car, visiting a house in Crewe where a young man let him in briefly, and then home. At least now they had more idea of the people Dyke knew and the places he went. That might come in useful later.

'I'm not going in his house,' Smith had said the previous night. 'We have no idea what it's like in there, whether he's got weapons or whatever … it's too risky. I'm going to take him down outside, in a public place where we're invisible but he's not.'

'We could just rud him ober,' Stevie had said. 'Ad accident.'

Smith had looked at him as if he'd crawled from under a stone.

'Don't over-exercise your brain cell,' he said. 'Leave the thinking to the grown-ups, okay?'

NOW STEVIE WAS sitting in the back seat of Jordan's Escort as if he didn't care where he was, his arms folded like a petulant child. Jordan had seen that look before. He'd find a way to get revenge, however petty. He'd said virtually nothing all morning since Jordan had picked him up from his mother's house at seven o'clock to bring them back from Chester to Crewe, and into another vigil. Jordan wondered whether Stevie would ever grow a pair of balls and fight back. Probably not.

'All right, big man,' Jordan said to Smith. 'What's the plan now?'

Smith's expression didn't change. 'We see what he does tonight. He must be hurting but he's not taking a holiday, is he? If he's still out somewhere tonight, we set up and I'll take my shot.'

Jordan put the car in gear and followed as Dyke's car pulled away from the kerb ahead of them. Part of him was curious about Smith's background but he didn't want to give the man the opportunity to talk and show off. He'd seen Smith fling a guitar case and a roll bag in the boot and they looked heavy, as if he was carrying an arsenal. His plan was to go to the train station as soon as the job was done, so this morning he'd come fully packed.

Usually Smith was either sarcastically critical or kept quiet. So Jordan wasn't surprised he was silent for five minutes as they worked their way out of Nantwich to head back to Crewe. But eventually he couldn't take the silence and said to Smith, 'So are you on drugs, or what? Your eyes are weird.'

He sensed the man turn towards him fractionally.

'You noticed. You're so observant. It's called myosis, or pinpoint pupils. Nothing I can do about it. Anything else?'

'Does it hurt?'

'Bright sunlight can be difficult.'

'Does it affect your, you know, your vision?'

'No. I'm a deadshot.'

Jordan nodded, taking it in, wondering how he'd got to this point where he was sitting in a car with a weird-eyed sharpshooter following a private detective through suburban Cheshire. Eighteen months previously he'd been dangling an East End nightclub owner out of the fifth storey of a car park and asking when he was going to pay up.

Things change.

Now Smith said, 'That's writing on your face, isn't it? I thought it was just random but now I look closer I can tell it's Japanese or Chinese or some shit like that.'

Jordan had never told anyone what the writing said. Now he found he couldn't help himself … he wanted to prove himself in some way to this man. He said, 'I got in trouble with a triad in London. I was doing bits of work for them, debt-collecting and stuff. They accused me of something I never did. I didn't give the right answers so they cut me.'

'So the writing's what … a warning?' There was interest in his voice for the first time.

'A message. It says, "Betrayed a Brother" in traditional Chinese. But it's not true. I turned up late to a meeting and the nephew of the boss got beaten up. They blamed me, said I'd taken money to turn up late. It was just fucking London traffic.'

'Fucking triads, I hate them. Got no sense of decency.'

'A lot of them went down, after I left. In my bit of the organisation, anyway. The boss's brother was turned by the cops. Had his day in court.'

'So he was the one who betrayed a brother. Nice. I like a bit of symmetry.'

Jordan said nothing. He didn't want to know what Smith liked or didn't like. He didn't trust him and didn't understand why Wolfe had brought him in. All he'd done so far was act superior and boss him and Stevie about. He wondered whether Smith was actually a deadshot or was like many of the men he'd met in the army, before he'd been pushed out: full of themselves because they could thump someone and not care about it afterwards. Go home and have a nice breakfast.

Although he had to admit, Smith was more like one of the officers. Kept himself to himself and didn't give anything away. Seemed to stay cool when things got difficult.

And always had a plan.

CHAPTER THIRTY-ONE

'So what do we do now?' Belinda asked. There was a catch in her voice and I knew she'd been affected by the Dhawans' story. 'You'll still want to talk to Nishi's mother, won't you?'

Doing this kind of work you developed an instinct for which conversations to have and which to ignore. She knew that I'd have to talk to Mrs Dhawan or the investigation would be incomplete, despite everything her daughter had told us.

I said, 'Of course. Is there any reason I shouldn't?'

'It's over fifteen years ago,' she said. 'That's a long time to pick up a trail, especially when it sounds as if the cops weren't particularly interested.'

'They'll have put in more effort than it appeared to Nishi. She was only ten—she wouldn't have been aware of what was happening behind the scenes.'

We both stared ahead at the road back to Crewe winding ahead of us. I knew what she was thinking but she said it anyway.

'Don't go off on a wild-goose chase, Sam.'

'Do you want that sandwich lunch or not?'

———

I DROVE US through Crewe and on to Sandbach, then parked in the Waitrose car park and we walked around to the fancy restaurant that had started up a year before. We wangled a table for two and sat in high buttoned chairs resting our arms on a thick wooden plank, as if the restaurant had magically transported us back in time five hundred years. Around us, Cheshire wannabes talked of babies and foreign holidays and the strains of their high-paying jobs. Belinda looked on approvingly.

'You kept this a secret.'

'My first time. I've driven past it once or twice and thought it looked interesting.'

'They don't do sandwiches, according to this menu.'

'Then go wild and choose something proper.'

She did, choosing courgette and lime soup to start, followed by roasted chicken with quinoa and wild rice. There may have been other ingredients I couldn't pronounce. It was good to see her enjoying herself. When I'd worked with Belinda in the past she'd been injured a couple of times and once nearly killed. And there was one time when she'd saved my life.

I realised I felt close to her, though there'd never been a suspicion of romance between us. It was a shared understanding of the compulsions we had to solve problems and try to put things right. I'd worked in government for several years, tracking smugglers, opening up the backs of container lorries to find a myriad startled eyes staring at me … but in that capacity I'd inured myself to the hurt I saw every day. It was the only way of coping.

Now, working under my own name, I had to remind myself I did it for money, and if I helped someone achieve an improvement in their condition it was a bonus.

And I had to admit to myself that part of how I operated was driven by guilt: I couldn't absolve myself of the fact I was a failure—as a husband, a father, a government bureaucrat. No one would give me a job based on the references I'd received from the former Customs & Excise department, so each morning I had to haul myself from bed and create a life I could live with, flying under my own flag. I wondered how it changed the decisions I made, the actions I took. At least I was learning to take responsibility for them.

I said to Belinda, 'Why do you do this?'

She had a face that was mostly oval and rarely still, her emotions visible as soon as she felt them, like a chameleon changing colour. Now there was enjoyment in her eyes because I'd asked a real question. She said, 'What, the life of the private investigator? Come on, Sam, you know as well as I do—it's the adrenaline. Walking into a room and not knowing what's going to happen. Even the boring stuff, the driving and the bodyguarding and the credit-checking … you never quite know if something dramatic is going to happen.'

I looked down at my roast beef and poked it with my fork. She was right, and I'd hidden that aspect of the work from myself. Perhaps I didn't want to think of myself as that shallow—or perhaps I was so used to the range of people, the different situations I found myself in, the varying levels of intensity, that I just didn't feel them as deeply as before. Perhaps I was getting jaded.

She stopped eating and directed her eyes towards my jacket.

'Isn't that your phone?'

It was. I answered and took it outside to talk without disturbing the other diners.

'At last you answer.'

It took me a moment but then I recognised Alistair Minton's youthful but resonant voice. I said, 'Have you been calling?'

'Look at your call history.'

'Sorry, I've been busy.'

'Okay, listen. I hear Sally Collins is dead. Is it anything to do with those two men who came after me?'

'I don't think anybody knows. What do you think?'

'Don't ask me. I didn't really know her.'

Neither of us said anything for a moment and I imagined him somewhere in a room, staring out of the window like his father, thinking about Sally Collins and wondering what the connection was to his own actions. He'd be fearful and probably annoyed at the same time, wishing it would all go away so he could return to some kind of normality.

I said, 'Thanks for calling. I wanted to talk to you about her. Is there anything at all you can tell me? Something you remember about her, perhaps when you were home and your dad was just starting his campaign? Was she there from the beginning?'

'I don't think so,' he said. 'The first thing that happened

was Dad meeting lots of people, the house was always full. The local party members, the selection committee. Then not long after that I kept seeing Tony Wolfe more often around the house, going home late after work but ringing the front doorbell at seven-thirty the next morning to come in ... at least till Mum gave him her office upstairs and they let him use one of the spare bedrooms to sleep. I didn't start seeing Sally regularly till a couple of months later.'

'You knew her at school ... was it strange to see her again?'

'Not really, I'd seen her around town when she came back from Uni. She knew Deborah better—they were big pals for a while.'

I waited but he didn't add anything. The line crackled and I wondered again where he was, this disembodied voice, what kind of place he'd found to stay now he'd abandoned Jack and their shared house. I was about to prompt him when he said, 'I didn't call to talk about Sally, anyway. I liked her, but there's something else I want to talk to you about. Can we meet again, tonight?'

I agreed and we decided on a place we both knew in Crewe. It was as though he didn't want me to venture into his life in Stafford. Or perhaps he would go and see his parents afterwards.

I said, 'Are you all right? Have you spoken to your mother or father?'

'Yes,' he said. 'I'm all right.'

That was as far as he was willing to go.

I WENT BACK inside and met Belinda's questioning gaze.

'Alistair,' I said. 'He's heard about Sally Collins and it's changed something for him. He wants to talk. Tonight.'

'Great. Can I come?'

'If you promise not to embarrass me with pertinent questions.'

'Hard, but I'll do my best.'

CHAPTER THIRTY-TWO

AFTER LUNCH I drove Belinda to see Dan and we sat around talking about the Mintons for a while. Dan told me what else he'd learned about Wolfe: we knew he'd been Carol's father's book-keeper for some years before progressing to become Giles and Carol's accountant. Dan found he'd always worked alone, never for a larger firm or even with a partner. In addition he was a big fan of military shows—the kind where they demonstrate their weaponry and other equipment to open-mouthed members of the public. In fact he'd once been the chair of a local group that organised military vehicle shows and liaised with local charities to distribute the earnings from entrance fees. And, as with his reputation amongst local farmers, he was well-known in military fandom but not particularly well-liked. 'He's not on Facebook but he does sign up for websites where people discuss the military and all its glories. Apparently he rubs people up the wrong way,' Dan said. 'The forums are full of people bad-mouthing his attitude.'

'So it's likely he knows military types online and maybe cultivated some relationships,' I said. 'People who are now out of the forces but still looking for an adrenaline hit.'

'Watch it,' Belinda said. 'You're talking about my people. Actually, you're talking about me.'

'Maybe—but you haven't got quite as much testosterone as some of these guys.'

'Says you.'

We discussed how likely it was that Wolfe would be able to recruit people he knew to carry out his dirty work. We thought that given his contacts and history, it was very likely. He might behave online like a wannabe soldier but wouldn't have the experience or physical expertise to threaten or cajole people in real life. Scarface and Yellow-hair would fit the bill ... though they seemed to be particularly poor examples of the kind of men he'd want.

———

EVENTUALLY THEY ASKED what had happened to me in the kidnapping and how I escaped and who I thought Scarface and Yellow-hair were working for. I told them in detail what happened, breaking into a sweat when I realised what my captors could have done to me while I was out. I knew they'd thrown me around, or kicked me, because I had bruises in the small of my back, my shoulders and thighs. And I was forced to catch my breath occasionally when I made a move my body didn't like.

'You should definitely report it to the cops,' Belinda said, though she said it as if by rote, knowing I wouldn't agree. 'If nothing else it would be on record for later on, if you needed proof of what these people had done to you.'

My stubbornness had got me in trouble before, and I could sense it rising in my chest now like indigestion. The kidnapping was something I wanted to keep to myself—not necessarily for the purposes of extracting my own revenge, but because it felt personal. I felt responsible for putting myself in the position of being kidnapped in the first place and I wanted to right that wrong on my own. I didn't want the policing system to take it away from me, interfere with my life, and possibly never prosecute the culprits. I said something non-committal, but both Dan and Belinda knew my refusal to report the crime meant I wanted to deal with it myself and not involve anyone else. Dan said, 'What would you have done if it was me?'

'Reported it straight away. Got some help.'

'So why won't you do it for yourself?'

'Because I know who did it. The one with yellow hair was checking on me while the one with the scarred face was downstairs, talking to someone else. I need to find out who he was, too, and the police won't help with that. They'll check their records, perhaps find the main two jokers from previous activities, and the third one, the one I don't know, will run away. I need to find him by myself and ask him whether he was involved. After I've talked to the other two first, of course.'

'This is sounding like a vendetta, Sam.' Belinda was laid out on Dan's sofa, staring at the ceiling, and she sounded weary. Perhaps she was tired of my self-aggrandisement. She added, 'When I first got into this business an old boy I knew told me I had to keep myself out of the case. Just collect the evidence and present it, that's what clients want. They don't want to feel they're responsible for us, or for anything we do. Now I haven't always followed that advice myself, but I do think about it from time to time.'

'We're not the same, Belinda.'

She didn't look at me but her words hit me hard: 'No, we're not. I try to think about the other people I might be putting in danger. I'm not sure you ever get that.'

The mood in the room had shifted quickly. I didn't think she was right, but it bothered me she thought she was.

Dan didn't like what was happening and he stood up, saying, 'I'm going to put the kettle on for tea.'

'Yes, please,' Belinda said, and as Dan walked from the room she turned her head and gave me a bleak smile in recognition of something I couldn't name, but seemed to be linked to a change in our relationship.

———

LATER I ORDERED us pizza to be delivered, though when it arrived Belinda waved it away and I had only one slice, the roast beef from lunch still weighing on my stomach, and at 8.45 Belinda and I climbed in my car for the short drive to the pub where we were going to meet Alistair.

The night was misty and cold and as so often I registered the streets of Crewe as distant and a little forbidding, a town that was inert and threatening at the same time, like a reluctant bully.

'Not very busy,' Belinda said as we took the back route through narrow Victorian streets filled with red-bricked terraced houses. Through drawn curtains, house after house, you could see the pale light of television screens. Nobody could afford to go out any more. Everyone stayed indoors with beer bought from the supermarket, watching family-friendly talent shows or dancing contests. The shows pretended they were bringing people together but in fact they kept them apart, nurturing them as captive purchasing-units in individual consuming-cells.

My mind went back to Aditya Dhawan's family, the wife and daughter. Nishi had seemed strong and purposeful, but I wondered what her father's absence had deprived her of. Was she resentful of those around her who had complete families? Did she blame anyone—or all of us—for taking him from her? Or, like many children in her position, did she blame herself for somehow driving him away?

Her family had been broken by the want of a father. And I was shortly to meet a son in the process of doing the same to his own family. Ironies like this were usually too subtle for me to spot but this one was inescapable.

'Deep thoughts,' Belinda said, and I sensed her looking at my profile.

'Indigestion,' I said, and then realised I wasn't lying. Nothing about this case sat well with me.

THE PUB WAS an adjunct to a modern estate opposite a Bombardier factory, closed for the night. The pub had a garden with a playground for children and was next door to a McDonalds, which didn't seem particularly busy. I drove the car to a corner of the half-empty car-park and we walked around to the front of the pub.

Inside the pub's bar, Alistair was sitting at a table with a fancy-looking burger and a silver mug full of fries in front of him. Definitely not a McDonald's take-away. He didn't stop eating when we sat opposite but looked at Belinda with hostility.

'She's a friend,' I said. 'In the same line of work as me.'

'Why is she here?'

'She's helping me out. Her name's Belinda, by the way.'

Belinda said hello but didn't reach out a hand. He said nothing and finished his burger, wiped his lips and sat back in his padded seat.

'What does she know?'

'Everything relevant.'

He'd tidied himself up since our meeting on Crewe platform. His hair was combed and he'd trimmed his beard to a close cut. Now I could see his resemblance to his father, especially in the hurt and distant look in his eyes. He wore a thick Aran-wool jumper.

He said, 'Do they know what happened to Sally yet?'

'Not as far as I know. But then I'm not privy to their thought-processes.'

'But what do *you* think happened to her?' he said. Despite the distance in his eyes, his voice seemed fearful, as if he might not like any answer I gave. I had to keep reminding myself he was twenty years old.

'I think she was murdered. She was wearing her underclothes, as if she'd stripped for a swim. But the night was cold and I just don't buy the idea she'd go for a swim in someone else's pool, at night, in the cold. It was too much of a dare for the young woman I met.'

Now he looked away, his eyes following the movements of other people in the bar.

Belinda said, 'How well did you know her?'

'I didn't *know* her at all. I used to see her around at school, she was older than me. And she visited us a couple of times when she was friends with Deborah. But they used to go up to Deborah's room, so I didn't really see her then. I don't think I ever had a proper conversation with her.'

'Even when she was working for your dad?'

'Especially then. She was always running after Tony Wolfe, fetching him coffee, typing things up for him.'

'You were both in a computer club at school, weren't you?'

He shook his head as if it were irrelevant. 'I did it because I was a gamer. She wasn't into esports, as far as I know, so I didn't have anything to do with her.'

He pushed his plate away from the edge of the table as if he were disgusted with himself for eating its contents. Then the energy seemed to leave him like an exhalation and he lowered his eyes to his lap.

'I want to tell you something. I don't know what it means, and I don't know if I should tell you. But I'm going to anyway. It's been preying on my mind for weeks now, and I haven't known what to do. I haven't told anyone else, not Jack, not Deborah, certainly not my mother and father. But it's got to the stage where I can't *not* say it. I've got to say it to someone. I've been reading pamphlets about … about students who self-harm. Suicides. And a lot of what they go through can be eased if they just talk to someone. It doesn't feel like it, and they don't want to do it, talk I mean—and I don't want to. But I have to. Otherwise I'll go nuts. It might hurt some people … in fact, I *know* it will hurt people. That's why I've kept it to myself. But I can't do it anymore, be quiet. Sally dying just proves how you never know … you never know when you're going to die. So I've got to get it off my chest. I don't know why I'm telling you but you're not the police, are you? You might help me understand it and give me some advice. It's going to hurt some people really badly.'

He paused but still didn't look at us, he had too much else to concentrate on.

'The problem with what I've got to say is that I don't know whether it's true or not. I think it is. I remember it as true. But I was very young. The memory I'm going to talk about is in flashes, like short clips from a video. A trailer. There's no structure or logic or coherence, just a number of scenes. They come to me when I'm not concentrating, when my mind is just floating around. It's like remembering bits from a film you saw years ago, but you can't remember the plot, just individual scenes.'

I glanced at Belinda and saw she was already looking at me, as if she were waiting for my reaction. I willed myself into stillness.

Alistair had lapsed into silence again but I said nothing. There was some music in the background, in the bar; it seemed as far away as Mexico.

Alistair began again. 'The first scene is … it's sunny and I've been left inside the house to read while my parents are outside, in the garden. I'm about five. My parents used to insist that I read at least an hour a day before I could play any computer games. So I finish reading and now I go outside, through the patio doors, into the back garden, on to the lawn. In those days it wasn't the same as it is now, with all the flower beds. It was mostly lawn. I used to play a kind of cricket with my dad, though my coordination wasn't very good. That's the first scene—me sliding back the patio doors and being blinded by the sun, looking over the garden, then walking outside.

'The next scene I remember is me lying on my back on the lawn, staring up at the sky. I hear birds singing. Everything's quiet and peaceful for a long time. And then I hear the sound of a shovel digging. I turn around … but before I see anything the scene ends.

'The last scene is me standing by the corner of the shed, looking at my mother and father. My mother's standing looking down, both hands to her face—no, to her mouth, as if she's trying to stuff her handkerchief in it. My father's in a long hole, his white shirt-sleeves rolled up, and he's digging. I can't see far around the corner of the shed and I know I shouldn't be there, so I don't move and I don't say anything. Then my dad climbs out of the hole and sticks the spade in the earth and moves to my left, out of sight. I can only see half of the hole. Then my dad jumps back into it and turns and reaches up and slides something down off the side, off the bank of the hole. It's wrapped up in one of my mother's table-cloths so I can't see what it is. As Dad carries on pulling on the object, the table-cloth comes partly unravelled and I see a brown arm fly upwards. My mother lets out a squeal and turns and runs back towards the house and then she sees me behind the shed and gathers me up and runs me back to the house. That's where the scene ends. That's the whole thing. Is it a memory or a dream? You tell me, you're the detective. I don't want it to be either.'

<hr>

WE WERE ALL silent for a while. I think we were waiting to see if Alistair had anything more to say.

245

Finally he looked up. 'I don't know what it means. It seems real to me, but I don't believe it. My sister talks about a memory she has of walking around the world—but obviously it's not a memory, it must be a dream. I don't know whether this thing is a memory or a dream. But whatever it is, it won't go away. And I'm scared of it.'

I said, 'You haven't told anyone about it? You didn't ask your mother or father what it might be?'

His eyes had dark half-moons beneath them now, as if the vision in his story had burned his eye-sockets. 'I went years without thinking about it, as if I'd forgotten. Then a couple of years ago it started to come back to me, in flashes. I want it to not be real, but I have a terrible feeling it is. I couldn't talk to them about it, because what if it *is* real? What can they say to me? Or do to me?'

'You think the man with the scarred face and his friend might have something to do with it? Who would have sent them?'

'How do I know? I don't think my mother would want me harmed … but Dad, he's different. We've had awful rows about his politics. I don't think he's ever liked me. He makes it hard to like him back.'

'You don't believe him,' I said. 'You think he's a fake.'

'I don't know what he is any more.' He hesitated and looked directly at me. 'Do you think I'm making it up, dreaming it into life?'

'No,' I said. 'I don't. Now I have a story to tell you.'

WHEN I'D FINISHED telling him about Aditya Dhawan his complexion had changed from student-pale to ashen.

'They did it,' he said. 'For some reason, they killed that man and buried him in the garden. I was five years old and they kept it from me. Of course they did. I didn't know anything about a gardener and I still can't remember him — I suppose I was at infant school or whatever when he came to the house to work. Except this was summer: perhaps I was on school holiday. So the gardener came and something happened and they killed him and buried him.'

I said, 'Was Tony Wolfe around at that time?'

'Yes. He used to come and try to play rough-and-tumble with me. But I hated him and used to run away. I remember he smelled of booze all the time.'

'Do you think he knew about Mr Dhawan? What your parents had done?'

'Why would he? Surely it's not the kind of thing they'd have told him?'

'There's a likelihood he and your mother had an affair.'

His eyes narrowed quickly. 'Fuck off, that would never happen.'

'There are letters, written by your mother to him when she was away in hospital.'

'It doesn't prove anything. I still don't believe it.'

'You believe she was involved in killing a man, but not that she and Tony Wolfe might have had an affair.'

'Well one's unlikely and the other's impossible. I'm not going to believe the impossible.'

We stared at each other, then I said, 'Your mother wants me to persuade you to come home. She wants you close by until after the election. She wants me to be a kind of mentor to you, whatever that means. Do you think she knows something she doesn't want to tell us?'

'I can't go back,' he said. 'There's nothing for me there. I can't do it any more … Shit, I've just realised something.'

'What?'

'I'm stupid … it's taken me this long to see it, to put it all together. Perhaps those counsellors are right—talking about something does help you see it more clearly.'

Then he told us.

CHAPTER THIRTY-THREE

I OFFERED ALISTAIR a lift to the train station but it turned out he'd brought his own car this time and wanted to stay until after we'd gone. We left him thinking about ordering a dessert, perusing a plasticated menu and looking exactly as old as he was.

Outside, Belinda said, 'So what do you think of his theory?'

I had to think about that for a long while. Alistair had told us his sudden realisation: he thought his father was claiming to be pro-immigration because he'd killed an immigrant. It was a kind of protective colouring—head off the posse by claiming to be one of them. Hide the guilt by burying it under a façade of Good Works.

I had my doubts.

Aditya Dhawan had gone missing fifteen years previously: why would Giles Minton suddenly decide to place himself in the spotlight while at the same time claiming a position likely to make him unappealing to voters—that's to say, supporting immigrants? Many people in his party had promoted the same position, but with disclaimers and qualifiers, effectively trying to ensure that only the brightest and the best—and whitest—immigrants should be allowed in. Minton's position seemed to be more inclusive, from what I'd heard. His argument was that any and all immigrants were a benefit to the country. This set him apart from the majority of his soon-to-be colleagues.

On the other hand, the psychology was compelling. Maybe Minton's passion for the rights of immigrants was born out of a deep psychological grief, a regret for what he and Carol had done. Fifteen years on, Minton's conscience had surfaced and was now persuading him to support a just cause.

This didn't explain Wolfe's involvement, however—it seemed he only acted in his own interests, not from any social obligation.

We'd arrived at the car and I was fumbling for my car key in my pocket, and looking at my Mondeo's side window, when it silently exploded. Glass shattered into small pieces and fell inside the car, and as I watched it happen in apparent slow motion I heard Belinda shout, 'Get down!' and felt a tug on my jacket.

I fell to my knees and then twisted so I was leaning with my back against the driver's door. I glanced to my right and Belinda was there, looking at me with a grim half-smile, as if something had been proved. There was no follow-up shot so we were evidently hidden from the shooter. The air around us was still and you could almost believe that my car window had exploded of its own free will, as if an internal tension had caused it to splinter.

We'd heard nothing, seen nothing, and even now, in the darkness of the car park, I could hear only the soft music emanating from the pub and the despairing sounds of people trying to have a good time. No one had come tearing through the front door to find out what had happened. No police sirens were sounding, or flashing lights arriving.

What I heard, apart from the pub sounds, was a car starting up a couple of hundred yards away, then roaring off back towards Crewe and anonymity. I guessed it was driven by Scarface and Yellow-hair, with the third man perhaps stowing away his rifle, cursing bitterly and planning when he was going to take his next shot.

I said, 'Are you all right?'

'Life with you is never boring,' Belinda said, and I heard her clothes rustle as she stood up. I followed and our eyes scanned the distance, beyond the car park, to see if we could spot a moving vehicle. We couldn't. My heart was beating a little fast but I seemed to be taking it quite calmly.

'We should report it,' Belinda said. 'We can't allow gunshots to go unreported in a pub car-park.'

I hesitated. She was right, but I couldn't see any advantages in doing so. I looked through the shattered window and saw that the passenger window on the far side was still intact. There was probably a shell in my car somewhere, but it would doubtless be untraceable. We hadn't seen the shooter or the vehicle and had no other witnesses.

'We've got them rattled,' I said.

'Great. They're rattled, we're nearly dead.'

'Did you see anything? Hear anything?'

'No,' she said, her voice quiet. 'I just don't like letting this stuff go—your kidnapping, now this shooting. We'll be in a lot of shit when it all comes out.'

I knew I should be concerned about my legal position, and I knew I should be worried about the assassin's attempt to drill a hole through me.

But I was still thinking about Sally Collins and what she had gone through. Someone had taken her to Ben Prescott's house—or had tricked her into going there—and had then drowned her. Her naivety and innocence had let her down, as they always did. I was neither of those things, though I was occasionally stupid, but I thought it was part of my role to extract some kind of reckoning for her death.

What that reckoning would be, I didn't yet know.

CHAPTER THIRTY-FOUR

JORDAN FOCUSED ON his view through the windscreen and tuned out Smith, who was still raging five minutes after taking his shot.

'You fucking touched me,' Smith said, not looking at either Jordan or Stevie but everyone knew who he meant. 'I was all set up, two hundred yards is nothing, and you fucking touched my elbow. I never miss at that range and you've ruined my record, now. And cost me a lot of money.'

'You're imagining things,' Jordan said. 'You missed, get over it.' He was focused on keeping his speed down as they sped west out of Crewe to join the Middlewich Road. He'd had the route planned out beforehand. They'd do a big loop and wind up back in Crewe later, much calmer and without any fear of being spotted.

Smith was in the passenger seat. He occasionally hammered the dashboard, getting his anger out, and then he'd produced the pistol he'd brandished the previous night, and which Jordan now recognised as a Glock, which he nursed in his left hand and rested on his lap. Jordan didn't like that development. After Smith's shot had gone wide, breaking Dyke's car window, Smith had stood upright, stunned, before turning towards Jordan who made himself express nothing through his body language. Perhaps a downturn of his lips, demonstrating a professional sympathy, bad luck, old chap …

Then Stevie had said, 'We'd bedder go dow, dey'll be looking for us,' and Smith had turned to stare at him accusingly before stalking to the boot, opening his roll-bag and throwing his specialist rifle in it while Jordan started the motor.

Since then Smith had shouted and raged and said the whole project was a waste of time and money anyway, that he wasn't getting paid enough for the shit he'd had to put up with, and that he was going straight home.

Jordan knew why Stevie had done it. Smith had gone too far, taunting Stevie about his smashed nose and his general lack of intelligence.

They'd both watched Smith setting up, laying a blanket on the top of the car to help steady the weapon, shaking his fingers out and taking deep breaths. They'd seen Dyke and the woman go inside and barely forty minutes later come out again, crossing the car park's tarmac as they talked to each other. Smith had been practising sighting his weapon on a spot a few yards in front of Dyke's car, so when Jordan said, 'Here they come,' he was already targeted and ready to lead Dyke, aiming for the central mass.

And Jordan had seen Stevie lean closer as if professionally interested, watching his finger, listening to his breathing become shallow … and then at the last minute allowing his elbow to touch Smith's shoulder just as the bullet was released.

Then Stevie had stood upright and grinned at Jordan behind Smith's back. He didn't care that he'd ruined the evening: he'd got his revenge for all Smith's insults.

Smith had turned on Stevie and would have hit him with the stock of his weapon if Jordan hadn't caught his arm. He'd pushed the rifle down, telling him quietly, 'Next time.'

'That's it,' Smith said now, 'I'm not dealing with amateurs again. You're fucked up. You cost me a lot of money tonight. Fucking amateurs. I should have you both put down, get some of my friends from London up to have a party on your fucking graves.'

From the back seat, Stevie said, 'Perhabs we'd hab a bedder chance in daylide.'

'Yeah, sure,' Smith said, 'when the world and his wife are out shopping. Got any more bright ideas?'

'You're always so fuddin degative,' Stevie said. 'Dry to look on de bride side dow and den.'

In the passenger seat, Smith looked down, drew a deep breath and then turned to the back seat. He raised his Glock and shot Stevie in the face. He said, 'Try to look on the bride side of that, bandage-boy.'

The car was suddenly filled with the pungent odour of fireworks. Jordan jammed on his brakes and pulled into the side of the road. He knew what Smith had done before he turned around to see Stevie's body slumped down in the middle of the back seat, his face now just a gaping hole and blood spatter dripping from the rear window.

'What the fuck!'

'He was getting on my nerves.'

'So you blew his fucking brains out?'

'It's my response to frustration. You're right, I need to deal with it.'

Jordan realised that the gun was still in Smith's left hand, lying casually in his lap, out of his own reach but leaving Smith the option of using it. Whatever he did, Smith would continue to have that advantage. He could try throwing a punch but it probably wouldn't knock Smith out, and as inevitably as sunrise his hand would lift just a few inches and the gun would tear a hole in his gut. Smith knew Jordan knew this and was calm.

He said, 'Get out of the car. We're going to dump the body, all right?'

Jordan looked behind him, through the bloody rear window. They were on the Nantwich bypass, a two-lane link road that wasn't busy at this time of night. There were narrow access lanes either side of the carriageway, and five yards ahead he saw a short path cut at right-angles into the grass verge that led directly into dense bushes. He pointed to it and said, 'I'm going there. Don't shoot me.'

He drove the five yards, then put on his flashing warning lights. Smith said, 'Turn them off. Turn everything off. We don't want to light up what we're doing.'

Jordan did as he was told then got out of the car. There was no traffic ahead or behind, just starlight overhead.

Smith joined him and they opened the rear door of the car and pulled Stevie out. Jordan couldn't look at him. He didn't know the younger man well but thought he was harmless, if a bit dim. It had been fun to have someone to boss around. He thought he probably wouldn't tell Stevie's mum what had happened.

They took one end each of Stevie's body and walked a few steps into the undergrowth. Jordan saw that in fact the cut in the verge was to allow access to some brick steps, leading upwards. He had no idea what they could lead to.

Smith said, 'Go round the side. I'm not carrying this wanker up any steps.'

Then they paused as two cars went by in either direction, their passing headlights casting oblique shadows on their task.

'Over here,' Smith said, suggesting by the way he was pulling Stevie's body that they should head to the right of the steps. He must have stuffed the gun in his pocket, Jordan thought, briefly wondering whether he'd have an opportunity to jump him ... Smith had gone in first, walking backwards, and Jordan heard him struggling against the stiff branches of the trees to make headway. 'Here,' Smith said, and Jordan felt the weight pull downwards as the other man let go of the body. He did the same and heard Stevie crash into the undergrowth.

'Shouldn't we do something to cover him up?'

'With what?' Smith said. 'The tears of angels? It'll be a few days before anyone finds him here and I'll be long gone. I suggest you do the same.'

He brushed past Jordan in the dark and climbed into the passenger seat again. The gun was back in his hand. Jordan got into the driver's seat. 'Christ, it smells,' he said.

'Your mate's brains,' Smith said. 'Don't worry, the smell won't last long. There weren't many of them.'

Jordan swallowed a reply and started the motor, then

pulled on to the road and continued on the slow loop back to Crewe railway station.

SMITH MADE JORDAN pull in around the corner from the station, near the football ground, then he bent under the boot-lid, taking the rifle from the roll-bag and breaking it down before placing the pieces in separate compartments inside a hard-shell guitar case. When he'd finished he picked up the case and the roll-bag and stood waiting for Jordan to close the boot.

He said, 'I'd ditch the car if I were you. You won't get the blood out. Wash it down as best you can then dent the wings and door with a hammer and drop it in a scrap yard. Tell them it's more expensive to fix than throw away. Tell Wolfe I think he's a wanker but he'd better send my money or he knows what'll happen to him.'

'Is that it?'

'No. The next time you or any of your mates pull any shit like that I'll staple you to a barn door and use you for target practice. Now get out of my fucking sight.'

He hefted his bags and walked back up to the corner before turning right towards the station.

Jordan stood for a while, considering his options.

CHAPTER THIRTY-FIVE

I DROVE US back to Dan's house so we could update him on what had happened. And calm down.

As soon as he opened the door he saw something in our faces and ushered us inside. He said, 'I've got beer and wine, if you want.'

I took a beer but Belinda was determined to drive home later and said water would do. We sat in Dan's living-room again like a sports team that had just taken a beating.

Belinda said, 'I'm shaking. I was all right at the time but it's catching up with me.'

'Adrenaline,' I said. 'You get all worked up and then there's nowhere for it to go.'

Dan said, 'So would you mind telling me what happened, exactly?'

I filled him in on what Alistair had told us and then what had happened in the car park. 'Bloody hell,' he said, when I mentioned my car's window shattering.

'Never heard a thing,' I said. 'And just one shot. He was so confident he wasn't prepared for a second pass.'

'I'd hauled your backside out of the way by then,'

Belinda said.

'Did you? I heard you shouting but I didn't know you'd pulled me down.'

'Face it, you're too stupid to duck.'

We grinned at each other across the room, perhaps beginning to feel a little celebratory, realising we'd cheated death.

Then Dan said, 'We still have no idea who these people are, have we? Who's so pissed off with you that they'd hire someone to shoot you?'

'Start a list.'

'No, Dad, seriously. Is it going to be these people again, the ones who kidnapped you? It's a bit of an escalation.'

'I'm in two minds,' I said. 'On the one hand I can't think of anyone else, from any other jobs I've been doing, that might want to go this far. On the other hand, I can't believe that anyone involved with Giles Minton or his wife or kids would lower themselves so far as to assassinate me. And the point is—what for?'

'Are you being deliberately obtuse, Sam, or what?' Belinda said. She turned to Dan. 'Alistair told us about a memory he has of seeing his parents burying someone in the garden. Someone with brown skin. Your father and I think it might be Aditya Dhawan.'

'That would be a hell of a reason to keep you out of their business,' Dan said. He thought of something else. 'Remember, Wolfe had all those documents about Dhawan on his computer.'

'Yes,' I said. 'But in a document that you say was originally opened by Carol Minton.'

'Why would she have done that?'

'Guilt,' I said.

———

'Let's go through the timeline,' Belinda said.

'Okay … So around fifteen years ago, the Mintons employed a local gardener, Aditya Dhawan, who cycled to his clients in and around Nantwich. One day he goes missing and is never heard from again.'

'Do we know that for sure?' Belinda asked.

'I checked,' Dan said. 'There's been no record of him since, as far as I can work out.'

'His daughter verified that,' I said, 'unless Dhawan has surfaced elsewhere and not gone back to his family. Not likely, I would think.'

'What's next?'

'Well at the same time, roughly, that Dhawan goes missing, young Alistair Minton, aged five, sees his parents digging a hole in their garden and apparently burying someone. He's so young he doesn't know what he's seeing and apparently forgets the event … but it's still in his head and in the last few months he's starting to think again about what he saw.'

'There's something else,' Belinda said. 'You told me Carol Minton spent some time in hospital with a mental problem. Could that be related to what she and Giles allegedly did all those years ago?'

'I've been thinking along the same lines,' I said. 'Unlike Alistair, she had to consciously repress the memory, bury it, because they couldn't give any hint of Aditya Dhawan's fate being tied to the Mintons. They would have had the police all over them, looking for evidence about Dhawan and his disappearance, so they would have needed to be tight as a drum with their stories. Maybe that was too much for Carol and a few years ago she started to crack.'

'So where do Wolfe and the letters from Carol come into the picture? What's his relationship with the whole thing? Did he know? Would the Mintons have let him in on the secret?'

I said, 'I think Wolfe is in it up to his elbows. He seems to have been hanging around Carol Minton almost from the beginning—first working for her father, then moving across to work for Giles. He seems to have been happy to get involved in shady dealings for Carol's father, so maybe he's temperamentally suited for criminal activity. What we in the business call A Crook.'

'Plus, he's involved in military paraphernalia, knows some people in that environment … perhaps he has contacts who have contacts.' Belinda rolled her neck. 'I hate white-collar criminals. Gutless cowards, the lot of them. If you're going to be a villain, at least come out and declare yourself.'

I said, 'All of that means we need to find out who Wolfe might have used.'

'Okay, I'll keep digging.'

I half-closed my eyes, thinking I could easily go to sleep. I forced them open and said, 'So, at the moment we've got a lot of supposition about Carol's behaviour and Wolfe's motives—but nothing about Giles Minton.'

'I still say you could take what you have to the cops. Get them to do the detail work.'

'I repeat,' I said, 'there's a lot of supposition but no real connection.'

'Okay,' Dan said, 'so what about the girl, Sally Collins? Why would she be murdered? What's she done wrong?'

I felt the tightness in my chest as I spoke: 'She was the one who told me about Minton and Wolfe plotting, and sent me the cuttings about Aditya Dhawan. If Wolfe is involved, perhaps he got rid of her because she was digging for information or had accidentally found the folder of information about Aditya, and he knew it … or she was just being too much of a pain in the neck for Wolfe and Minton to handle. If it was them, they took a big risk in getting rid of her. If it wasn't them, then there are more crooks involved than I thought. I hope this whole thing isn't running out of control.'

'Too late,' Belinda said. 'Brakes are no use now. Best to go with the flow and see where you wind up. Any ideas?'

'Yes,' I said. 'But they'll keep. Go home and I'll see you tomorrow morning, if you're still willing.'

'And leave you to get your backside shot up again? Not likely.'

CHAPTER THIRTY-SIX

JORDAN HAD SLEPT in his car the night before and knew he probably stank. He didn't care. He couldn't face the drive back to Chester and he didn't have enough money to pay for a hotel. He'd found a blanket in his boot and laid it on the back seat, grateful it was too dark to see Stevie's blood—and maybe some of his brains—scattered over the seat.

It didn't matter: he couldn't sleep. He kept thinking he might be lying on some of Stevie's skull, or a bit of an eye, or his nose …

So he got out of the back and climbed in the front passenger seat and wound it as far towards horizontal as it would go and closed his eyes … and still nothing. His brain was whirring, hearing the sound of the gun-shot, remembering the weight of Stevie's body as they'd hauled it into the roadside verge, smelling the coppery odour of Stevie's blood congealing on his clothes and in the car …

AT EIGHT O'CLOCK he phoned Wolfe's burner phone. Wolfe

replied cagily.

'Is it done?'

'Fuck no. Your man missed. He's fucked off back to London or wherever. He says you'd better pay him or there'll be trouble.'

'What the hell happened?'

'We were too far away. It was dark. He was overconfident. He did a great job of killing Dyke's car, though.'

'Jesus Christ on a bike. I'm going to advertise for help in the War Cry, I'd getter better recruits.'

'What's that, one of them military magazines?'

'No, you halfwit, it's the Salvation Army's rag. Don't you know anything?'

Jordan bit his lip. He said, 'So where are you? I need to talk to you.'

'No you don't. This is us, talking. Stay the fuck away from me and from Minton. Tell the yellow-haired moron the same thing.'

'I can't.'

'What do you mean?'

'I'm not saying anything else over the phone. Where will you be in an hour?'

Wolfe went quiet for a few seconds, then said, 'Giles is giving another of his sparkling speeches.'

'Where?'

Wolfe told him reluctantly and Jordan thought for a moment until he remembered where it was. Not far. In the countryside. Nice and quiet.

HE ENTERED THE grounds between tall stone pillars and drove along the gravelled track towards Crewe Hall. He knew nothing about its past except it was now a hotel. It looked exactly like he expected a Victorian country house to appear. It had dozens of tall windows reflecting the sky, and a large stone fountain in front of steps that went up to the entrance doors. Cars were parked in bays to either side of the steps so he rounded the fountain and pulled into an empty slot. Looking down at himself, at his filthy jeans and dirty hands, and knowing that he definitely needed a shower and a shave, he decided to call Wolfe out rather than go inside.

When Wolfe answered, he said, 'I'm here. In the car park. If you don't come out, I'm coming in.'

'Fuck sake, I'm in the middle of something.'

'Finish it, cancel it, I don't care.'

He hung up and leaned back, resting his head against the car seat. He had no plan. He didn't know what he wanted from Wolfe, except to tell him about Stevie and the fuck-up last night. He'd known Wolfe since he was a teenager, and there were times he counted him as a friend and times he saw him as a user. He didn't really mind. He'd realised when he was in London that he liked to be useful. He'd given himself to the triads because they needed someone like him, someone from outside their set who had no fear and would do more or less what was asked. He'd threatened and bullied and beaten people up … but he'd never had to kill anyone. That's why the events of last night had finally pushed him too far. He'd thought he could manage the situation because Smith was the one who was going to pull the trigger, but in the end he couldn't allow it to happen. He let Stevie nudge Smith before he did it himself.

———

THROUGH THE WINDSCREEN Jordan could see Wolfe waddling towards the car. He was wearing one of his best suits but it still didn't fit: as usual his shirt was venturing from the front of his trousers, struggling to escape. The thickness of his legs turned his feet out and he moved from side to side as he walked rather than walking straight. What a dickhead.

Wolfe opened the passenger door and ducked inside. As his weight hit the seat, the car gave in and sank lower into the gravel.

'What's so fucking important?' he said.

'Your man Smith's a fucking psychopath, that's what.'

'Good. He'll get himself beaten up or shot and we won't have to worry about him.'

'He shot Stevie. In the face. Turn around and you'll see his brains all over the back window.'

Unable to help himself, Wolfe did just that. Jordan watched the side of his face as he did so, saw the glossy round cheeks, the sunken eyes, the unconscious pout of his lips as he realised what he was looking at. His eyelids flickered once.

He said, 'What have you done with him?'

'We threw him into a hedge. Out of sight. He won't be found for days, maybe weeks.'

'Did he have any ID on him?'

Fuck, Jordan thought. *We forgot to check.* But he said, 'We took it. I burned it all last night.'

Wolfe turned back to him. 'So what do you want? I told you to keep away from us. If Dyke sees you, we're screwed. He'll put two and two together.'

'My money would be a good start. I've seen nothing from you except promises. Get your man to put his hand in his pocket and I'm gone. I don't want anything to do with you or Giles Minton any more.'

Wolfe was looking out of the windscreen at the monstrous red-brick building in front of them. 'Four hundred years old, this thing,' he said. 'I was reading the history. They used it as a place to repatriate men who'd come back from Dunkirk, then turned it into a prisoner of war camp for Germans. Afterwards it became a science lab.'

'Interesting, I'm sure.'

'Now it's a fucking hotel and here we are, two squits, sitting in a car park talking about blackmail money.'

'Who's blackmailing? You owe me money for what I've done for you.'

'True. But you've got a sword hanging over my head, haven't you?'

They turned and looked at each other and Jordan felt a tremor of fear pass through him—the first in years. Wolfe had something inside him that could turn your blood cold. He wished he had a weapon with him.

Wolfe said, 'I haven't got your money here, have I, so you'll have to hang around until I can get it.'

'When will that be?'

'A day or so.' He reached into his pocket and pulled out his wallet. He took £150 in notes from it and handed them to Jordan. 'Tide you over. Put petrol in the car. Buy yourself a car wash, inside and out.'

'Smith said I should get rid of the car, take it to a scrap yard.'

'You'll be able to buy a new one when I get your money.'

'Anything to get me away from you and this shit-hole.'

'I might have a use for you later, when we get to London.'

'I don't care. I've been there, done that. Learned some Chinese. I didn't like it. Neither will you.'

'Why's that?'

'Because they're all bullies down there. You won't be able to do it to other people because they'll see you coming a mile off. Small fish in a big pond.'

'That's where you're wrong,' Wolfe said. 'I intend to make myself a bigger fish, then the size of the fucking pond won't matter, will it?'

CHAPTER THIRTY-SEVEN

THE NEXT MORNING was Sunday, dry and clear and cold as a penguin's breath. I made breakfast slowly, my bruises coming out in force now, making certain movements difficult, and sat and read a couple of pages of a Sunday paper.

My eyes drifted from the page. My concentration was shot.

I couldn't see where I was going with the work I was doing for Carol Minton. Alistair had said he wouldn't return home, and I couldn't blame him. If ever there was a dysfunctional family, this was it. There was no chance he'd go back to live with his parents.

So what did I have left to do? I was convinced by now that Tony Wolfe had set the two men on Alistair and then on to me, and had probably hired the third man, the shooter, to try to finish the job. The simple act of finding and talking to Alistair was a threat, and I didn't know why.

I wondered how the shooter had missed me. I was in a well-lit car park, probably no more than two hundred yards away—chicken feed for a professional with a long rifle.

And there'd been no second shot, even though he would have had time to fire again before I realised what was happening and ducked down behind the shelter of other cars. Had he panicked? Not much of a professional if he had.

Of course I couldn't tie Wolfe or Minton to anyone. And besides, the question of their motive was still unanswered. What was I doing that was so dangerous to them? What were they doing that I might uncover? And was it linked to Sally Collins' death? Two possible murders fifteen years apart seemed to be connected by the Mintons and Tony Wolfe, and I had no idea how. It was all speculation, presumption and guesswork.

Which led back to the dream or vision that Alistair had seen. A brown body being buried in the garden, behind the shed, next to a tree ... It was undoubtedly Aditya Dhawan, but I had no proof except the hazy memory of a five-year-old boy. I couldn't go to the police without at least a hint of evidence, especially when I would be launching action against a prospective Member of Parliament in the run-up to an election.

I needed to go back to sources.

I FOUND MY wallet and took out the Post-It note Nishi Dhawan had given me. I phoned the number and after a couple of rings a voice older than Nishi's answered. Her mother. She sounded severe and matter-of-fact and recognised my name when I gave it.

'Mr Dyke, you came yesterday and talked to Nishi, didn't you?' Her voice was clipped and without accent.

I said that I did, and that I'd like the opportunity to talk to her in person, today if possible.

'And what good will that do?' she said. 'Aditya left fifteen years ago and we have carried on together, Nishi and I. We are strong and we don't need him back.'

'I understand that, Mrs Dhawan. But forgive me, if he's not able to come back, if something happened to him … wouldn't you want to know?'

'You mean if someone killed him, my Adi?'

'I'm sorry, yes, that's what I mean.'

'Do you have information about this?'

'Not yet.' I wanted to keep Alistair out of it for the moment—and maybe permanently, if possible. 'I want to hear you talk about it and see if you have any information that ties in with what I know.'

'And who do you work for? Nishi said you were a private detective. I don't understand what you do.'

'I can't tell you the name of my client, because I'm not allowed to. But it's a private person with an interest in this.'

The line went quiet for a moment. During the silence I realised the client I'd mentioned was me.

'You can see me at twelve o'clock today, for no more than an hour. Then I have to go to work.'

'It's Sunday.'

'I know that, but the shop doesn't.'

She hung up.

———

I PHONED BELINDA and an hour later she was knocking on my front door, looking youthful and fresh despite the previous late night and the stress of standing next to a moving target.

I'd told her about the phone conversation with Mrs Dhawan and she was eager to come along. I'd found some pieces of cardboard to put in my car's side window—I'd found the bullet underneath the passenger seat—and I'd phoned a local garage to ask whether they could replace it. In the meantime, Belinda had offered herself as chauffeur.

Now she said, 'Do you want me to lead the questions?'

'Don't you think I can be sensitive and delicate?'

Her smile didn't falter but neither did she say anything.

'I'll chip in,' I said, 'if I think you're going off track.'

'Yes, perhaps you can explain to her what I mean to say.'

'I'm sure it won't come to that.'

'Get in the car.'

ADITYA DHAWAN'S WIFE was small, wore large glasses with blue frames, and was very fierce. Her hair was set in dark waves. When she opened the door she looked us up and down as if considering whether to slam it right back in our faces, but finally she pursed her lips and nodded us inside.

When we were seated I thanked her for talking to us but she waved this away impatiently.

'I don't need thanks,' she said. 'You're doing what someone else should have done years ago. You know I can't pay you, don't you?'

'What for?'

'For looking for my husband. I assume that's what you're here to do, isn't it?' Belinda and I glanced at each other and she saw it. 'What? Have I made a mistake? I thought you wanted information to help you find Aditya.'

'That's true,' I said, 'but I won't take any money for it.'

'Why not? Is someone else paying?'

'Not directly. Look, Mrs Dhawan, let's forget the subject of money. It's not an issue.'

She sat back in her chair and folded her hands as if not entirely satisfied and pursed her lips again.

I said, 'Is there anything you'd like to tell me about the way your husband went missing? Anything you haven't told anyone else, or anything strange or unusual about the day he went.'

'He didn't go,' she said immediately, as though she'd had to say this many times before. 'He was taken. Adi would never just leave like that. He loved his family. He loved this house. He even loved his job.'

'So there's no reason he would have left without saying anything.'

'Absolutely not.'

I suppose I'd partly expected to find someone in widow's weeds, grieving and sorrowful. But of course her husband had been missing for fifteen years. She'd had time to recover from the shock and find some kind of equilibrium, though something seemed to have been taken from her spirit. She held herself as though a physical pain was being kept in check.

I was wondering how to bring up the subject of the Mintons when she got there ahead of me.

'Have you talked to that family?' she asked. 'Mr Giles Minton and his wife?'

'Why do you bring them up?'

'Because they were the last house in his routine. The

police told me that Adi had been to Mr and Mrs Millar and had been seen leaving it by several people. His next visit was the Mintons, but they told the police he never arrived. They didn't report it because they didn't think anything of it.'

'Do you think they're lying?'

She was suddenly suffused with anger, her eyes turning dark. 'Someone is lying,' she said coldly. 'If he didn't reach them, where did he go? No one saw him again.'

We were all quiet for a moment, then I said, 'What kind of man was he, Mrs Dhawan?'

I expected her face to soften as she remembered him, but she remained stern.

'He was a good man. A quiet man. He had skin like butter and a smile that would light up any room.' She stared at us as though we might contradict her. 'My husband would never do a wrong thing, it wasn't in his nature. Women found him attractive, I know that. I didn't hold him responsible for it. You don't blame a man for being attractive to women — it's not his fault.'

'Your daughter told us the police made some suggestions to you about him ...'

'They were false. The police were not on our side. He would not look at another woman.'

'Do you know whether they questioned Giles and Carol Minton?'

'I assume so. Nobody told me anything, I'm just a Paki woman to them. Our family is not from Pakistan, but we're all the same. They use that name because it's easy.'

Belinda leaned forward. 'Did *you* speak to them — the Mintons?'

'Not since that day. I knew them before. I met them once when I was out with Adi and he introduced me to them in the street. They looked down their noses at me, especially that woman.'

'Do you think they're racists?'

She turned her head to one side. 'Who is not?' she said. 'But I can't bear to see him, Giles Minton, on the television now, talking about immigrants and how lovely all brown people are. I don't believe him.'

'He might have changed,' I said, but she carried on as though she hadn't heard me.

'I have friends who knew them, people who worked, who served them food. They were all together, the Mintons and the policemen … eating food being served by the sons and daughters of immigrants. They heard what was said between them.'

'What kind of things?'

'You can guess. They didn't like immigrants coming into their white towns and villages. Giles Minton was there, he was in that group, at the golf club. So now I don't believe him when he blows hot air into the ears of the people who listen.'

'That's a strong allegation to make. Have you said this to anyone else?'

'What would be the point? No one listens.'

'Perhaps these days they would.'

She turned back to me and now her eyes were moist, dipped in grief.

'Find my husband, Mr Dyke. I will pay you if you do. I don't care about Giles Minton or his wife. I just want to know what happened to Adi.'

'We'll do our best.'

'There's one thing I would like you to do especially.'

'What's that?'

'Find his bicycle. He loved his bicycle and the trailer, as he called it. It was never found. I would like to have it back.'

CHAPTER THIRTY-EIGHT

BELINDA DROVE US back to Crewe and we had a sandwich in my kitchen for Sunday lunch. I think she'd been moved by the interview with Mrs Dhawan and had lost some of her energy and enthusiasm. She ate a chicken sandwich as if it were cardboard.

She said, 'Do you think the police were complicit? Do you think they didn't do their job?'

This had been weighing on my mind, too. I'd worked cases where the police had been worse than complicit—had been the actual villains—but I still held to the view that most of them knew they were public servants and worked hard to justify the public's faith. In cases like this, though, where racial prejudice seemed to be at the heart of a severe malpractice, it was difficult to be non-judgemental.

I said, 'I can't go into that now. I've got to focus on finding Aditya Dhawan.'

'But you can't let it go.'

'It was fifteen years ago—those cops have either left or been promoted. It would be hard to track them down.'

'Sam—'

'First things first, Belinda.'

I realised I'd said this in a stronger voice than I'd intended and I saw her eyes draw inward. Not long afterwards she finished the sandwich, thanked me for lunch, and left. I stood in the doorway as she turned her car in the driveway and roared off, spitting gravel.

SEBASTIAN ROBERTS' FARM office was down a long muddy track that passed between open fields in which a few desultory cows clustered together for warmth. I guided Dan's old Escort down the track, trying not to get stuck in the path's deep ruts. I'd borrowed the car with the promise I wouldn't hurt it.

I'd had Dan find the address for me and he'd supplied the phone number as well, but I didn't want to give Roberts the opportunity to say no to a meeting. As it happened, he was standing outside a single-storey, square building when I rolled up. Opposite this building was a more imposing farm house with a single barn making the third side of a square. Despite its rural setting, this was the administrative hub for his farming business and, I guessed, gave little idea of the business's actual scope.

Roberts was a tall man with an imposing bearing. His hair still had yellow streaks amongst the grey and looked set in place, as immovable as the expression in his eyes. He must have been around seventy but stood upright in well-pressed jeans and a Barbour jacket. As I climbed out of my car he didn't move or, apparently, blink.

I approached him and held out my hand and smiled. He looked at the hand as though it harboured typhoid and said, 'Who are you? Don't you know it's Sunday afternoon?'

I gave him my name and said I was working for his daughter.

'Give her my best,' he said, and turned abruptly in the doorway and went inside.

I waited for a moment, noting that he hadn't closed the door behind him. I stepped inside to find him sitting behind a wide office desk containing a wide-screen laptop. There were piles of paper on the desk and behind him, open cabinets containing neatly organised Lever-arch files. The walls contained calendars and graphs. The floor was concrete and bare. He ran a tight ship.

'So what does Carol want from me?' he asked. 'Does she need me to lend her more money so she can buy more clothes?'

'Your grandson, Alistair, has refused to talk to his parents for over a month,' I said, recognising that directness was the way to his heart. 'She wants me to find him and bring him home.'

He shook his head dismissively. 'She smothers that boy,' he said. 'I'm not surprised he wants some time to himself. But what do you expect me to do about it? I haven't seen him since last Christmas, and that wasn't a bundle of fun.'

'Why?'

'None of your business. It's personal. What I will say is that if you ask me, that husband of hers has lost his mind.'

'Because he's standing for election?'

'He had a perfectly good job, although bankers are not my favourite people. Christ knows why he'd give it up to become a bloody politician. I've seen them up close—it's not worth the effort. And besides, he's too weak in character to survive, even if he does win.'

I looked for another chair in the office but there wasn't one. I had the feeling Roberts came here to escape all the ways in which the world disappointed him, and didn't want any company while he luxuriated in that disappointment.

I said, 'Your daughter's husband seems very reliant on Tony Wolfe. Have you noticed that?'

He looked up at me from under his fierce brows. He'd settled at the desk like a stone statue.

'What of it?'

'Is Wolfe a good influence, in your opinion? I understand he used to work for you, so you probably know him quite well.'

'He's very good at what he does.'

'Keeping the books.'

Roberts didn't answer but looked at me as though the statement didn't even require an acknowledgement, as though I'd not actually uttered a word.

I said, 'Why did he stop working for you?'

'How is this relevant to Alistair?'

I tried to make my face appear open. 'I'm just getting to know the family, the context.'

He waited a moment, then said, 'He left on my suggestion. When Carol married Minton I wanted her interests to be looked after properly, not by a banker. I continued to pay him a full stipend while he worked for Carol a couple of days a week. She built her own landscaping design business and he looked after the accounts and dealt with her portfolio. Eventually he started working on Minton's private accounts, too, and I stopped paying for his keep.'

'What kind of accounts did Giles have that were private?'

'You'd have to ask him. I assumed they were share investments not related to his work. At least I hope so.'

I put my hands in my pockets and glanced at the various calendars and timetables on the walls, giving me time to think. I didn't know whether what I was hearing was important or not, or just a typical set-up for someone in Minton's financial position.

I said, 'Wolfe lives alone, doesn't he?'

'Why do you ask?'

'I heard he was married but when his wife died he didn't take up with anyone else.'

Roberts barked out a short laugh. 'Have you seen him? Love's young dream?' Then he narrowed his eyebrows again and turned serious. 'When his wife died he went to pieces. I'm not surprised he didn't want another woman. If I'm brutally honest, I always suspected he was keen on Carol.'

'Did he ever act on it?'

'That's a question you'd have to ask her, isn't it? And another question that seems to have very little to do with my grandson's absence from the family hearth.'

'In my line of work,' I said, 'little is ever wasted.'

I thought this would close off the conversation but Roberts seemed to relax and leaned back in his chair. I think he'd now begun to find the situation slightly comic, and me faintly ridiculous. Given that, he could be more open and chatty. He said, 'Wolfe has an odd side to his character—have you noticed?'

'In what way?'

'He likes the company of men who I suppose I'd call rogues—men who were macho, tough, swore a lot, that kind of thing. Almost as if he was topping up his testosterone level by associating with them. He collects replica guns—has them hanging on the walls of his house— he goes to military fairs. I believe he was even involved in organising something of that nature.'

'Military vehicle shows.'

'Correct. He used to have a young friend hanging around him all the time. He went and joined the army but was drummed out in short order for some disciplinary lapse. He went to London after that and vanished. I haven't seen him around for a while, but then I haven't seen Tony Wolfe in many months either.'

'Do you know what this other man was called?'

'Jordan something. I don't know that I ever knew his surname. Grew into a big chap, and quite argumentative. I wonder whatever happened to him.'

CHAPTER THIRTY-NINE

I WAS SITTING in the Escort on the road outside Sebastian Roberts' farm track, watching the sun fade into an orange puddle on the far side of the horizon. It was late Sunday afternoon and I had the sense I needed to do something rather than go home to an empty house and brood on failure.

I still had Jack's phone number and he answered on the second ring.

'I didn't want to talk to you again,' he said.

'And yet you answered the phone. Admit it, you can't help yourself. You can't live without me.'

'What do you want?'

'I know you can't contact Alistair and have no idea where he is or how to get hold of him … but tell him I'll be at your place in about forty-five minutes to pick up the key to his parents' house that he's going to drop off for you. I'm assuming he has one because why wouldn't he?'

'If I can't contact him and have no idea where he is, how will I get this message to him?'

'I know you. You'll find a way.'

THE DRIVE WAS quiet, even on the motorway, so I made it more quickly than I thought and parked outside the house. I had no thoughts of parking in the separate car park after what had happened to me the last time I'd done that.

When Jack opened the door he stepped back immediately so I would follow him inside. He stood in the hall outside the sitting room and directed me inside.

Alistair was standing close to the wall, inspecting the poster of van Gogh's Sunflowers I'd seen on my first visit. He seemed younger each time I saw him, as though he was sloughing off protective skins designed to make him look older and less vulnerable. I heard Jack taking the stairs behind me two at a time, as if he didn't want to be in the vicinity when I met Alistair again.

'You didn't have to stay,' I said. 'You could have left the key with Jack.'

He continued staring at the poster for a while, making his point, then turned to me.

'Why do you want the key to the house?'

'It's probably better you don't know. I'm not going to steal or break anything.'

'You want to look inside, then.'

'I've looked inside.'

He gave up and reached out a hand containing a single Yale key. I could have broken in if that's all it took, but I thought it better to at least pretend I had Alistair's permission: I remembered the security camera over the Mintons' front door, though I had no idea whether it was connected.

I considered telling him about the attempt on my life when Belinda and I had left the pub two nights before — but I thought it might worry him even further. If he thought Scarface and Yellow-hair were resorting to rifle-fire he might disappear altogether, never to be found again.

Instead I said, 'I spoke to your grandfather this afternoon. He sends his regards.'

'You bloody liar — he wouldn't say that in a million years.'

I shrugged. 'You're right, he didn't. But he did seem mildly concerned about you when I told him you weren't speaking to your mother.'

'"Mildly concerned"? That's extravagantly emotional for him.'

'He says he hadn't spoken to you since last Christmas, when there was some kind of problem.'

His eyes had been in shadow, the only light coming from a single standard lamp in the corner of the room. Now a gleam of thoughtfulness appeared in them as he turned fully from the poster and moved to the centre of the room. It was as if he wanted to show he still controlled this space even though he didn't live here any more.

'Christmas, eh?' he said. 'The absolute worst time for happy families. He and Dad started a huge row and my mum ran upstairs, covering her ears with her hands. I stayed and watched, for the fun of it. It was like a stage play, a horror piece.'

'What was the row about?'

'What do you think?'

'Knowing your family, it concerned either your mother's health or your father's politics.'

'Both, in a way.' He ran a hand over his face and when he removed it his cheeks were red and raw, as though slapped. 'It's all connected, isn't it? I don't think he ever wanted Dad to marry his precious daughter and he made it pretty plain every time we saw him. My grandmother died a few years ago and he's been a lonely and grumpy old sod since then. Buries himself in his farm books and working in local charities. The Lions, Rotary Club, stuff like that.'

'He said your mother borrowed money from him.'

'Did he? I don't know anything about that. I don't know why she'd need to borrow anything. Dad earned more money than he could spend — not that he spent it on anything. Same car for five years. Hardly ever goes on holiday. Not interested in clothes or gadgets or anything like that.'

'He's paid for half of this house and your education, presumably.'

He reacted as though I'd insulted him … which, in a way, I had. His eyes glittered in the half-light. 'He'll get the money back when we sell it. It's an investment, like me.'

'Is that how you see yourself?'

'It's hard not to when your father has used that language about you to your face.' I said nothing and he went on. 'He hated that I didn't want to go to Oxford or any of the fancy universities. It was like I was spurning him, personally. He's taken the opportunity more than once to tell me I was letting him down and letting myself down. I was like a portfolio that wasn't performing well.'

'So why didn't you? Want to go, I mean.'

He had moved to sit on a large bean bag next to the television. He crossed his legs and looked down at the carpet.

'I don't like big institutions which have grand ideas about themselves. Whether it's universities or banks or supermarkets. I didn't want to be a "customer". I didn't want to get lost in the crowds.'

'And Stafford is different?'

'Yes.'

He didn't elaborate but offered the word as a full-stop to the conversation. I was beginning to have a sense of him as an individual with his own tastes and inclinations and not just the product of his parents and the requirements of their social class. It had taken a long time for me to get past my own prejudices.

'I talked to your grandfather about Wolfe. He said he liked the company of macho men, rogues. What do you know about that?'

'Nothing. I never saw him with anyone like that.'

'So you don't know anyone called Jordan?'

'No, why?'

'No particular reason, the name just came up.'

I think Alistair was frightened to ask me any further questions along this line in case he didn't like the answers. He sat on the bean bag, cross-legged like a young, slim Buddha, his breathing shallow. I felt he was willing me to leave, but then he looked at me curiously and said, 'When you use the key and go into the house, what are you looking for?'

'As I said earlier, it's better you don't know.'

Quiet descended in the room again and I turned to leave. I'd opened the door when Alistair asked, 'How is my mother?'

It was the first time he'd enquired about any member of his family.

'I haven't seen her in a while. The last time I saw her she was fine.'

'If she's hiding from you, that's not good. She stays away from people when she's heading downwards. It's like part of her knows what's happening and she wants to spare other people from the consequences.'

'What kind of consequences?'

'It's better you don't know.'

CHAPTER FORTY

LATE SUNDAY NIGHT I had Dan track down Tony Wolfe's
address, and at 8.30 Monday morning I was standing
outside his cottage using his elaborate, lion's head door-
knocker. Around us the Cheshire countryside was pristine
and innocent in the early morning sunshine.

When he finally opened the door he looked as though
he was ready to leave the house—suited, shaved, briefcase
in hand. His face broke into a scowl as soon as he saw me.
'You're worse than a bad smell,' he said.

'What do you know about Aditya Dhawan?' I said,
trying to surprise him with bluntness.

'Who?'

He was good: his face had stayed neutral, with perhaps
a slight frown forming between his eyebrows.

'The Mintons' gardener who went missing fifteen years
ago. You must remember, it was in all the papers.'

'I remember the man going missing. I didn't know his
name.'

'So you never met him?'

'What's this about? I've got to be at the Mintons' in

twenty minutes.'

'His name popped up. He worked for the Mintons as a gardener but then went missing one day when he was travelling from one client to the next—Carol Minton. The police never found out what happened to him. Never found his body, or his bike.'

'This is all fascinating, but nothing to do with me and, as far as I can tell, nothing to do with what Carol hired you to do in respect of Alistair. Does she know you're asking these questions?'

'She will soon. I daresay you'll tell her.'

'I might do. Now, can you shift out of the way, and move your car so I can go?'

He bustled forward and turned to close the door behind him. There was an air of unreality about his behaviour, as if he were putting on an act of normalcy—his actions were slightly exaggerated and deliberate, and when he turned towards me again he refused to look at me but tried to brush past.

I said, 'Have you seen your friend Jordan lately?'

He surprised me by not denying he knew the man.

'Not in a long time,' he said, lifting his car keys from a pocket. 'He went down to London years ago and I haven't seen him since.'

'So he wasn't one of the men who tried to beat me up outside my house, then kidnapped me and kept me in Chester?'

He stopped by his car door and looked me up and down. A number of fugitive emotions passed across his features, none of them settling until he said, 'I have no idea what you're talking about. Even if he were back up here, why would he do that?'

'I thought you might know the answer to that very question. I thought you might have hired him and a friend to keep me out of the picture for a while, to stop me finding Alistair because of what he might say.'

'What might he say?'

'Who knows? Perhaps it's something related to the disappearance of Aditya Dhawan. Perhaps he saw something as a child, something he'd forgotten until recently but which is now making his life a misery. Perhaps he dislikes his father's politics so much he might start telling everyone what he remembers.'

He opened the rear door of his BMW to throw his briefcase inside. I could tell he was thinking furiously, trying out various responses.

He closed the rear door then opened the driver's door and stood for a moment, holding on to the door and looking down like a parachutist deciding whether to jump or not. Then he slammed the door and walked back towards me.

'Ever since Carol hired you my life has been a nightmare,' he said. 'God knows, the Mintons aren't easy to manage—she's nuts and he's a stranger from another planet. You've talked to them, you know all this. I'm working as his agent. That means I do what I can to make sure he gets elected by spending the campaign money wisely. That's it. That's all I do. You keep coming to me with these bullshit stories that you seem to be pulling out of your backside and I'm left thinking, Why are you doing this? What do you get out of it? And the only conclusion I can come to is that you are, in fact, working for our opposition. Your plan is to disrupt us, to upset our smoothly-running applecart so that Giles Minton never has the opportunity to prove his worth to this community. Am I right? You can tell me. I won't let your secret out.'

'The point of an applecart is to be upset.'

'Answer the question.'

'Okay, cards on the table,' I said. 'You've had your say, now it's my turn. I think the Mintons, one or the other of them, or both acting together, killed Aditya Dhawan and buried him in their back garden. I don't know why or how, or whether it was deliberate or accidental. I'm not *certain* you knew, but I'm pretty sure that you did. So you're an accessory. The fact that Minton says he's pro-immigrant is a blind—there's some kind of weird psychological transference going on in his head, almost as though he's trying to work off the sin he and his wife committed with the murder. Alistair doesn't know all the details yet, but he's working on them. Giles knows that—has known it for the last fifteen years—and it's driving him further and further inside himself and away from his family. How does that sound so far?'

Wolfe stared at me for another beat, then turned and climbed into his BMW. It started up with a sophisticated roar but he couldn't leave because I was parked on the drive behind him.

I walked slowly past him, looking down through the window at his profile. His round face, half in shadow, refused to acknowledge my presence.

I reversed into the street and he came out after me and drove off, expelling smoke that hit the cold air and immediately turned as dark as his thoughts.

CHAPTER FORTY-ONE

THE DRIVE BETWEEN his own house and the Mintons' wasn't long enough for Wolfe to think through his anger and work out what to do next.

So when he arrived he was in a foul mood and finding Giles Minton lounging casually in the sitting room reading a newspaper threw him into a rage. He tore the newspaper from Minton's grasp and flung it to the ground.

'He knows everything!' he said. 'That fucker Dyke knows about that wog gardener and Jordan and for all I know he could make a good guess about how often you've screwed Carol.'

Minton stared up at him, his features only mildly concerned. 'Who's Jordan?' he said.

'Stan fucking Laurel. One of my genius employees who's been doing his best to see you and me buried under a ton of shit.'

'Then you should sack him.'

'Did you hear what I said? Dyke knows everything. He's made the link between you and that gardener. All your precious concern for our brown brothers probably tuned him in to what you were up to.'

'What am I up to?'

'Are you on drugs?'

'Of course not. Though I am slightly in shock at your appearance. I have to give a speech this morning to a very influential group of people and you come in here stomping around like Nellie the Elephant who's trodden on a tack. Now calm the fuck down and tell me what Dyke think he knows.'

Wolfe felt his anger travel through his body and come to rest in his extremities—his fingers began clenching uncontrollably and he prowled back and forth behind the blue sofa, feeling the strength in his thighs and calf-muscles. He sensed he had to hold on to the emotion he felt because it might help him think clearly. He hadn't been thinking clearly of late—he'd been too influenced by Minton's calmness.

He ordered his thoughts and then told Minton what Dyke had said—he knew the name of the gardener and that Alistair was remembering what happened in the garden fifteen years ago. He also knew Jordan's name and that he was probably involved in the attempted beating up and kidnapping.

He didn't tell Minton about the failed assassination by his man Smith. No need to burden him ...

'But he didn't say anything about proof?' Minton asked.

'No, but I hardly think—'

'Which means he doesn't have it yet, just speculation and guesswork. He was trying to scare you, and it seems to have worked.'

'If by "scare me" you mean he's told me about all the

crimes we've committed in the last fifteen years, you're right. Should I be feeling something else? Exhilarated? Delighted?'

'Try and be serious, man.'

'Listen, your wife has got us into this mess and she can get us out of it. Tell her to drop Dyke. Pay him off and dispense with him. If we've got some client relationship with him he probably can't talk to anyone.'

'You forget, Carol's his client now, not us.'

'But the original hire was done by you.'

Wolfe let the implication hang there for Minton to think through. He knew Minton would be wondering where the money came from … whose account had been tapped to pay for it? It couldn't be the campaign fund, could it, surely …?

Wolfe kept his face neutral while Minton put his slow thinking process into gear. He watched as the other man stood up and went to the patio window, looking once more down the length of the garden towards the shed that had been there for as long as Wolfe could remember.

'This has irritated Carol beyond measure,' Minton said. 'With her interest in landscape gardening, as you know, but not being able to change anything. Oh, the change of a shrub or a plant here and there … but nothing serious. Nothing *landscapey*. Always having it remain the same as it was fifteen years ago, for obvious reasons.'

'Quite frankly, I don't give a shit whether Carol's a bit irritated right now. We need a plan of action. We need to *do* something to get Dyke out of our hair.'

Minton turned from the window, his eyebrows raised as though baffled by Wolfe's statement. Wolfe hated the simplicity of Minton's emotional range—he put on an expression of confusion, anger or attentiveness as easily as swapping a mask. And in between there was nothing, a blank. He would, in fact, be a perfect politician. Now Minton said, 'I thought you were taking care of the Dyke problem. Forgive me, I don't remember the details but I thought you took it upon your ever-broadening shoulders.'

'I can only do so much,' Wolfe said, 'being your humble servant.'

'Didn't you tell me he was in, ah, captivity? What happened?'

'It didn't last.'

'I'm sorry if I seem simple, but if he escaped, and he knows—or thinks he knows—that it was we who were responsible for his incarceration ... shouldn't we be expecting a visit from the police?'

Before Wolfe could answer, the front doorbell rang.

———

MINTON SAID, 'SEE who it is, will you? Send them away. We have to leave soon and Carol's sleeping upstairs, drugged to the eyeballs.'

Still seething, Wolfe went through the house to the front door and wrenched it open.

At first he couldn't make sense of what he was seeing— it was out of context and bizarre. Then he realised he was looking at Jordan, who was wearing a cap with long flaps that came down over his ears like a deerstalker.

He was just thinking about closing the door in Jordan's face when the other man stepped forward and barged into the house. 'Nice place,' he said. 'Why don't you show me around?'

MINTON WAS STILL standing in front of the patio doors when Wolfe returned with Jordan. He turned and frowned when he saw Wolfe had brought someone with him, but he was too well-bred to complain or to exhibit any shock at Jordan's appearance.

Wolfe said, 'Giles Minton, meet Stan Laurel.'

If Jordan was offended by the insult he said nothing. Wolfe thought he'd dressed up for the occasion, wearing proper shoes instead of boots and corduroy instead of jeans. He had an idea what Jordan wanted but waited for it to be confirmed.

Which happened very quickly.

Jordan said, 'Mr Minton, I'm sorry to come to your place like this but I'm pretty desperate. I need money. I don't know how much Mr Wolfe has told you but I've been working for you in the background, if you like. Mr Wolfe has promised various payments but they've been late or non-existent, so I've taken the liberty of coming here today to ask for payment.'

Minton coughed genteelly, as though he was equally embarrassed. Wolfe noticed that he hadn't looked at Jordan's face since the first glance. Gentility included not staring at another person's disfigurement.

Minton said, 'Do you have invoices to hand?'

Now Jordan let a slow vulpine grin spread over his face. 'I work in a cash environment, Mr Minton. Very few records. It helps all of us, one way or the other—know what I mean?'

'I'm sorry, I can't see what I can do for you without

some indication of monies owed and for which services.'

Wolfe started to cut in. 'Giles—'

'No, Tony, I'm sorry. From what I've heard from you, Jordan here hasn't exactly been successful in any of the operations he's carried out for us. What's more, he placed us in great legal jeopardy by taking Mr Dyke by force and keeping him against his will. I can't condone that kind of activity, especially when there are no written records to go by.'

Wolfe saw that Jordan was taking this badly. A muscle in his neck began to thicken and he straightened his spine to stand tall.

Jordan said, 'I'm trying to be polite here, Mr Minton. I've been patient for weeks now, waiting for this man here to hand over payment. And it still hasn't come. I need a new car because of work I've done for you—let him explain it afterwards—and I've got out-of-pocket expenses that I wouldn't have run up if it wasn't for doing your dirty work. I'll take a cheque if that's all you have, though cash is better. I'm looking at fifteen thousand pounds, give or take.'

Minton almost staggered, but turned it into a pivot and walked towards the far end of the room. Wolfe thought he'd blanched. Served him right.

'Fifteen thousand?' Minton said in a quiet voice, as though repeating the amount might make it appear less. 'I can't believe your failures could be so expensive.'

Jordan walked towards him and stood three feet away, raising a fist that turned into a pointing finger.

'Shocked, aren't you? That's nothing compared to what'll happen next time. I'll give you a day to get over your heart-attack.'

'You can't say anything to anyone—you're as implicated as we are.'

'But if I'm the one that tells the tale, I get a better cell, don't I?'

He turned away and walked from the room, glaring at Wolfe as he did so.

Minton recovered himself and went to the sideboard, where he poured himself a whisky and drank it, shuddering slightly. Wolfe noticed that he wasn't offered one.

Minton said, 'I never knew politics was such a dangerous business. The characters you have to deal with are positively Dickensian.'

'Wait till you meet the other politicians,' Wolfe said.

CHAPTER FORTY-TWO

As I ARRIVED I saw a battered Ford come out of Giles Minton's driveway and head in the opposite direction. I'd have liked to have followed it but I couldn't afford the time. Ten minutes later I watched from the end of the street as Minton's Mercedes and Wolfe's BMW came out of the driveway and headed towards Crewe. If cars could be angry, these were furious. Assuming Wolfe had told Minton what I'd said, I suspected that they were both in some kind of funk. They'd be worrying what I was going to do, who I'd spoken to, what would happen next … Good. I hoped it wouldn't be long before I had real evidence and I could say goodbye to all of them.

I drove up to the house and got the equipment out of the boot. I'd hired it half an hour previously from a small company located just outside Nantwich, who'd also given me a short lesson in how to use it.

At the door I hesitated, then rang the bell. I didn't have a story ready if Carol or Deborah Minton came to the door but I expected Carol to have gone with her husband to his meeting. As for Deborah … I had no idea where she might be.

In fact no one answered the bell so I used the key I'd got from Alistair and let myself in.

The house was quiet but I stood in the foyer for a moment and listened anyway. The atmosphere was expectant, as though someone might come through the front door any moment. It was probably the after-image of Wolfe and Minton's exit because as I waited, the air seemed to change, becoming still and almost deathly.

I walked through the house to the living room and its patio doors, which I slid open. The day was still bright, a crisp November morning whose sun gave light but no warmth. I walked out of the house, across the paved patio and on to the grass.

I put my arm in the device's handle, then switched it on and fiddled with the controls as the man had instructed me, setting the sensitivity. I walked past the wooden garden shed to the large flower bed beyond it and stood at its edge. The bed contained at its centre a large rose bush whose blooms had long gone. The ground beneath it had been turned over recently but was hard, as if a crust had formed.

The device had a long shaft which ended in an oval head my instructor had called the loop. I reached out the long shaft of the device and passed the loop over the ground.

There was no response, no sound, no flicker of the lights on the device's control panel.

I swayed the shaft to the left of the rose bush … and the machine bleeped, once. At the same time an orange light lit up on the control. I moved the loop further and the instrument bleeped once more.

I moved the loop in a series of sweeps until I could

assess the extent of the find. Taking note of when the machine bleeped, I measured an area roughly two feet by four.

About the size of a bicycle, if it were deconstructed and the pieces laid on top of each other.

I SWITCHED OFF the device and took its cradle from around my arm. I paused a moment to look at the garden. It was the expression of a calm and ordered mind—neat, regular and aesthetically pleasing, with curves and right-angles echoing each other in the cut of the lawn or the shape of a low incidental wall. Carol had designed this garden, presumably, and used Aditya Dhawan to help her make it. It would have been intended to be a showpiece for her business, something to put in her catalogue and on her website.

Instead it had become an over-elaborate cemetery that she could never leave behind.

A MOVEMENT AT the house drew my attention. Carol Minton had appeared at the patio door, looking out at me with a hand shading her eyes. This lifted the shape of her body and I saw again the sexuality in it.

She called, 'Mr Dyke, is that you?'

I walked towards her, feeling slightly embarrassed by what I was carrying.

She said, 'What are you doing in my garden? And what is that thing?'

'It's a metal detector,' I said. 'I'm sorry, I didn't know

you were in.'

She became vague and I realised there was a distant, half-asleep look in her eyes. She was wearing what appeared to be a kaftan and I wondered if she'd just woken up. I'd expected her to be worried or annoyed by the metal detector but she seemed to have forgotten it already. She stepped back into the room and I followed her through, wiping my feet on the small mat just inside. I closed the sliding door behind me.

'I've been sleeping very badly,' she explained. 'I'm having dark dreams and they wake me up in a cold sweat. So now I'm a drug addict just to help me sleep.'

'I'm sorry to hear that.'

'Well thank you, that's very kind.' She sat on the sofa and talked into the air, as if I weren't in the room with her. 'My father used to say that dreams are the films we make of our lives when we're not looking. What on earth do you think he meant by that? Have you met my father?'

'I met him yesterday for the first time. He sends his regards.'

'He's a very strong man, a very … political man. He's extremely calculating about what he wants and what he has to do to get it.' She sighed. 'We didn't really get on, though I think he wished me well. The only way I know that is because he didn't like Giles. Oh he was polite and quite helpful when we first got married, but he's become more and more critical, especially with the politics thing. He doesn't believe Giles has the moral fibre to be a good politician. What did he say to you?'

'We talked about different topics.'

'Really? What topics?'

'I really should go, Mrs Minton. I'm sure I'm dropping all kinds of mud on your carpet here.'

A kind of steeliness came into her posture now, as if she wasn't going to let me change the conversation without a fight.

'No,' she said. 'Tell me what my father said to you yesterday, on a Sunday afternoon. I insist. Treat it as a report to your client.'

As I began to speak, I wondered whether I wanted to punish her — for being beautiful but innocent, wealthy but naive, frail but dangerous. I said, 'He thinks you smother Alistair — that's his word, not mine. And he thinks that your husband is crazy for wanting to become an MP.'

'Is that it?'

'He also said he thought Wolfe had a crush on you.'

At this she smiled and raised an eyebrow, as if I'd confirmed something she'd suspected but hadn't known for sure.

'I led that man on,' she said, surprising me. 'I wrote to him, you know, when I was … away. I couldn't write to Giles because for one thing I was seeing him every day, and for another he didn't know how to respond to expressions of emotion. I rather used Tony as a surrogate. Very mean of me.'

A tear formed in the corner of her eye and she wiped it away as brusquely as she might an ugly thought. Then she sighed and looked at me almost for the first time.

'Why did you bring a metal detector into my garden? What were you hoping to find?'

'I wasn't sure.'

'So did you find it?'

'Perhaps.'

Now she closed her eyes and leaned back on the sofa. Her kaftan had a square, scooped neck and I saw the first rawness and wrinkles across the top of her chest. She spread her arms wide in a gesture of some kind of acceptance.

'I wish I could sleep, and when I slept I wish I could stop dreaming. The dream is always the same. I'm on one of those rides in a funfair that goes to a great height and then plunges down through water before rising again. The difference is that in my dream I never rise. I reach the first pinnacle and then fall downwards, everyone in the carriage screaming, arms in the air, and we dive into the water but then we keep on going down—not into the water, you understand, just on the track, descending and descending and gathering speed, our arms waving like lunatics as we continue our descent into … I don't know what. I wake up in a cold sweat, thinking that I've done something momentous but I can't remember what. Do you have dreams like that?'

'My dreams are those of an alien picking over the remains of a damaged landscape.'

She lowered her head to look at me. 'What a very peculiar thing to say.' She laughed briefly, an unpleasant sound. 'You and I have seen too much.'

'And understood too little,' I said.

'We're all heading for a lonely grave,' she said, 'like that poor girl Sally.'

And Aditya Dhawan, I thought.

'We can never predict the hour of our death,' I said, adding pointedly, 'Or anyone else's.'

She didn't reply to this but drew in a deep breath.

'I think I'd like you to leave, now. You haven't said anything about your quest to find Alistair, so am I to assume there's no news?'

'Not in relation to him,' I said.

'Then I await your first report with anticipation and trepidation. Can you see yourself out?'

OUTSIDE, PACKING THE detector into the boot of my car, I went over the conversation again in my head. It seemed to me that Carol Minton had been trying to communicate something to me, but I didn't know what it might be.

However, I was certain she was heading for another breakdown unless she received urgent treatment.

I should have acted on that certainty.

CHAPTER FORTY-THREE

By now it was lunch-time and I still had plenty to do before the end of the day. First I drove home and scavenged in my fridge for something to eat, then I made three phone calls.

The first was to Forster, the journalist who'd given me Ben Prescott's history. He answered breathlessly, as if he'd raced to answer the phone. 'Mr Detective!' he said. 'Are you ready to talk to me yet?'

'Not me. How interested are you in police corruption?'

'As interested as the next hack. Why?'

I told him the story Mrs Dhawan had told me—about the cosy relationship between Giles Minton and the police officers who'd been in charge of the search for her husband.

'Are you suggesting he bribed them or something?'

'No, not at all. But there was some evidence they might have been prejudiced against Indians and Pakistanis and might not have been as thorough as they could have been.'

'How long ago was this?' he said. I could tell by his voice he was doubtful.

'Fifteen years. Does that make a difference?'

'No, of course not … It's finding the people, getting hold of any evidence. People's memories aren't what they were. You must have the same problem in your line of work.'

'Yes,' I said. 'But that doesn't mean I give up.'

I broke the connection while he was thinking of a reply.

SAWYER, THE DETECTIVE investigating Sally Collins' death, was more difficult to get hold of. Eventually he answered with a curt, 'Who is this?'

I gave him my name and explained how we knew each other.

'I remember,' he said. 'What can I do for you?'

'I've got some information for you,' I said. 'And a question.'

'I don't do swaps.'

'It's up to you. I'll give you the information anyway.'

'Okay, go ahead.'

'Sally Collins worked for Giles and Carol Minton.'

'I hope that wasn't it.'

'I know you spoke to them. You might want to consider searching their garden.'

'What the hell for?'

'Let me tell you a story …'

For the second time in ten minutes I told a story about Aditya Dhawan, but this time with a different emphasis. Sawyer didn't know of or remember the case and he didn't seem interested, as though I was complicating one straightforward investigation by adding another.

He said, 'I can't go in there without some suspicion of a

crime, or if we thought it was a crime scene. You're making it sound as if you've had a bright idea and you want me to check it out for you.'

'I'm not making this up.'

'I need proof.'

'Take a metal detector.'

'Why?'

'I did. I think I found his bike. Or maybe it's an unexploded bomb nestling underneath Carol Minton's rose bush.'

<hr>

WE WENT BACK and forth for a while and eventually he said he'd think about it. He added, 'So what was the question? Not that I'm promising to answer it.'

'I presume you did a full forensic investigation at Ben Prescott's swimming pool.'

'Well that's a stupid question.'

'That wasn't it. You think she was murdered, don't you?'

'No comment.'

'Okay. Did you find anything that was out of place in a swimming pool, or nearby?'

'What, like a bicycle?'

'Serious question.'

'What if we did? Like what?'

'Something small and colourful.'

'What are you not telling me?'

'The things I'm unsure about. At the moment.'

He hesitated for a moment, then gave me the answer I expected.

I wasn't happy about it.

<hr>

MY FINAL PHONE call was speculative—I didn't expect it to be answered at all. In fact the number rang for thirty seconds before it was finally answered.

'What do you want?' Deborah asked. There was a high, distracted tone to her voice, as though she was watching a high-wire act and couldn't be disturbed for fear of calamity.

'I want to talk to you,' I said.

'What about?'

'There's a lot to choose from.'

'Don't be so fucking cryptic. Is it Mum, Dad or Alistair?'

'None of them,' I said.

'Do you want a date, old man, is that what this is?'

'You've missed your opportunity on that. I had a very short window.'

'You think a lot of yourself, don't you?'

'Someone has to.'

'Give me a good reason why I should talk to you.'

'You can talk to me about Sally Collins.'

CHAPTER FORTY-FOUR

WE MET IN Queens Park, in Crewe, an old Victorian park that had been recently renovated. Although it was a cold November, there were still visitors walking, taking the air, catching the last of the year's sunshine before grey winter descended.

I found her on a bench facing the lake, watching ducks and geese skimming the surface and squawking and screeching into the dry air. The trees were still shedding and the grass banks were covered in crisp layers of yellow and russet leaves. As I sat next to her, more yellow leaves fell around me.

Deborah was turning a large ring on her finger and didn't look at me when I sat down. Although I was barely a foot from her on the bench, it seemed to me a gulf as wide as the Pacific separated us now. It was as though the peak of our relationship had been that first night, leaning together side-by-side on my car and making jokes at each other's expense. Since then we'd been growing further apart as we learned more of the other's foibles. It had been like being married, without the fun.

Deborah offered no greeting, but said, 'What about Sally?'

'She was a young woman. You're a young woman. I thought you might have insights that could help me.'

Now she turned to me with a half-fretful, half-inquisitive look on her face. 'I thought the police were handling all that. You're not involved, are you?'

I shrugged, casting aside the burden she'd implied. 'I found the body. I feel involved.'

'"The body",' she said in a flat voice. 'Is that what we all become to you detectives, in the end? Pieces of meat?'

I ignored the question because it was evident she was trying to goad me into an argument. I said, 'You told me Sally came to see you when your mother was away in hospital.'

'What of it?'

'What did you talk about?'

'It was five years ago. How am I supposed to remember?'

'I thought you might have a general impression or memory.'

'What are you trying to get at?'

This was a good question to which I didn't have an answer. I wanted her to say something but I didn't know what it was. I'd thought if we spoke to each other long enough it would emerge, but I didn't know how to prompt it.

Thankfully, she came to my rescue. Perhaps she thought I was trying to trick her, so instead she put her cards on the table.

She said, 'You found out I'm bisexual, didn't you, and

you want to know whether Sally and I had a thing.'

'Did you?'

Strangely, she coloured and turned away again. 'I was fourteen years old. I didn't know what I felt then.'

'Do you know how Sally felt about you?'

'She pitied me. But she liked me. I was funny. We had more fun at my place than she ever did with her troglodyte parents.'

'She was pretty, wasn't she? Didn't she have boyfriends?'

'I think she scared boys off. She was clever and she could be quite direct and cutting. There wasn't really anyone in her year who could stand up to her. That made her even lonelier, which is why she came to visit me. We laughed. We made up rap lyrics about people at school, teachers. Perhaps I was in love with her, a bit.'

'But nothing happened between you?'

Now she was quiet, turning her ring, watching the ducks on the lake.

Eventually she said, 'Not then. Mum came back from the hospital and Sally stopped coming around. And besides, she was going away, to university. Kent, of all places. Miles away. So we just stopped.'

'Then she came back, after university.'

'She never even told me. I was at a party and she turned up looking exactly the same, same hair, same faintly out-of-it expression. Sat in a corner by herself, frightened of life. Took her a minute to recognise me when I went up to her — I used to be as girly as she was when I was younger, believe it or not. Skirts, long hair, make up. Here I was with a blue edge, short hair and a nose stud … I must have been like a different person.'

'Did she like the new you?'

'She said she did. We met up a few times afterwards, went out to bars, even up to Manchester, Canal Street, you know? But it frightened her. She wasn't really out. She wasn't really anything. She didn't know what she wanted, even after three years when she had the chance to find out.'

'You accused Alistair of wasting his time at university—do you think Sally did, too?'

'She got her degree, didn't she? She could speak French and Spanish like a bastard.' She caught herself and was quiet for a moment. Then she said, 'The shit hit the fan when she found out about Ben.'

'You were still going out with him at that time?'

'Monogamy's never been something I'm good at.'

'Did you tell her about him?'

She looked at me and for once she was smiling, but it was a bitter grimace. 'No, my mother did. How do you like that?'

<hr>

'Why would she do such a thing?'

'Another excellent question. You're good at this game, aren't you? My guess is that she thought Sally and I were too close. She'd never have said it out loud ... she might not even have thought about it in those terms. But I think she guessed something was happening between us—Sally and me—and she wanted to nip it in the bud. Plus, the Ben stuff was just coming out. There'd been an article in the paper that mentioned an anonymous student and teacher—which was sneaky in itself—and my parents had found out it was me and then found out it was Ben and been to see him to warn him off. My mother has always been more protective of the blessèd Alistair, but this time I think she was trying to look after me. I wasn't supposed to be seeing an older man, and I certainly wasn't supposed to be seeing another woman.'

'You must have felt like you were trapped on all sides.'

'Since I was about ten years old.'

The sun was setting now and throwing long shadows like the ghosts of dead men through the trees and over the lake. What Deborah was telling me had the outline of an ancient family tragedy—the older generation fearful for the lives of the younger—but Deborah had the stoic, pragmatic air of a doctor serving in a field hospital: nothing could shock her now.

I said, 'So your parents stopped you seeing Ben Prescott, because they could. And then Sally dropped you as well?'

'She said I obviously wasn't committed to us. It had been a big step for her to admit to herself what she was and of course she became a zealot then and couldn't let me be what I wanted to be. We broke up.'

'And then she started working for your father.'

Deborah arched her back as if to release some kind of tension. 'Yes, you can imagine how well that went down. At least at first. But then we kind of got over it and stayed friends. We didn't see much of each other because she was kept busy by Wolfe—just occasionally we met in the kitchen or passing in the corridor. We didn't talk about anything serious.'

'Still, it must have been tough.'

'I got over it.'

'But you don't know how she felt about it, seeing you every day.'

'We'll never know, will we?' she said, and for once I couldn't read the emotion in her voice.

CHAPTER FORTY-FIVE

BY THE TIME I arrived back at the Mintons' house it was almost dark, the sky turning into a navy blue shroud with an orange fringe on the horizon.

Giles Minton answered the door with a bored expression that didn't change when he saw me. He said, 'Mr Indefatigable. Come in and give me some shit, why don't you?'

'Is your wife in?'

'No. I have no idea where she is. I left her sleeping the sleep of the dead this morning. Now she's off somewhere haunting the Crewe and Nantwich district like the ghost of Christmas past.'

I noticed the whisky glass in his hand but said nothing.

He said, 'So are you coming in, or do you need to speak to both of us?'

'I can talk to you alone.'

'Great news! Come on in …'

He turned and left me to enter and close the door behind us. Then I followed him along the usual path down a short corridor and into the large sitting room at the rear of the house. Through the patio windows I could see the solar lights just flickering on in the garden. Given my discovery that morning, I realised why he spent so long looking through the window at the garden. I think he saw the past there … or the future we all faced. He'd been brought face-to-face with it more starkly than most, shovel in hand.

'So,' he said, turning almost flamboyantly, the whisky glass held out to prevent spillage. 'What do you have to ask me, or tell me? I have to tell *you* that this whole experience has been a revelation to me. I've been brought to confront myself as though a veil has been drawn back from a mirror. I thought going into politics was self-revelatory at a fundamental level. But it doesn't compare with having your own private detective shred your privacy. Is that where the "private" comes from, do you think? You investigate the private corners of your clients' psyches like a cut-rate psychoanalyst.'

'I'm sorry if I've given you that impression. In my mind I'm just asking questions.'

'Well that's the thing, isn't it? Nobody does that any more. We're all so confident in our own views because of Google and Facebook and all that Internet shit … what do they call it? A bubble? Our views are constantly validated by the friends we keep. Nobody questions anything because that would be too threatening.'

'Is that how I've made you feel? Threatened?'

'Don't be naive, of course I am. That's been part of your ploy from the beginning. Perhaps you don't like my politics. Perhaps you don't like me personally. I don't know which—but then I can't separate one from the other nowadays. Anyway, you've run through this household like a tornado, tearing things apart. Please don't deny it.'

He subsided into an armchair and I sat on the blue sofa. I became conscious of the fact that I'd been talking to his wife in the same location earlier in the day, and it bothered me for an unspecified reason.

Now Minton raised his glass and said, 'So go ahead. Fire away. Say what you came here to say, several days after I told you I didn't want to see you again.'

———

I said, 'As you know, your wife hired me to continue looking for Alistair.'

'Don't state the bloody obvious, man, get on with it.'

'I've talked to Alistair and he doesn't want to come back.'

'I told you not to repeat the obvious.' He said this with a bitter twist on his lips. But his eyes were shadowed with pain. It was as if he were harbouring two contradictory emotions at the same time.

I said, 'He also told me some things that led me to ask questions elsewhere. I learned about the disappearance of a man you used to have as a gardener —'

'Aditya Dhawan, yes, I know. Move on.'

I paused. I'd expected him to feign memory-loss or ignorance about Dhawan. I moved on. 'Alistair told me of a memory he had. A memory that implicated you and your wife.'

Minton took a sip from his drink, then placed it carefully on a side table, as if he needed two free hands to fight this accusation.

He said, 'Mr Dyke, my family has gradually been going

mad around me. I'd hoped you'd find that out for yourself without my having to point it out. You know my wife's history because I told you. I think you know about Deborah and her unsavoury relationships with older men. I thought Alistair was free of this taint, but apparently not. The gardener went missing fifteen years ago, if I'm not mistaken. Alistair would have been five years old. If I were you, I wouldn't take his word on the absolute veracity of his memory. Can you honestly say you can remember clearly things that happened when you were five years old?'

'I didn't have anything quite so dramatic happen to me when I was that age.'

'Well good luck persuading any judge or jury that his memory is to be believed.'

He leaned back and folded his fighting hands together on his stomach. There was something in the casual nature of this gesture that convinced me he'd murdered Aditya Dhawan and buried him in the garden.

———

'One more thing,' I said.

'Believe it or not, I'm enjoying these Arabian Nights tales—they're keeping me awake. Although if truth were told, I should try to get some sleep. I suppose it's too early, isn't it?'

'Did you know that your wife wrote to Tony Wolfe when she was in care for that month?'

His face didn't change, but red patches appeared at the corners of his mouth. He said, 'Why are you telling me this? Are you trying to be deliberately cruel?'

'I know you put a lot of store by Wolfe's advice.'

'And so what? You wanted to shake my faith in him and his counsel? That's a very childish thing for you to do.'

He stared at me as though willing me to retract what I'd said. In a way I wished I could—I'd taken no pleasure in saying it and now wondered why I had.

I said, 'I think your election campaign has run its course. You should withdraw your candidacy.'

'Out of the question.'

'Then things are going to get difficult for you.'

'You think it's been easy so far?'

I said nothing.

CHAPTER FORTY-SIX

AFTER DYKE LEFT, Giles returned to the sitting room and sat for a while staring into space and drinking whisky. He knew he should be working, visiting his staff in the office or writing a position paper or talking to a prospective local donor … but he was tired of the race, tired of the play-acting. And he couldn't help thinking about what Dyke had said to him—he knew about the gardener, he should withdraw his candidacy … Perhaps, after all, it was finished. He was finished. His grand bluff had been called and he'd lost. He could never tell a lie with a straight face, so what on earth had convinced him he'd get away with it this time, on a far larger stage than he'd ever been on before?

It was Tony Wolfe.

Wolfe had been the one who'd planted the first seed, all those months ago. He was the one who'd suggested there was a future for him in politics, especially as Brexit went through … Wolfe saw everything in monetary terms and he was very convincing when he started talking about the finances, how he, Giles Minton, could make a fortune through clever investments in companies which were well placed to capitalise on the move out of the EU—specifically, asset management firms based in Dublin. He'd empowered Wolfe to rent office space eighteen months previously and had begun quietly talking to colleagues in his bank, sounding out whether they'd like to join a new venture that was bound to make them a fortune.

He had a list of ten people who'd come on board when the time was right, bringing expertise and, in some cases, clients with them.

Stage two had been the campaign itself, raising his profile as a candidate friendly to business but with an ethical backbone inimical to anti-immigration sentiment—someone with whom companies could do business without feeling ashamed. He was aware there was an element of guilt relating to Dhawan playing out in his speeches and in his professed attitude to immigrants, but the fundamental goal was to appear balanced and sensible in his public persona. He would work for a couple of years as an MP, then resign on some trumped-up principle before joining Wolfe in Dublin to expand the business there.

HE FOUND HIMSELF troubled, though, by what Dyke had said about Wolfe and Carol. He'd always suspected Wolfe had a kind of sublimated yearning for Carol, begun when he'd worked for her father and would have seen her around the house or in his office. When they'd played foursome tennis, along with Wolfe's wife, he'd always thought Wolfe was more attentive to Carol than he was to his own wife. He'd put it down to the fact that Carol was something of a beauty when younger and attracted male admiration anyway.

But now he realised it had gone further than that. If Dyke was telling the truth, and Carol had written to Wolfe when she was under supervision in hospital, what did it mean? Had they been engaging in subterfuge all these years? Was their relationship full-blown, and still continuing? Wolfe was often scathing about Carol and her influence on him, but that could easily be a front, a way of concealing a harder truth.

———

HE WAS DEEP in contemplation of the maze that Dyke had presented to him when the doorbell rang again. He pulled himself back into the room, switched on a desk light as it was now completely dark outside, and went to answer the door.

The man confronting him was dark-faced and angry, his eyes like chips of coal.

'You'd forgotten I was coming, hadn't you?' Jordan said, and pushed his way into the house.

Minton found himself following the man through his own house, wondering what he intended to do. He felt a little worried but he also realised the whisky had emboldened him. He said to the man's back, 'Where do you think you're going?'

Jordan turned in the narrow corridor and loomed several inches over Minton, who forced himself to stand his ground.

'I'm going where I fucking well like,' he said, then turned and went through to the sitting room, bursting into it like a sudden spasm of energy. He strode to the middle of the room and looked around. It seemed to Giles that the man was barely containing himself, like someone who'd found a purpose and couldn't wait for an opportunity to express it.

The man said, 'So, have you got my money?'

'Have you got the invoice?'

Jordan took a step forward. 'Fuck you. I've known Tony Wolfe longer than I've had short and curlies—invoices make him want to throw up. If he'd wanted invoices he'd have asked for them. He didn't, so there aren't any. Just a gentleman's agreement. Do you know what one of those is?'

'I think so.'

'It's when both fuckers in a contract know they're fucked if it gets out.' He paused, staring down at Minton with his eyes moving back and forth over his face, as if looking for a modicum of understanding. 'What you probably don't know—because Tony won't have told you—is that my mate Stevie is dead. He wasn't too bright, and he should have kept his trap shut, to be honest, but that man Smith wasn't someone you wanted to play around with. Anyway, long story short, Smith shot him in the face and that's on me, and it's on you and Tony, too. I'll take Stevie's share and give it to his mum. It's the least I can do.'

Minton knew his own expression was a mixture of incomprehension and horror, as if he were watching a caged animal eat its own young. The man Jordan was saying things that seemed to have no meaning—except they were obviously true.

For the second time in a few minutes he brought himself back into the room and started thinking more clearly.

Eventually he said, 'I … I didn't know you'd come back here. I gave Tony a cheque for him to cash for you.'

'A cheque?'

'He was supposed to cash it for you, so you'd have the money in cash.'

Jordan seemed to accept this. 'All right. So where is he now?'

'What are you going to do?'

'What do you think I'm going to do? I'm going to get it and tell him what I really think of the lying bastard, then I'm going away.'

'What if Tony hasn't got the money yet?'

'Well I'll burn that bridge when I get to it, won't I?'

Minton thought for a moment, then said, 'Do you know where he lives?'

AFTER JORDAN HAD left, Giles wondered whether he should phone Wolfe to tell him that Jordan was on his way and was likely to be in a bad mood … and, he told himself, would be worse when he found out Wolfe didn't have the money.

Then the thought of Carol and Wolfe talking to each other on the quiet for all these years, or perhaps doing even more, stung the back of his eyes. He felt his heart harden.

No, he said to himself. Jordan is Tony Wolfe's responsibility. He can deal with it, whatever *it* turns out to be.

After thinking this through, he felt a little better and not at all guilty.

CHAPTER FORTY-SEVEN

JORDAN WAS ON his way to Tony Wolfe's house when he realised he'd drive past the end of the road where the man Dyke lived. He could do something there, really mess Dyke up for all the shit he'd been put through.

He slowed down, indicated carefully and turned down the road that went past the football ground. It was well-lit here but as he reached the more rural stretch it got darker and Jordan switched off his headlights before turning into the end of Dyke's track. He swung the car so it was facing outwards, then climbed out quietly and closed the door without slamming it. He took some leather gloves from his jacket pocket and put them on, partly as protection against the cold and partly so he could feel more comfortable when fighting. He considered putting on his knuckles again but thought better of it: he wanted this to be a fair fight, one he could look back on with an element of pride.

The air was clear and the sky was black as velvet and he breathed deeply and looked around to get his bearings. As he moved cautiously down the track he saw that Dyke was in—house lights were on and his car was parked at an angle outside his front door.

This could be easy.

HE KNOCKED ON the door and waited. A few seconds later it opened and Dyke stood there, a piece of toast in his hand. He looked Jordan up and down, then said, 'Come in, Jordan,' and stood back.

Jordan felt a buzzing in his head, as though a fly were trapped in his ear canals. How did Dyke know his name? He wanted to do something decisive and something violent but he was on the back foot. He sensed his hands bunching into fists and stepped forward, but Dyke turned and went inside.

He followed him into a small sitting room that looked like a show-home—everything seemed new, bought in a modern furniture store, something like IKEA. It was the exact opposite of the Mintons' place but reminded him somehow of Tony Wolfe's cottage.

Dyke was facing him square on now and the toast had disappeared. He realised that Dyke was maybe an inch or so shorter than him and thick set across the chest. When he and Stevie had bundled him out of the car, Dyke had been crumpled up and barely able to walk so he had a false sense of the man's size.

Before he could say anything, Dyke said, 'On your own this time? Not brought your mate with the wooden stick?'

Jordan hesitated for a second over how to respond, but then said, 'I don't need a partner for this.'

'What's "this"?'

'I've come to have a word, haven't I?'

'Has Wolfe sent you to have another go? I suppose the shooter's gone home—he took his shot and missed.'

Again Jordan was surprised by what Dyke knew and it confused him. He thought he was going to have the upper hand here but Dyke was talking to him as if he knew everything he'd done in the last week. He stood there, casual but somehow solid, his face neutral in its expression but slightly amused, too. He also had a Yorkshire accent that was distracting because he wasn't expecting it. Jordan felt himself getting wound up and he knew there was going to come a point when he'd have to find his balance and leap forward.

Now Dyke said, 'What you probably don't know is that Wolfe and Minton are in deep shit for a crime they committed fifteen years ago. They've been using you to contain it, to take me out of the picture not because of the politics, but because they're scared of being caught.'

'I don't know what you're talking about. You've lost me.'

Dyke assessed this, then said, 'You were in the army, weren't you?'

'Till I kicked it in the head, yeah.'

'People I've met who were in the forces are usually calm and rational, but you're not like that, are you?'

'What do you mean?'

'You're all choked up inside. Wolfe saw that and used it. He's taken you for a ride, Jordan, used you against yourself.'

'He's looked after me, money-wise. I just do jobs for him.'

'Not exactly a bit of plumbing or carpentry, though, is

it? Beating up people? Throwing a scare in them? You can't have been happy doing that. You're a big bloke and it's easy for you to do it, but I bet nine times out of ten you didn't enjoy it. Most people don't. I've met some headbangers in my time and I don't think one of them really enjoyed beating up other people. It's unsatisfying, isn't it?'

'You know fuck all about me so stop pretending you do.'

Jordan suddenly felt overwhelmed with grief and sadness … he didn't know where it came from and it made him mad: he didn't want to feel sorry for himself, it never helped. He sensed the skin around his eyes pulling tight and knew the whiteness of his scars would be showing even paler than usual against his dark complexion. His angry face, Stevie had called it.

Stevie. That fucker Smith had shot him in the face without thinking twice. Just lifted his gun and pulled the trigger …

It happened so fast, he couldn't remember afterwards who'd moved first.

He knew he'd stepped forward, left foot, so he could swing his right fist at Dyke's face.

But even while he was shifting his weight, Dyke had shifted his own weight and parried Jordan's fist with his left and swung his right into Jordan's stomach.

Before he knew he'd done it, he'd fallen to his knees and was breathing heavily, clutching his stomach. He never saw the man move, it was just a blur and then a whoomp of pain and he was falling, banging his knees on the wooden floor.

Dyke said, 'You didn't box in the army, then. You gave it all away with your eyes. Now stand up.'

Jordan reached upwards as if trying to grasp a chair arm—but instead made a lunge for Dyke's midriff with both arms.

Again a fist came down like a hammer on the side of his head, above his ear, and the buzzing grew louder.

Now his hands were on the floor and he was staring at the grain of the wooden floorboards, tracing its movement around the knots ...

'Be sensible,' he heard Dyke say. 'It's over, Jordan. Wolfe and Minton have had it and I'm afraid you're next on the list. Look at you, you haven't got any energy left, have you? Your heart's not in it.'

Jordan moved his tongue in his mouth before he spoke. 'I'm going to fucking get you. And Wolfe. He owes me money.'

He felt a hand grasping his collar and lifting him and wondered where all his strength to resist had gone. Perhaps Dyke was right—perhaps his heart wasn't in it any more. He didn't like being the heavy. Dyke had said it: he didn't see himself that way. It was an act he played to earn money but he'd never really been any good at fighting. He was too lazy to learn any proper technique. That's what got him booted out of the army, after all. Resistance to authority, not because he was a rebel but because he couldn't be bothered.

He let himself be frog-marched to the front door. Dyke let go of his collar and opened the door and gave him a shove in the back. He stumbled down the step and on to the gravel.

Behind him, Dyke said, 'You can expect a visit from the cops pretty soon. Be honest and tell them everything. Don't let Wolfe or Minton's lawyers screw you out of a fair hearing.'

Jordan turned, then, and said, 'Why are you talking to me like that? I don't need your advice.'

'Oh but you do, Jordan,' Dyke said. 'I recommend you take it. Hard as it is to believe, you're a victim too.'

CHAPTER FORTY-EIGHT

Wolfe heard the loud rapping of his lion's head door knocker and had a bad feeling. It couldn't be the police, surely? It was way too soon for anything to have happened. He hoped to god it wasn't the cops because he wasn't ready. He had a bag packed in case, but he hadn't been to the bank and had barely a couple of hundred in the house.

Thinking about the money reminded him of Jordan. He and Giles had completely forgotten Jordan's threat of the day before. What if he'd come here to collect? What could he tell him?

The door was rapped again, with even more malevolence.

'All right, all right!' Wolfe called, and walked from his kitchen to answer it.

As he thought, it was Jordan, looking as though he'd had an argument with some farm machinery. It wasn't that he was cut or bruised—though there was a slender cut above his left temple—but he seemed defeated and bedraggled.

And angry.

Wolfe stood back, saying, 'What the fuck's happened to you?'

'Doesn't matter,' Jordan said. 'I've come for my money.'

'What money's that?'

Jordan closed the door behind him and leaned back against it, closing his eyes. He said, 'I hoped you weren't going to say something like that. I hoped you were going to say, "Yeah, sure, I've got it right here." Then we could all go home happy. But you've got to come up with the bullshit, haven't you? As long as I've known you, the bullshit is flowing. You can't help yourself. I used to think it was aimed just at other people. *I* was in on the joke. But I see now it's aimed at everyone, including me. I'm just one of the dummies you have to deal with, aren't I?'

Wolfe didn't like the direction the conversation was heading and began to inch back towards the kitchen. There was more space there, and perhaps something he could use as a weapon if Jordan turned violent. Which he might; Wolfe had seen it happen before, almost like a switch being flipped. The switch that went from placid to mind-numbingly violent in less than a second.

He said, 'Have you talked to Giles? He hasn't given me authorization yet. It probably slipped his mind.'

'Of course it did,' Jordan said, pushing himself away from the front door and walking towards the living room. Wolfe followed him as if connected by a thread.

Once in the room Jordan didn't seem to know what to do next. He stood in the centre of the room and looked at the collection of replica guns Wolfe had displayed on the wall.

Wolfe followed his gaze and said, 'All fake. You knew

that, didn't you? I just like the look of them.'

Jordan turned back to him, the white lines on his face almost shining in the table lamps Wolfe had switched on earlier. He was like a parchment that people had written on, Wolfe thought. Poor bastard had taken orders all his life, disobeyed a few—maybe the writing on his face was an instruction manual. He didn't know how to operate by himself, that was for sure. He always needed pointing in the right direction first.

Jordan said, 'Everything about you is fake, isn't it, Tony? You can't take a shit without it coming out in a corkscrew. Everything you've ever done is bent in some way.'

'Now look—'

'Oh shut the fuck up, will you? Just tell me where the money is or I might have to get violent.'

As if to illustrate exactly what he meant, he stepped forward and slapped Wolfe hard on the cheek. Wolfe raised his hand and rubbed his cheek vigorously. It was a moment that had been coming a long time but he knew it was a precursor to something else. Wolfe had wondered how long it would be before Jordan took that step and lifted his hand in anger—he'd seen it in his mind's eye for a while.

Wolfe said, 'I've got some upstairs. I'll go fetch it.'

'Do that.'

Wolfe turned and left the room, then headed up the narrow semi-spiral staircase to the first floor. His heart was thumping because he'd remembered something. It was true he had a lot of replica rifles and pistols in the house ... but there was a real one, too.

He went into the second bedroom, the one where Carol

Minton had slept the day she and Giles had come here to avoid reporters after Sally's death. The eiderdown was still rumpled and Wolfe could just about discern the shape of Carol's body, turned sideways, knees drawn up, head on the pillow. He hadn't touched the bedclothes since she'd left. Seeing her profile there had given him some kind of comfort.

His hands trembling, he turned to the chest of drawers at the end of the bed. He pulled open the top right drawer and felt around amongst his socks and handkerchiefs.

There was nothing there.

He moved closer and moved more of the socks aside, lifting them out and throwing them on the bed.

He opened the top left drawer now, trying to calm his breathing, telling himself it must be in here, he knew he hadn't moved it …

But it wasn't there.

He tried all the other drawers, trying to be both quiet and thorough at the same time.

But he slammed the bottom drawer closed on its runners and the whole chest rattled. The pistol was gone. It was a Glock 17 4th Generation he'd had for a while, bought from another man he'd met at a military show, a man like Smith, with no scruples but plenty of gear. He knew he should have kept it in a safe somewhere, but he liked its weight and from time to time he would take it out and walk around the cottage pointing it, unloaded, at imaginary invaders.

Now it was gone, and he knew where. Carol and Giles Minton had both spent time in this room. Either one of them could have found it and taken it, though he didn't know why. Neither of them had shown any interest in his collection before.

Panic wrapped around his chest like a cold bandage. He had no money—or not enough to satisfy Jordan. He had no weapon. Worse, he couldn't think of an argument.

And he knew Jordan was in an unrelenting frame of mind.

From the doorway to the bedroom, Jordan said, 'Have you found it?'

'No! Give me a minute ...'

'Sorry, time's up.'

Wolfe felt Jordan detach himself from the doorway and come towards him like an elongated shadow.

He turned and charged, trying to use his girth and his weight to barge Jordan out of the room, but the other man was too agile. He side-stepped and Wolfe felt a crushing blow on his wind-pipe as Jordan raised his arm like a steel bar.

He struggled to breathe, lifting his hands to his throat. But then those hands were brushed aside as Jordan's fingers crept to his neck and insinuated themselves under his chin and on to his Adam's apple.

Wolfe tried to lash out at the man behind him, wriggling his torso and trying to kick backwards, which was hopeless.

The pain in his neck grew worse and then he realised that he couldn't actually draw breath in. The pressure was so great on his windpipe that he couldn't force the muscles in his neck and throat to flex and let air pass through.

His vision was beginning to blur and lose focus and he realised his mind was becoming detached from his body.

He was seeing himself from the outside, a useless blob of flesh. It was only because Jordan had taken his weight that he was still upright.

He decided to go with it, just aim for sleep, let the blackness take over because it was easier than fighting.

He was tired of fighting.

CHAPTER FORTY-NINE

JORDAN HAD BEEN gone about ten minutes when my phone rang. It was Nishi Dhawan, speaking quietly.

'I think I should tell you,' she said, 'that we've had a visit from Carol Minton. She's been talking to my mother all afternoon. Now we're driving back to her house.'

'Do you know what she's said to her?'

'No, she wanted to talk to her alone. I had the day off work and came down to visit and she turned up in the middle of the afternoon. She seems … odd.'

'Can she hear you?'

'No, we stopped for petrol … she's coming back, got to go.'

The line went dead and I hunted down my jacket.

———

THE RUSH HOUR traffic out of Crewe meant it took me longer than usual to reach the Mintons' house. Pulling into the drive I saw their Mercedes parked right in front of the entrance to the house, as though Carol wanted to deliver her passengers directly, without even having to walk the last ten metres.

The door was locked but I still had Alistair's Yale on my key-ring, so I let myself in. I called out a Hello, but there was no reply. All the lights were on but the atmosphere hadn't changed since I'd been there earlier, talking to Giles. I wondered what he'd done in the intervening hours — called a lawyer, packed a bag, booked a cruise ... or just waited for his wife to return home, the faithful husband.

I went into the sitting-room and through the patio windows I could see a little scene playing out: four figures given texture and form by the dim light emitted by the solar lamps Carol had stuck in the soil. The figures stood in a circle, as though discussing what to do next. They were still on the lawn and were not looking at the rose bush flower bed where I'd found a resonance of what I thought was Aditya Dhawan's bicycle.

I slid the door open and went out to join them. Before I arrived I could hear the voices of Giles and Carol in strained argument with each other. Given what Nishi had told me on the phone, I could guess the subject of the disagreement.

All four of them turned to me as I approached, Carol and Giles breaking off their row to watch me. They were all in shadow and while I could make out their faces, I couldn't discern their expressions. We were like players in some kind of kabuki drama, our meanings unknown even while our gestures could be observed.

Perhaps the most desperate of the four, Giles broke first and turned to Carol, saying, 'This isn't the place, sweetheart. You shouldn't be doing this here, it's too cold. Let's go inside ...'

Beneath a knee-length coat, Carol wore the same roll-neck sweater as when she visited my office, with the addition of a long-strapped handbag draped over her shoulder. She said, 'We're doing this now, Giles. Apologising to Mrs Dhawan for what we did.'

Nishi and her mother stood close together and I had the sense that Nishi was protecting her mother and was ready to move at any moment. Her mother on the other hand seemed immovable, as though planted in the ground.

Nishi said to Carol, 'It's not necessary, Mrs Minton. Really.'

'It *is!*' Carol said sharply. 'It was fifteen years ago and I've never forgotten. I've lived through it time and time again and it's broken up our family and no one understands. It's made me ill …'

Giles Minton seemed alert to this, as if he'd been given a prompt. His gaze moved to take us all in, though he would only have seen a glint in our eyes. He said, 'I should explain … my wife's had some problems. Mental problems. She was diagnosed about five years ago and I'm afraid she hasn't been remembering things as they really were.'

'Tell them, Giles,' Carol said quietly. She'd wrapped her arms around herself against the cold and was staring at the ground.

Minton cleared his throat, as if about to make a campaign speech, and said, 'My wife used to work very closely with Mr Dhawan—Aditya. He seemed to be a very nice man and very helpful when Carol began to remake the garden as a showcase for her business.'

I glanced at Aditya Dhawan's widow. Her face, what I could see of it, was set in stone, as if the words meant to smooth away the harshness of what he said had simply bounced off her.

Giles continued: 'Carol told me, however, that Mr Dhawan was being too attentive. He seemed to want something from her, and she was growing afraid of being alone with him, in case he … he decided to take matters further.'

'A lie,' Mrs Dhawan said quietly.

'I'm sorry to have to say it, but you know he had a reputation. The police officers on the case told me as much. They'd had complaints about him, but nothing provable.'

I said, 'Were these the police officers you played golf with? Who were well-known for their racist views?'

Giles turned towards me. 'I don't know where you heard that and I don't think it's true.'

'From what I've heard you're not an unbiased judge.'

'It doesn't change the fact that I came home one day to find my wife being attacked here, in this garden, by Mr Dhawan. He was lying on top of her, trying to kiss her, while my five-year-old son, Alistair, looked on from the patio windows back there. I'd come home early and I found this … this action going on in my garden. I ran towards them and pulled him off, rolled him over on the ground. And he laughed at me. He opened his mouth and he looked up and laughed at me. I didn't know what to do. I'm not a physical man and I didn't want to hit him or punch him. So we stared at each other, until he started laughing again. That's when Carol hit him in the the head with a spade … and kept on hitting him. I'm sorry to say I watched until it was too late … the blood was everywhere. He stopped laughing. He stopped breathing. Carol put the spade down and we fell into each other's arms. We've lived with that incident ever since, the greatest tragedy of our lives. I've been racked with guilt, Carol has suffered dreadfully. And I'm afraid she might even have been responsible for the death of that poor girl Sally Collins. I don't know why, but I think Carol is still suffering and doesn't always know what she's doing ... I just want the time to look after her now.'

Carol had been looking down with a hand to her brow. Now she began to shake her head from side to side, murmuring, 'No, no, no ... that's not it, that's not right, no, no ...'

When she raised her head it was to look directly at her husband and even in the dark I could see the expression on her face: a clouded mixture of anger and hatred.

And then I noticed a dull glint from her right hand — she was holding a gun, and was raising it even as I saw what it was. She must have slipped it from her handbag.

I said, 'Carol ...'

She stepped back one pace from the group and we were all now staring at the gun, it's barrel moving back and forth between us.

'It wasn't like that,' she said.

'Carol—'

'Shut up!' she said to Giles, with some authority: her voice had gained strength, probably because she was angry. She turned to Mrs Dhawan, who raised her hands defensively. 'It's true I had an affair with your husband. I wanted to tell you this afternoon but I couldn't bear to do it. He was such a nice man, so pleasant to work with, and very good looking.'

'Please don't talk to me about him,' Mrs Dhawan said. She shifted her posture to stand more upright and I saw that she'd raised her chin to look Carol Minton in the eye. Carol stared straight back at her, oblivious to any sense of shame.

'I worked with him and I enjoyed it, and we laughed. And then … one thing led to another and we ended up in bed. Please don't blame him—'

'I don't.'

'—I needed something and I thought your husband could provide it. An imitation of love, perhaps. Tenderness. Some feeling of some kind.'

'The things your husband couldn't give you,' Mrs Dhawan said, and was shushed quietly by her daughter.

'That's right,' Carol said. 'You understand. I knew you would. You knew what Aditya was like, what he could do for you.'

Mrs Dhawan started to cry, gently and without much noise. Nishi leaned sideways, her long hair drifting like a black waterfall, and put her arm around her mother's shoulders.

Carol Minton said, 'The second time it happened, Giles came home early and ran straight upstairs to change and found me in bed with Aditya. There was a horrible scene and then he left and Aditya got out of bed and put on his trousers and ran downstairs and I ran after him. I got into the garden just in time to see Giles hit him with a pickaxe.'

Mrs Dhawan drew in a horrified breath. I was still watching Carol closely but she was too far from me to risk stepping towards her. If she didn't shoot me, she might hit one of the others.

'Aditya fell down but he was still alive and Giles hit him again, and again, and I threw myself at him but it was too late. We buried him there—' she pointed to the rose bush behind her '—and then we buried his bicycle with him. We took his little trailer apart and Giles sawed up some of it and we dropped it in the rubbish tip piece by piece. Tony Wolfe came over that night and helped us rearrange the garden and dig more beds. I hated him knowing but we didn't know what to do.' She shuddered with a long sigh. 'I wish I could take it all back, everything, and not go through the hell I've been in for the last fifteen years, wanting to tell someone but not being able to. Knowing that Alistair knew but we couldn't talk about it. Wanting to relive my life and stop Alistair worrying about his.' She looked at us all in turn. 'For years my husband's been trying to tell me I'm not well, that I'm going mad, I'm not remembering things clearly. He even persuaded me to spend a month in that horrible place, talking to people who didn't know why they were there, or what they'd done wrong. I think he hoped I'd forget, or think I'd been dreaming. But I remember everything. It's been in my head like a film, over and over again. I loved Aditya and Giles took him from me. I'll never forgive him.' She looked at us all again. 'I'm not going mad, am I?'

'Carol,' Giles said, taking a step towards his wife. And she shot him in the stomach. Giles stumbled backwards and fell to the ground as the sound of the shot echoed through the garden.

Mrs Dhawan started screaming.

———

NOW I LEAPED forward and knocked the gun from Carol's hand and grabbed her around the arms. She made no effort to shrug me off and seemed to welcome the support. She relaxed into me. She seemed as fragile and broken as a bird that's flown into a plate-glass window.

I said to Nishi, 'Go inside and call an ambulance and the police. Look after your mother.'

Nishi said nothing but hurried off, taking her mother, now quietened, by the arm.

I bent down next to Giles Minton but I knew he was dead. He'd been too close and the bullet had ripped out his insides. The odour of blood and human lights began to rise in the air.

Carol Minton said, 'Did you find Alistair again?'

I stood up. 'Yes. He asked after you.'

'Oh! What did you tell him?'

'I said you were doing well.'

She laughed softly. 'You little liar. Still, at least you've done what we paid you for, haven't you? Another successful case?'

I looked away and said nothing. It seemed to me that I'd done nothing but seize a hornets' nest and shake it until its inhabitants were crazed and blind to consequences. I couldn't call that a success by any measure.

Then Carol was quiet by my side and we waited there, listening to the traffic on the road and watching a low-hanging moon gradually ascend into the black sky.

CHAPTER FIFTY

THE FUNERAL WAS held at a small church in a village outside Nantwich. The last time I'd been there was for the interment of another client. Halfway through that service, the grieving widow on the front row had turned to leave the church and I realised it was my ex-wife, remarried for a while and now widowed.

All of this came back to me like an uncertain memory and left me wondering whether it was true or not. Having known the Mintons, I was beginning to doubt my own powers of recall.

They permitted Carol to come and stand at the back of the church with her police handlers, and afterwards she watched as the coffin was led through the cold graveyard to a family plot: Giles' family hadn't been as prestigious as Carol's, but they'd been foresighted enough to reserve space for the only son.

AFTER THE VICAR had said a few words at the graveside, and the coffin had been lowered in, the crowds began to disperse. Minton's newly-elevated status as potential Member of Parliament for the constituency meant that the press and TV were there, as well as sightseers and locals drawn in to see how a celebrity was buried.

Alistair and Deborah, both dressed neatly in matching dark blue suits, had been standing with some distant family relations, neither of them catching my eye nor, as far as I could tell, willing to talk to their mother. They seemed pointedly to stand with their back to wherever she stood so they weren't obliged to see her.

At the end, Alistair came over and shook my hand, practically the first adult thing I'd seen him do.

He said, 'I suppose I should say thanks for coming.'

'Have you spoken to your mother?'

'They won't let me see her—the lawyers, I mean. Apparently we're biding our time.'

'Do you know how she is?'

'We're going for "delusional", though I don't know if that's the technical term. I suppose they won't let her out of hospital after this, will they?'

'Hard to know,' I said. 'I don't have any experience in this area.'

'I would have thought everybody you met was crazy to some extent. Why else would people commit crime?'

'Usually because they think they don't have any choice.'

He nodded but I think he was unconvinced. The thought led him to say, 'Have they found the man with the scars, or his friend?'

'Jordan and Stevie. They picked up Jordan for speeding while he was driving Tony Wolfe's BMW. He's saying Stevie was shot by another man in the back of his own car, so he'd taken his boss's as compensation. It was only right, he said.'

'Was he the one who killed Tony Wolfe?'

'It looks like it.'

'And it said in the paper they think Wolfe was defrauding my dad as well.'

'I heard the same. I don't know anything about that except Wolfe was supposed to be the financial whiz. It wouldn't surprise me.'

'Nor me.' He glanced around at the people slowly filtering from the graveyard, then lowered his voice. 'So I don't have to be scared any more?'

'You didn't have to be scared in the first place,' I said, 'though you had no way of knowing that. Excuse me, I have to talk to your sister.'

He drifted away to rejoin family and I headed for the churchyard gates, where Deborah was standing with a placid if rather forlorn expression. I approached her and said, 'Walk with me, will you?'

She'd washed out the blue edge from her hair so it was all black now and, together with the dark suit, it gave her a more adult demeanour. She glanced up and down the road, then let her eyes rest on me. I couldn't see in them any feeling of sadness or pity or regret, just an acceptance of the day for what it was.

She said, 'Okay,' and walked alongside me towards the centre of the village.

As casually as I could, I said, 'Why did you drown Sally?'

She stopped and I stopped with her, ready to seize her arm if she ran. She looked at me again, but this time there was a glint of interest in her pupils.

She said, 'How do you come to that conclusion? I thought my mother did it.'

I continued walking and she came with me.

I said, 'For a while I thought it was your mother, too. But her anger didn't seem to extend to Sally. And then there was the phone call we've already talked about, when you called Sally Sweetie. That was an alarm bell. And I noticed after she died you stopped wearing that blue nose stud. I started wondering about it and checked with the officer in charge of the investigation into Sally's murder. They found a blue nose stud in the bottom of Ben Prescott's swimming-pool.'

'That was probably Sally's. She wore one from time to time. Just not when she was working for Tony Wolfe. She was the reason I had mine put in, if you must know.'

'Too much of a coincidence, Deborah — it was found in the swimming-pool of the man you'd had an affair with, whose house you visited, and to which you still had a key. I talked to him, incidentally, after he came back from Greece. He told me you had a key and came over to swim now and then. You told me you were doing a lot of swimming, remember?'

I sensed she was getting more agitated, looking back down the street, standing a little further away from me. She had the nervousness of a wild animal who'd been domesticated but still didn't trust her captors. Then she seemed to come to a shuddering decision and grabbed my arm, halting us again. Her eyes were now intensely focused, and she spoke as if she thought she could convince me with the strength of her anger.

'She couldn't keep her fucking mouth shut, could she?'

'About what?'

She sighed and the action released a tumble of words. 'She was the first one I told about Ben. I thought I could trust her but I was stupid … she was jealous. She rang up the newspaper and told them about us without mentioning our names, just enough to get them interested. Then she emailed my mum and dad using a fake email address.'

'So you were lying when you said it was your mother who told Sally about your affair with Prescott. You wanted me to think she was trying to make Sally jealous.'

'So what if I did?' Her eyes were the darkest I'd ever seen them. 'Face it, Sally was a cow, wasn't she? She told you about Mum and that turd Wolfe. She was doing it just to embarrass me, because she knew I hated him. I suppose you fell for the dumb angelic blonde act, didn't you? God, men are so stupid.' She looked down the street again but didn't see the houses or the road. 'She was a hero to me when I was younger and I suppose I was the jealous one. She was pretty, had a degree, could go on and do anything. I couldn't understand why she hung around me. I didn't feel like I deserved the attention and eventually I despised her for making me feel second-rate. Fuck, that must be exactly how Mum felt.' She paused a moment to consider her own insight, then continued. 'Of course she got catty when I started seeing Ben—that's when she sent the anonymous email to my parents and called the newspaper and my life turned to shit for several months.'

'Did you know at the time it was Sally who'd told all these people?'

'No. She told me later.'

'When you got back together, afterwards.'

'Yeah, I suppose I tricked her into telling me. Chalk one up for me. We were talking about the whole business, how it got blown up in the press and so on, and I told her I didn't care who ratted on me and she said it was her. She seemed proud of the fact she'd screwed up my life.' Deborah grinned at me, and I was suddenly reminded of her mother's switches of mood. I'd seen the physical resemblances between them before—but maybe the similarities were more than merely physical. She said, 'So I listened and said nothing. I'd grown up. Learned some strategy. I talked her into coming to Ben's house, to see where it all happened. Like a tour. We'd have a laugh. I knew he was away. She agreed to come and I met her in Crewe and we left her car there and I drove her to Ben's house, then let us in with the key.'

She went silent and I could tell she was living it again, seeing herself and Sally wandering through Prescott's house, looking at the film and theatre books on his shelves. Laughing. Perhaps suggesting they take a dip in the heated pool …

She knew what I was thinking and said, 'I got in the water first and persuaded her to come in after me. Once she was in I said I needed to get out again to fetch my phone to take a photo, so I climbed out and went round the side of the pool and knelt down behind her, saying I was going to give her a massage first … and instead I pressed down and held her under. It was surprisingly easy, though she did flail about a bit and she must have knocked my nose stud out, which isn't easy. She was feeble, though, and I'm strong in the arms. All that swimming.'

'Why do you think you did it?'

She gave it some thought, then said, 'It was revenge, wasn't it? She talked to people about me, and then told other people about me and Ben. I trusted her and she screwed me. I was embarrassed, and angry. Those are the default emotions in our family, by the way. At the time when it happened I couldn't do anything about it, but eventually I could, so I did. Like Mum taking it out on Dad, fifteen years too late. Seems I am my mother's daughter, after all.'

Another grin, but this time there was terror behind it.

A black car passed us and pulled in. I said, 'Deborah, that's an unmarked police car. A man called Sawyer is going to ask you to repeat all that while someone writes it down or records it. They'll make sure you have a lawyer with you.'

She drew a deep breath and her features softened, as if she might cry, but she made no attempt to run. She said, 'Poor old Alistair's going to be all alone in that big old house now. We couldn't get him to come back and now he can, we're not going to be there for him, are we? I hope he's going to be all right, by himself.'

I said, 'Well, your family's living proof there are many different ways you can be lonely.'

The police car doors opened and two officers came towards us, followed by Inspector Sawyer.

We nodded at each other.

ALSO BY KEITH DIXON

The Sam Dyke Series

Altered Life
The Private Lie
The Hard Swim
The Bleak
The Strange Girl
The Secret Sharers
The Innocent Dead
The Second Guess (short story)

Paul Storey Crime Thrillers

Storey
One Punch
The Song of Geneva Chance

Standalone Novels

A French Darcy – a Romance
Actress – a Contemporary novel

Essays on Writing

The Idle Writer
Crime Writing Confidential

Blog

www.cwconfidential.blogspot.com

Webpage

http://www.keithdixonnovels.com

ABOUT THE AUTHOR

Keith Dixon was born in Yorkshire and grew up in the Midlands. He's been writing since he was thirteen years old in a number of different genres: thriller, espionage, science fiction, literary. He's the author of eight novels and a short story in the Sam Dyke Investigations series and two other non-crime works, as well as two collections of blog posts on the craft of writing. When he's not writing he enjoys reading, learning the guitar, watching movies and binge-inhaling great TV series. He's currently spending more time in France than is probably good for him.

Learn more about Keith by following him on Twitter @keithyd6, by reading his blog at cwconfidential.blogspot.com or connect with him on Facebook at facebook.com/SamDykeInvestigations/ On his website you can find out more about his other novels and current news: keithdixonnovels.com.